Twenty-Six Miles

ibooks

Habent Sua Fata Libelli

ibooks
1230 Park Avenue
New York, New York 10128
Tel: 212-427-7139
bricktower@aol.com • www.ibooksinc.com

Library of Congress Cataloging-in-Publication Data

Twenty-Six Miles
Andrew Spencer
p. cm.

1. Fiction—General 2. Fiction—Thriller 3. Fiction—Mystery
Fiction, I. Title.

978-1-59687-968-3, Trade Paper

July 2013

Twenty-Six Miles

by Andrew Spencer

For Niki,
the love of my life and the best editor I could have ever hoped for

Je t'aime, mon amour.

Acknowledgements

I would like to thank John Colby of Brick Tower Press for his ongoing professional guidance and belief in my work. Without his willingness to support this project, it all would have been just another idea percolating in the overcrowded part of my brain that houses those things.

My parents first brought me to visit Nantucket when I was in diapers, and their love and support – though tested often by me – have been unwavering since those earliest days. Dick Cumbie has provided me with more than I can ever repay, and I will be forever grateful to him for his friendship. Arnold Spencer, Mark Junell, and Jamie Ranney all proved yet again how valuable they are in the role of unpaid legal counsel. Mike Slizewski provided his expert copyediting skills. Mair Downing never censored herself when offering her opinions on the manuscript in progress. Caroline Miller didn't know it at the time, but her comment one afternoon before a University of Virginia football game gave me the spark I needed to finish writing this book. The island of Nantucket and my many friends there have served as equal parts inspiration and salvation over the years. My sincerest thanks to you all.

And most importantly, my never-ending love and thanks to Niki, whom I happened to meet as the result of a chance encounter one day when I was a high school student at Woodberry Forest. Twenty years later, she did me the incredible honor of becoming my wife. It's been said that good things come to those who wait. Apparently if you're willing to wait twenty years, those things are indescribably amazing.

Although inspired by true events, the story you are about
to read is a work of fiction.

All characters and incidents are products of the author's imagination.

"Telling the truth is one of the best ways to disguise a lie."

—Adam Langer
The Thieves of Manhattan

CHAPTER ONE

All my friends call me Billy, and even though you and I just now met for the first time, I think we're going to be friends. So go ahead and call me Billy. I was born Adam William Faulkner, and that name always got me linked with the author William Faulkner, which got me in good with my high school English teachers. I never read a thing the guy ever wrote, but they tell me he was pretty good. Maybe one of these days I'll get around to it. Just not right now. Other than that, the name didn't get me far in life.

Actually, you know what? I take that back. It got me here, but more on that later. One step at a time.

I'm a small-town kid from Vermont, the only child of a couple of hippie farmers who scratched out a living in a town called Eden. Right in the heart of the Northeast Kingdom. That's what they call the region. The Northeast Kingdom. Sounds a lot better, I guess, than calling it "that place where it's cold as a motherfucker and where there's not a damn thing to do." It was full of kids that dreamed of one day getting away, getting out, getting to the big city, and living the dream of success and wealth and luxury. All those glamorous things we saw on TV.

The problem was, we didn't know the first thing about life in those big cities we'd heard so much about. But that didn't stop us. We'd seen the places on reality shows and we'd seen the pictures in magazines, and that was enough research for us. We knew we wanted to get the hell out of Eden, and the life we thought we could have in those faraway places was hard to resist. Those of us who did manage to get out more often than not ended up right back where we started, though, once we'd figured out what we didn't know. The big city wasn't designed for kids from Eden, Vermont.

The path my life has taken to today has been what you might call a bumpy ride, so long as you're being nice in how you describe it. I'm sure there were warning signs from my earliest days, but nobody thought enough about what I did back then to really pay attention. For me, it all really started the day I graduated from high school. It was on that day that I made the fateful decision to start my own business, and nothing would ever be the same again.

College wasn't in my future, and I didn't want to work for Franklin's Hardware Store in downtown Eden, or some other mom-and-pop operation. And I absolutely refused to work with my parents on their farm. So my choices were starve to death or start my own business. Starvation wasn't the most appealing option; I kind of like to eat, you know? So I decided to tap into my entrepreneurial instincts and see where they led me. And where they led me was down a dangerous path that started an avalanche.

I came up with an idea to market organic maple syrup to the tourists that came to Vermont to experience all that Norman Rockwell New England crap, an experience that included Vermont maple syrup. No vacation to Vermont was complete without it. It was a pretty simple business plan, actually. I got a friend who was an artist —God only knows there are enough starving artists in Vermont—to design a label for me, and I found a company online to print stickers for pretty cheap. From there, all I had to do was get myself some maple syrup, and I was in business.

To accomplish that little logistical requirement, I'd drive to Burlington once a week, a trip that took me just over an hour each way, and go to the local wholesale warehouse club. It was a thirty-five-dollar membership fee, plus about twenty bucks in gas per trip. I bought cases and cases of this knockoff syrup they had in the place, some stuff they marketed under the name "Vermont Maid." It came in the standard plastic squeeze bottle, but at the warehouse club, they were huge bottles that held the equivalent of about four regular-sized ones. I'd also get a few cases of Mason jars. All told, my overhead costs were under $500 a month.

Back in my apartment in Eden, I'd put the labels on the jars and fill each one with the chemical crap that they were passing off as syrup, some formula I imagined that had been developed by a chemist in a lab somewhere in California. I screwed the tops on the jars and that was that. Voilà. Genuine, organic Vermont maple syrup. Twenty-five bucks a jar. I almost felt guilty about how easy it was. Almost.

The power of suggestion, I figured out pretty quick, is a pretty amazing thing. Just by telling people that this stuff was organic, they immediately trusted me, because I was doing something good for the environment. And of course telling them it was genuine Vermont maple syrup made it almost too easy to sell.

I sold the stuff out of my truck on the side of the road, which added to the whole earthy-crunchy nature of the thing. Free samples for everyone. People bought it up as quickly as I could get it in the jar. They'd ask me about the process, and I'd read enough about making syrup to be able to talk about it. Let me tell you, you don't live your life in Vermont without learning at least a little bit about they how make the state's number-one export.

Of course, none of the tourists knew anything about it, so I could have told them that I drilled a hole in the ground and watched it come bubbling up like oil, and they would have believed every line of it. Probably would have gone home and told their friends that the shows they watched on public television were all wrong. There weren't any trees involved at all. Real Vermonters got it right out of the ground. They'd gotten it firsthand from a reliable source, so it had to be true, right? People will believe anything you tell them.

My customers raved about how much better my syrup was than what they got back home, the syrup that came out of the bottle that talked to people on TV. It's that power-of-suggestion idea. If they think they're getting something special, their mind believes it, and the rest of their senses just follow along, like little soldiers following orders. Easy as that. Like I said, they'll believe whatever you tell them, so long as you sound convincing enough.

Things were going great. I was selling out of my stock every week and making a pretty tidy profit that was keeping the rent paid and the bill collectors at bay. I had my own little territory staked out, right on the side of Route 12 near the entrance to Elmore State Park. The whole scene did nothing but make me look even more like the nature-loving hippie trying to make an honest living peddling nature's gifts that I wanted them to think of me as. And my spot was far enough away from

Eden to make sure that I wouldn't run into anyone who might know me from there. Nobody from Eden ever came up to commune with nature in the state forest.

Then one morning, I had six or eight people lined up to buy syrup from me. I'd just set up for the day, and I took it as a great omen that people were already around to buy my syrup this early in the day. And then a state trooper rolled up in his cruiser. He got out of his car and tipped his hat to the tourists. To serve and protect, plus make nice with the people who come and support the local economy.

"Sorry, folks. No maple syrup today," he announced very officially. "I've been ordered to shut this guy down." He pointed at me, then looked me up and down, trying to figure out just how dangerous I really might be.

The would-be customers pleaded with him to let them buy their syrup first. They'd heard such great things about it from their friends, and they'd even sampled it and just had to have it. But the statie was not going to budge on this one.

He shook his head. "I'm really sorry," he said in an almost sincere voice. "Official orders. Just doing my job. Plenty of other places to get syrup. *Real* Vermont maple syrup," he added with a sideways glare at me that added a whole new dimension to the emphasis he'd placed on the word "real."

When I heard that, I knew the gig was up. Somebody had ratted me out. The tourists left slowly, looking suspiciously over their shoulders at me. Was I a rapist? Maybe a murderer? A fugitive from the long arm of the Vermont law?

When the crowd had left, the trooper turned to me. Gone was the friendly attitude he'd had a second ago. Now he was all business.

"You're done selling this shit," he said to me. "You're under arrest."

And that was that. I asked him what I'd done, and all he said was, "Selling counterfeit goods." I had to laugh. I wasn't selling counterfeit anything. I was selling syrup. Maybe there was a little bit of liberty taken in the description of the actual syrup, but counterfeit? Please.

But he didn't want to hear my side of the story. No, sir. He kept talking about the Department of Agriculture and mentioned federal charges. Then he pushed me up against the side of my truck with my hands on my head and frisked me down. Wallet, truck keys, wad of bills wrapped in a rubber band. Nothing that qualified as a dangerous weapon. All of it came out of my pockets, though, and went into a plastic bag that he told me would be evidence. I didn't think it would be terribly smart of me at that point to suggest that I was pretty sure that the key ring with the bottle opener was genuine.

He slapped a pair of handcuffs on me and put me in the back of his car, then told me my truck would be towed, and I might be able to get it later, if the judge was nice enough to let me go without keeping me in custody. He was actually pretty straightforward about the whole thing, like he was explaining to me the process of making cookies. I was going to be taken to the jail in Morrisville, which was the closest town with an actual police station. Eden was that small. We didn't even have our own police department. Instead, we had to share with our friendly neighbors to the south.

*   *   *

We drove to Morrisville in complete silence. I'd seen enough TV shows to know that I wasn't supposed to say anything to the cops before I talked to a lawyer, so I just sat there and kept my mouth shut. Once we got to Morrisville, a couple more officers came out, and they unloaded me and took me inside. The outside of the place looked more like somebody's house than a police station. The only sign you could see that might have told you it was a police station was the pack of four police cruisers in the parking lot.

The Morrisville County Jail is a pretty compact affair, and to be totally honest with you, they use the space they've got pretty efficiently. They're not set up for any kind of psycho killer that might need what you'd call special attention, but for the average drunk driver or wife-beater, they've got everything they need in that little building. Granted, I don't like to consider myself an authority on the interior of American jails, you know? But from what I could tell, this one seemed like a pretty well-run outfit.

The state trooper that had originally put me in handcuffs held me by the arm as he walked me in, my hands still cuffed behind my back, and told the dispatcher who I was. Apparently they were expecting me; I was something of a minor celebrity because of the fact that I'd done something beyond taking a joyride in Dad's pickup after shotgunning a couple of beers. I was an actual criminal. I guess they didn't get a lot of those in Morrisville. The way he announced my name, though, it was like he was showing off for his little entourage that had followed me in. I was the day's entertainment.

First they took all of my personal possessions from the trooper, then they took my belt away from me, just in case I lost all hope and decided to try and hang myself in my cell rather than face the wrath of the Morrisville Police Department. At least I didn't have to wear one of those jumpsuits, so I figured I was doing okay so far. And they finally took off the handcuffs, which were really starting to hurt.

They fingerprinted me and took my mug shot, front and profile, before putting me in a holding cell. The whole process was, I guess, exactly the way I would have imagined it to be. The cell was one of four they had in the basement of the building. There were two cells per side, and I was the only prisoner—they seemed they like they really enjoyed calling me "the prisoner" while I was there—in the place.

I have no idea how long I was in that cell, because they took my watch as soon as they had brought me inside. It could have been a few hours or it could have been fifteen minutes. I didn't have any way of really knowing for sure. However long it was, one of the local guys eventually came in with a different state trooper right behind him. The local cop told me to turn around and face the wall while he unlocked the cell. I did, then he told me to put my hands behind my back, which I also did. He cinched a pair of handcuffs on tighter than I thought was necessary, then jerked me around so I was facing him.

"You're headed up to Hyde Park," the statie told me. "The Lamoille County Courthouse." He said it in the same tone of voice that you might imagine a judge using to tell you that you were going to Alcatraz for the rest of your life. I had no idea what it meant, but the way he said it gave me a pretty serious shiver down my back. This was starting to sound serious.

After that, I was led outside again and back into another state trooper's car. It looked just about the same as the first one on the inside. The only difference was the guy driving. It was only about ten minutes up the highway to Hyde Park. When we pulled up to the courthouse, I honestly thought we were in the wrong place. This courthouse, such as it was, was red brick, with a spire on one side and a nice little covered porch out front. It even had the requisite white picket fence. It was just so Vermont-ish, you know? Like a postcard.

The exterior façade, though, was just that. A façade. Inside, it was all business. And not any kind of good business, either. I didn't know it at the time, but this place was going to become the starting line for a series of events that would drastically alter the course of my life.

CHAPTER TWO

From the parking lot, they took me inside. Another parade. But this time, at least, they didn't seem quite as impressed with me. A woman behind the desk started processing me into the system. I was handcuffed the whole time, and when she had all my information, they led me down to yet another cell. Apparently we were going to skip the fingerprints and photo shoot.

The cell they put me in had a few other people in it, most of whom looked like they had no place better to go, so they figured that jail was as good a place to spend the day as any. At least they got fed and stayed warm inside. This was what my life had become. I was under arrest, sitting in a holding cell with a bunch of homeless men whose survival instincts had told them that their best option was getting arrested so they could get the old "three hots and a cot."

I took a seat against the cinder-block wall on a bench that was bolted to both the floor underneath it and the wall next to it. This place might get destroyed in an earthquake, but by God this bench would not be going anywhere if the men who'd installed it had anything to say in the matter. I closed my eyes and rubbed my temples. A dull pain that had been sitting in the back of my head like a rain cloud since they first took me into custody was now starting to grow into a full-blown migraine.

I started to think about my options, but given that I didn't have a lawyer, I wasn't sure exactly what my options were. My mind kept going back to something I'd heard one of the state troopers say to one of his buddies, something about federal labeling laws. He'd actually used the word felonies to talk about the supposed crimes I'd committed.

Seriously? They were going to charge me with a felony for making a few bucks off syrup? And what did it mean that I'd supposedly broken federal laws? I didn't know a lot about the legal system, but I knew enough to know that a felony conviction would screw me for the rest of my life. I needed a lawyer. But I had no idea where to even start in terms of getting one.

I had plenty of time to toss these worries around inside my skull. One of my real character flaws, I guess you'd say, is the fact that I can take a problem and, with just a little bit of thought, come up with enough doomsday scenarios to last a few lifetimes. In other words, I can take any situation and, within about five minutes, tell you exactly how it's going to result in my dying an unimaginably painful death. This little situation in which I found myself didn't even take that long to turn into me spending the rest of my miserable life in prison, living as the boyfriend to some big, fat murderer named Bubba.

Every so often the door would open, and either some new lawbreaker was shoved inside the room, or a uniformed officer would call somebody's name, which was followed by that particular person groaning to stand, and then shuffling slowly across the floor to be led up to his arraignment. For that poor bastard, the free ride inside the holding cell was over.

But I was different. I actually wanted to get out. I wanted a chance to explain that this whole thing had been a big misunderstanding. I'd promise to never do it again if they'd just let me go this one time. I began looking towards the door whenever it opened, hoping maybe it was my time to go. Regardless of what the next phase of this nightmare was, I figured that I'd rather get it over with than sit in here worrying about what might happen. My mother always used to tell me that the devil you knew wasn't as bad as the devil you didn't. I was beginning to see how right she had been.

Finally my turn came around. The door opened and an officer yelled out, "Faulkner!" I skipped the groan and the shuffle. I jumped up like I was on fire and just about ran to get the hell out of that cell, away from those people. The officer handcuffed me again, this time with my hands in front of me, and led me by the arm down a long hallway, through a door, then up a flight of stairs. We came out into a completely empty room without any kind of decoration at all, not even an American flag like you'd always see on TV. There were a bunch of plastic chairs bolted to the floor. They all faced a large wooden podium kind of thing that looked like some kind of church altar. Behind the podium sat the woman who was going to be determining what happened to me next.

She was a mean-looking woman. Sort of like a school principal. Gray hair, black-framed glasses that sat on her nose, wearing one of those black gowns judges wear.

"Mr. Faulkner, I am Judge Evelyn Cory. You have been charged with violating Vermont Title Six, Chapter Thirty-Two, Section Four-Eighty-One, Subsection Seventeen. That's a long way of saying that you illegally labeled syrup as being made in Vermont when it was not. Do you understand this charge?" She looked down her nose at me. I could feel her eyes shooting out little spears.

I looked at the floor and nodded my head.

"I need you to give me a verbal answer, Mr. Faulkner," she said. "Again I ask you, do you understand the charges as I've read them to you?"

"Yes," I said quietly.

"Very well then. Do you have legal counsel to represent you?" she asked.

"No."

"Can you afford an attorney, Mr. Faulkner?"

"No." I suddenly realized that, for the first time that I could ever remember in my life, I was really terrified. Scared out of my mind. I had no idea what was happening, and it was like there was some other part of my body that was answering this woman, some part I wasn't in control of.

"The court will appoint you an attorney, then. I suggest you speak to him as soon as possible. In the interim, I will enter a plea of not guilty on your behalf." She hit the table in front of her with a little wooden hammer.

And that was it. Before I had a chance to offer up my deal about never doing it again, I was taken out the same door I'd entered through. They took me to another cell, this one a single-occupancy unit. A metal bed bolted to the wall, a metal toilet bolted to another wall. For some reason, those bolts became the only thing I could even kind of focus on. There were a hell of a lot of bolts in this place. If only I'd gone into the bolt-making business, I probably could have made more money than I did with fake maple syrup, and I could have avoided the whole counterfeit issue.

Maybe it was some kind of psychological thing—you know, the whole focusing on ridiculous things that I saw around me. Like the bolts. It was all new to me—being arrested, being in jail, being scared half to death.

I sat down on the bed and leaned back against the cinder blocks of the wall. There was all kinds of graffiti on the wall, some of it just initials scratched into the stone and some of it gang tags. Apparently somebody who'd been in my position at some point earlier was something of a philosopher; he'd written in black pen, "If you find yourself at the end of your rope, tie a noose and hang yourself. It's not going to get any easier from here on out." Even though I laughed a little, the sentiment hit me pretty hard. This was, for better or worse, my life. There was no escaping that. This was all too real. And from where I sat right then, it looked like this current reality was going to be a part of my future too.

I lay down on the bed and began thinking about my life to this point. You know, sort of going back over everything I'd done, trying to figure out where everything had gone so damn wrong. Of all the possible plans I'd played out in my head over the years of how my life would go—and there had been a lot of them—none of them involved my sitting in a jail cell. I actually started to cry as I saw my whole world falling down around me. I was a failure, plain and simple. A complete failure.

After a while, a tall man in a dark business suit appeared outside my cell, with a guard standing next to him. He looked like he was about thirty, blonde hair, wire-rimmed glasses, carrying a dark-brown leather briefcase. He introduced himself as Mark Sandell, my court-appointed attorney. The guard opened the cell, and told me to stand up and turn around. I did, and he cuffed me. Then the three of us walked down yet another hallway, this one lined with a few empty cells, down to a conference room. The guard waited outside while my attorney and I got down to business.

"Okay, I'm not going to mince words here," he began. "You're in some trouble. You happened to violate a law that a lot of Vermonters hold very sacred, namely selling fake maple syrup. In the most basic sense, the brand that is Vermont maple syrup has effectively been trademarked by the state as a way of protecting that brand. So in the state of Vermont, you'd probably have been better off beating a puppy to death using somebody's grandmother as a club than selling fake maple syrup."

I laughed. I know it wasn't the time or the place, but I really found what he'd said funny. For one thing, it was the first time anybody had talked to me like a regular person since this whole situation had started, and it felt good to react like a normal person, even just for a second. And I also thought it was a pretty funny mental image that he'd described.

"Don't laugh, Mr. Faulkner. This is many things, but a joke is not one of them. You're also facing federal charges for violating labeling laws. And that's just for the syrup part of it. The organic thing is going to be a whole other set of issues," he said. "But you're lucky there, in that the laws haven't quite caught up with the organic food movement just yet." Even though he'd said that I was lucky, his voice didn't seem to sound quite as sure of himself as it had when he'd talked about killing puppies. Now he sounded much more serious. Kind of like he didn't want to give me too much hope, just in case things didn't work out for me.

I looked across the table at him. "Look," I said, "I honestly didn't mean to hurt anybody. I was just trying to make a living. You know, I'm not some rich kid, and I'm really not a smart guy. I'm just a poor, dumb farm kid from Vermont. I was just trying to eat, man."

"Of course you didn't mean to hurt anybody. I know that. And the fact that you don't have a prior record is going to help you," he said. "But before you start making any plans to get out of here, we need to see the judge again to talk about bail. I'm optimistic, given your lack of a record, that you won't have to stay in here until we can work out a deal. But for now, you're going to go back to your cell, and I'm going to go meet with the district attorney and the judge. I'll see what we can work out."

When he'd finished killing any hope I had, the guard took me back to my cell. When he slammed the door behind me, hearing it clang like it did it set off a whole bunch of emotions inside of me. On the one hand, I was still scared as anything about what might happen to me, especially if the charges were as serious as he'd made them sound. But on the other, I was holding on to the hope that the system would be kind to me, since I was a first-time offender. I lay back down on the bed and closed my eyes for what seemed liked just a second.

The next thing I knew, the same guard was at the door of my cell, calling my name, my lawyer behind him. I stood up and turned around, waiting for the command to turn around and face the wall, and then the pain of the handcuffs digging into my wrists again. I was like a dog that had been trained to respond to its master's commands. I was already used to the jailhouse routine. "No cuffs. You're out on bail," the guard said.

I turned to face my attorney. "What does that mean?"

"They're letting you out on personal recognizance," he said. "You don't have to pay anything, which is pretty fortunate. But you'll have to come back to court when they tell you to. Otherwise, you'll get slapped with a warrant for your arrest. And you don't want that, trust me."

The guard told me to exit the cell, which I did without him having to tell me twice. I followed both of them as they walked towards the front of the building, where I had to sign the paperwork promising to return at the appointed date for my trial, and to pick up my stuff that had been confiscated from me when I was first arrested. Sandell gave me his business card and told me to call him in the next couple of days to talk about the case, and he asked me if I needed anything.

"I could use a ride to go pick up my truck," I said as I put my watch back on my wrist. It felt good to have something on there besides handcuffs for a change. "They towed it when they arrested me." I had no idea where it had been taken, though, so he asked the clerk to find out which impound yard had received my vehicle. She punched a few buttons on her computer and pulled up my information.

"Looks like they took it to Morrisville," she said. "The Morrisville Police Department."

Sandell turned to me and said, "It's on my way home. Come on. I'll give you a ride."

We walked outside, and I was totally thrown off by the fact that it was nearly dark. I'd spent the entire day going through all the different parts of the legal system that I'd been involved with, and by then, the day was basically a blur in my overcrowded brain. I looked at my watch for the first time; it was after five o'clock. Sandell pointed out his car in the parking lot, and I got in. As we pulled out of the lot, I let myself relax for just a second. It was the first time I'd really been able to do that in a long time. I had to admit that it felt good to be riding in the front seat of a car again, and without wearing handcuffs.

That moment of relaxation started me to thinking again, as I had done a lot that day, about the last year of my life. I realized then that I'd spent that time constantly nervous, constantly looking over my shoulder, constantly afraid that I'd be caught doing what I was doing. I knew it was wrong. As for the fact that it was a felony, I have to plead ignorance, no pun intended. But I did know that what I was doing by selling fake maple syrup was wrong, if nothing else.

And I think that knowledge was one of the reasons why I was so sure that I'd eventually get caught. There was no way I could keep on doing what I'd been doing forever, no matter what I might have convinced myself. In all honesty, you know, I didn't really think much about the future. My only real concern was getting through each day. But when I really thought about it, I realized there was no way I could have kept it going. So on some level, the fact that I'd gotten caught was actually kind of a relief to me. I didn't have to worry anymore about when it was going to happen. It had happened. Now at least I knew the devil I was dealing with. I just had to worry about how to get out of the trouble I'd gotten into.

We rode back to the Morrisville Police Station without talking. I was cool with that. I'd had a hell of a day, and I really wasn't in the mood. Music from the car's radio filled the silence inside the car with background noise. I was only half-conscious that a Gin Blossoms song was playing. When the lyrics hit my brain, though, I had a moment of sudden clarity. "If you don't expect too much from me, you might not be let down," Jesse Valenzuela sang as the guitar chords backed up his vocals. I had never heard a more perfect way to describe my attitude about my own life. You know what I mean? If all those people would just lower their expectations of me, I'd be a success in their eyes. It was as simple as that. If everybody around me would just quit expecting me to be someone I clearly wasn't cut out to be, I'd be fine. And the sooner they got that through their collective heads, the better off we'd all be.

As the song ended, we pulled into the Morrisville Police Station parking lot. I said good-bye to my new attorney, and promised him that I'd call him in the next couple of days. I got out and walked inside to pay whatever bill they were going to hit me with for towing my car, and to get back the keys to my truck. It had been a long day, and I had a feeling there were going to be a lot of those long days in my future before this whole thing was done.

CHAPTER THREE

There's a thing about the English language that I have always thought was funny. I'm the first one to admit that I'm no English scholar, but I've noticed in my time that language can work in some pretty funny ways. The state charges filed against me were pretty much based on the fact that I was selling maple syrup labeled as Vermont maple syrup. The argument against me was that I was claiming to people that the syrup itself was made in the state. The statute I was accused of breaking had all kinds of really complex descriptions about the requirements for when you were and when you weren't allowed to call something Vermont maple syrup. But basically it came down to the fact that the syrup had to have been made entirely in the state from maple sap harvested in the state. Blah, blah, blah. A bunch of legalese that made no sense to me.

But my lawyer's eyes lit up during one of our first meetings. He'd asked me about the specifics of the business, and I told him everything I've told you so far. The only thing I didn't think about was the kind of syrup I was actually buying. But he was all about the details like that. He asked me what it was and I told him, and that was when he got excited. Looked like a kid opening his birthday presents. Because the fake syrup I'd been selling was called "Vermont Maid," I had what he called a justifiable argument that I'd thought it was made in Vermont.

So in other words, I was as much of a victim in this whole thing as anybody else. I was a victim of some major food corporation's clever marketing team that had come up with a way to make money off the reputation of the Green Mountain State by playing a little game with the English language. Imagine the nerve of those people. You've gotta love it.

That little language hiccup made the state charges pretty easy to beat. The federal charges were a little tougher, basically because the folks throwing the accusations around had the backing of the United States government, which was enough to scare the bejeezus out of me. But once the state charges fell apart, the feds didn't seem to be too terribly excited about coming after me. I guess they had bigger fish to fry.

I won't bore you with all of the details about the whole affair, but let's just say that it was a long, strange trip through both the Vermont state and the United States federal legal systems. Thank God for my attorney, who actually believed in the fact that I was, underneath it all, a good guy who'd just done a stupid thing. More proof that there's a sucker born every minute, but I needed his support and I needed him to keep on believing in me, at least until I was free and clear. And thank God, too, for that language thing. What did my English teachers call those? Homophones? Something like that. Whatever they're called, thank God for them.

So between my lawyer's magic moves and the goofiness of how English happens to work, I managed to skate by with probation and a fine. The Department of Agriculture also issued me a cease-and-desist order, which meant my organic maple syrup days were over.

I was okay with that. Like I said earlier, I was relieved, in a way, that I didn't have to worry about getting caught anymore. I never found out who it was that had turned me in, but to this day I have a sneaking suspicion that it was my artist friend. She'd started dating a real maple syrup maker who no doubt wasn't happy to learn about my chosen occupation, especially after the check I'd written his girlfriend to pay for her artistic services bounced. Oh well. Buyer beware, as they say.

Eden is not a big town, and when you find your name on the front page of the local paper, you can bet it's not because you won the Congressional Medal of Honor. It's usually because you're this week's Public Enemy Number One, and when your name is a headline repeatedly like mine had been recently, you can't hide from it. Gossip spreads like chicken pox in a town that size, and before you even have a chance to explain to people your side of things, the story has changed so many times that you don't know where to start with defending yourself. And that assumes, of course, that you actually have a life worth defending. And a defense that's worth arguing in the first place, for that matter. That was all a lot of assumptions that I didn't want to deal with.

I had basically turned into a leper in Eden. My friends deserted me, my landlord canceled my lease. There was no way that I was going to be able to get a new job or a new apartment. I was branded. It was like I had a big sign around my neck that told everybody I was a criminal, wherever I went in town. People talked about me, and they'd point me out when they saw me. I was a con man. I was a counterfeiter. Worse. I was *the* con man, *the* counterfeiter. I'd broken the code. I'd ruined Vermont's fair reputation by selling a fake version of the state's most important export.

And of course, because I was such an outcast, the place I called home and the people I called my friends and family were also branded just like me. They'd had the horrible luck to be associated with me. So they did whatever they had to do in order to get away from me. I couldn't go anywhere or do anything. So I did what any self-respecting vagrant would do.

I made a plan to run away from home.

Yeah, I admit it. I was going to run away from home, but I was going to do it right. No bullshit. I planned to leave in the middle of the night without saying good-bye to anyone. I figured they'd all basically turned their backs on me when I was in trouble, so I wasn't going to give them the satisfaction of seeing me leave, of seeing me run away from home and all my problems. Maybe they'd miss me then. Maybe then they'd feel bad about how they'd treated me.

When I finally made the decision to haul ass, the only issue I could see that might screw it up was that I was leaving without giving my probation officer any notice. Technically, I wasn't allowed to leave the state without letting him know, and if I did, the court would immediately issue a warrant for my arrest. I hated to put myself back in that position of constantly worrying, but I had to get out just the same. I didn't have a choice in the matter.

I had debated with myself about whether to talk to my probation officer and tell him I was planning to leave Vermont. I figured that if I explained the circumstances, maybe he'd grant me permission, and all would be well. I went back and forth with myself, one day ready to pick up the phone, the next swearing myself to secrecy.

In the end, I decided against calling him and asking permission. While I would have liked nothing more than to have gotten his official permission to leave and do the whole thing legally, I was more worried about him not allowing me to go, which would have meant that I would either be stuck in Vermont or, if I still decided to leave, on a watch list as a possible flight risk.

But after all was said and done, I decided that what he didn't know wouldn't hurt him, and I left it at that. I wasn't supposed to check in with him for several weeks, and by that time, I hoped I'd be too hard to find to make it worth their while to come after me.

And then there was my family to think about. Of course, I didn't think too long about them. Just like everybody else in Eden, they'd more or less started to pretend they didn't know who I was, let alone that they were actually related to me. So I just wiped them off my radar altogether. We weren't real close to begin with, even though they were my parents. Now it was like they didn't even exist.

I knew I would need cash, though, because using my credit card was going to be like wearing a tracking device to help them find me. And my whole strategy about staying hidden relied on the fact that I wasn't that important for them to go to any real trouble to locate me. But if I just planned to paint a big target on myself that they could see from space, I might as well just give up now. So I schemed a way to do it a little less obviously; my con man's brain was still alive and well inside my head, still messing with how I thought and how I acted.

I had about $3,000 in the bank at the time, but I knew that if I went in and drained my account all at once, they'd probably get a little suspicious. And since I was who I was—the Notorious Billy Faulkner—I didn't even want to go in and face the tellers in person. So I decided to do it through the ATM.

I was only allowed to take out $400 from an ATM in any single day, so I did just that. I took out $400 every day for a week, socking it away underneath a little flap of carpeting behind the seat in the cab of my truck. For some reason, I thought it would be safer there than in the apartment I was getting kicked out of. Sure, I was a little scared somebody might break into my truck, but that was a risk I was willing to take.

It wasn't like I had any kind of strict schedule to stick to, but I did want to get the hell out of town as quickly as I could. So as soon as I had emptied my account, I packed up the truck with the few things I owned, bid a fond farewell to my hometown, and started driving. I didn't have a specific destination in mind, but I knew I needed to go south. North was Canada, and that didn't help. I didn't even have a passport, so leaving the country was out.

So south it was. I picked up Interstate 91 just east of Irasburg and turned right. South. Away from Eden, away from the Northeast Kingdom, away from Vermont.

Three hours later, I'd crossed into Massachusetts. I was now officially a fugitive, because I'd illegally left the state of Vermont. There was nothing I could do about it now, though, so I just kept looking straight ahead. But I was eventually going to have to stop. I was getting tired, and I needed to eat. And besides, it was getting close to ten o'clock.

I found a cheap motel off the highway in Greenfield. I went inside to the front desk, where I found a kid who couldn't have been more than eighteen. Bloodshot eyes, kind of a stupid grin on his face. Stoned out of his mind. I had to laugh.

"You got a room I can get for the night?" I asked.

"Yeah, dude. Fifty bucks. No pets, checkout is eleven in the morning." He ended his little speech with a cough that he tried to cover up, followed by a laugh that he also tried to hide. It was a good try, but it was still pretty obvious that he was high.

I told him that would be fine, and I paid for the room in cash. After he told me about what was going to be available for breakfast and the location of my room, he gave me a plastic key card for the room. I drove around to the back side of the property, where I'd been told I would find my room. Single king bed, smoking, cable TV included.

It was a pretty standard motel room. A bed with a thin brown comforter, cheap art prints on the wall, cheap furniture. It reeked of stale cigarettes, and the carpet had a bunch of burn marks. The key card advertised a local pizza delivery place on it, and as soon as I got inside the room, I cranked up the air conditioning, and then called to order dinner.

I showered while I waited for the pizza to arrive. The hot water pounding down on my head and back felt really good. When the delivery guy finally showed up, I was starving. I scarfed down the whole thing in about five minutes, then collapsed into the bed. I hadn't realized how tired my body really was. I guess it was a combination of the stress of running away and the driving, plus the fact that it was late. That whole combination had finally gotten to me, and I could barely stay upright. But it was weird, you know, because I wasn't all that sleepy. It was a strange feeling to have my body be totally physically exhausted, but to have my brain be still kind of awake at the same time.

I flipped on the television to see what was on. I figured I was paying for it, since it was included in the price of the room, so I should take advantage of it. Scrolling through the channels, I stopped on a commercial for some ambulance-chasing lawyer. It was one of those terribly dramatic scenes. You know what I'm talking about, right? Sirens and a hospital emergency room, then a cutaway to a guy in a tie who was supposed to be the lawyer that would be coming to visit you in the hospital and sit by your bedside while you were recovering. He said something about fighting the insurance companies on your behalf, and the scene changed to a bunch of guys in a big conference room, all of them talking about screwing over this client who'd been in a car accident.

It was, at the time, nothing more than a commercial, really, and one that I'd seen a thousand times before. Something that flashed on the screen that I normally would have forgotten about as soon as it was over. Just a thirty-second space filler that interrupted an otherwise perfectly good television show, a way for the network to pay for the airtime. But what I was beginning to figure out for the first time—or maybe what I'd known all along, but was just now beginning to realize—was that everything I did, every single moment of my life, seemed to have an impact on my future, no matter how insignificant those moments seemed at the time. And my choice to stop pushing the channel-change button on the remote right then was yet another single action that seemed so small by itself at the time. But it was one that would end up having pretty serious, far-reaching effects on my life.

It didn't so much register in my brain right then, though. The regularly scheduled programming came back on, and the moment was gone. The current offering was some cop show that you had to be following from the beginning in order to truly appreciate, and my mind started to wander. Gradually my eyelids began to get heavy, and I couldn't keep them open. I drifted off to sleep, and as I did, the image of the insurance agents in that commercial started to dance around in my mind.

*   *   *

The next morning, I woke up early, even though I was still tired from a horrible night's sleep. But I knew that the sooner I got going, the sooner I could be farther away from Vermont. And I wanted to get far away fast. So I fought the urge to go back to sleep, and instead pulled myself up and out of the bed. I decided against a shower; I just pulled on the same clothes I'd worn the day before and ran my fingers through my hair, trying to push it down a little.

I skipped the free breakfast in the lobby of the motel. From what I'd seen last night, what they were trying to pass off as breakfast wasn't much more than a rotten apple and a stale piece of toast. I'd grab something later if I got hungry. After a quick look around the room to make sure I hadn't forgotten anything, I walked out of my room into the early morning air. The sun was just starting to come up over the trees that had been planted in what was basically a failed attempt to hide the motel's parking area. A quick stop at the gas station to fill up the truck, and I was back on the highway, driving south.

As I drove, it occurred to me that this road trip I was on didn't have quite the romance I'd always thought that cross-country trips had. I mean, Massachusetts is actually a pretty nice state when you think about all the scenery. It's got nice beaches, and there are lots of trees and flowers and historic buildings. But when all you see is the side of the interstate, you know, it looks pretty much like every other place in the world when you see it from the highway. There's no romance, there's no culture. There's Texaco and there's McDonald's and there's Travel Plaza exits. But that's it. I doubted there was an artist anywhere, dead or alive, that could make this scenery interesting.

By the time I got to Connecticut, I'd only been driving an hour, but I felt like I'd been on the road for days. I hadn't slept well the night before, and I was definitely feeling the effects of the stress of the last several weeks of my life. I needed to take a day—or a week or a month— and relax. I needed to stop somewhere soon and start to make a new life.

I drove into the city of Hartford, and I just made the decision all of a sudden to stop running.

To tell you the God's honest truth, I'm not entirely sure what it was that made me choose to stop in Hartford. I do know that I'd always liked the idea of living in Connecticut, because it had always seemed very nice, very upscale. So many of the tourists that came to Vermont during foliage season were from Connecticut, and they were always beautiful people with beautiful wives and beautiful children and beautiful cars. I was sure they lived beautiful lives back home in Connecticut, and that image had always stuck with me. I wanted to be one of those beautiful people and live that life.

Once I got into the actual city limits, it seemed like the number of billboards I saw advertising insurance agencies increased. My mind sort of clicked back to that commercial I'd been watching on TV, and again I saw myself sitting in that conference room. An honest-to-God professional, making an honest-to-God living in a legitimate profession. A profession that didn't require me to look over my shoulder the whole time. A profession that didn't also include the title of con man as a part of the job description.

The more I thought about it, the more I liked the idea. As I hit the city limits, I had made my mind up. I was going to get a job selling insurance. If I could sell maple syrup, I could sell insurance. I was sure of it. That was going to be my ticket to a legitimate life.

I found a little roadside motel, and I got a room at a cheap weekly rate. I went to the convenience store at the end of the block and bought a newspaper, then went back to my room and opened the paper straight to the classifieds. I was going to do this the right way this time around. Find people looking for employees, and then present myself as the answer to their Human Resources prayers. I scanned the help-wanted ads, circling insurance sales jobs that looked promising. My prerequisites were pretty basic. I looked for ads that included "will train the right person," or "no experience necessary." My ideal job listings included both of those phrases. If I was anything, it was inexperienced, at least in terms of the qualifications I had to offer. But I was willing to play the part of being the right person, no matter what that person looked or sounded like. I could be him.

I ended up with five possibilities, which sounded to me like a pretty good start to my search. Maybe this whole new life of mine was going to work out after all. All of a sudden, pieces were falling into place. In fact, maybe they were falling into place too quickly. Looking back on it, maybe I should have seen that as a problem. But I didn't think about it too much, so it didn't bother me. I was too busy planning how I was going to spend my six-figure salary to worry about it. Ski weekends in Aspen and trips to Anguilla sounded like the perfect way to reward myself for working as an honest businessman and earning a huge income for all of my hard work.

It was Sunday, so there was no point in calling offices. I decided instead to take a walk, just to get my bearings, you know. Just a chance to figure out where I was, and kind of get the lay of the land. A few blocks away from the motel was a pretty run-down-looking church, and the black sign outside announced in white plastic letters that those seeking new direction in their lives were welcome inside. Some kind of force compelled me to walk in. Maybe it was the hand of God Himself guiding me; maybe it was just the fact that I couldn't think of any other way to kill an hour. Or maybe it was just a big coincidence. Whatever the reason, I walked in.

The service had already started, and I slid myself into an empty pew in the back row. I immediately felt anything but welcome. I didn't care what the sign outside said. The church was filled with black faces, the women wearing some of the most outrageous hats I'd ever seen in my life. A few people shot confused looks in my general direction, and I could feel the blood rising up into my face.

The whole thing reminded of a scene from *The Lords of Discipline*. It was a movie I'd loved since the first time I saw it. The story was about the integration of The Citadel, a military college in Charleston, South Carolina. In the scene I was thinking of, one of the students is talking to the commandant of cadets, who says that he is looking for "the fly shit in the sugar." What it is that he's actually looking for is the first black cadet in the middle of the crowd of new freshmen that are arriving on campus for the first day of the fall semester. For the first time in my life, I could relate to what that first black cadet felt like on that first day of school. It was a really bizarre feeling.

Somebody a lot smarter than me once told me that being white was what he called an invisible marker. What he meant by that was that you don't notice white people, because they're the standard. You know? They're everywhere, so you get used to seeing them, and you get to where you don't even notice that they're white. It's not an issue. So either you're white or you're not. You're either white or you're other. That's how it usually is, anyway. But just at that moment in time in that small church, it was actually blackness that was the invisible marker. As the only white guy in the place, I was alone. I was the other. I was the albino fly shit in the bowl of brown sugar.

The preacher—I guess that's what they would call the guy who was speaking, though I'm not totally sure what his title was—was nearly screaming at his audience. They were all staring at him like he was God himself. He was holding a Bible in his hand, and every once in a while, he would open it and quote some passage that proved the point he was making.

"Brothers and sisters, the Good Book tells us that we must work hard to gain favor in the eyes of the Lord," he screamed. He flipped open the Bible and read: "Work hard and become a leader; be lazy and never succeed." He gasped for air, letting that little bit of wisdom sink in. He dabbed the sweat from his huge forehead with a handkerchief that he pulled out of his front pants pocket. Heads nodded and hands were raised, and an occasional "Amen" came out from somewhere in front of me as the true believers were moved to speak.

After a too-long dramatic pause on his part, the preacher continued. "Brothers and sisters, the Lord wants us to work hard. If we work hard, we will achieve the Kingdom. Hard work is our insurance of eternal glory."

That sank in with me. It was another hand-of-God moment. Or maybe it was the first hand-of-God moment. Or maybe still it was just another of those random moments in time that I didn't see as very important, that might turn out to be important after all. My decision to try out this new life had just been shown to me to be a go, compliments of this man's dramatic speech. I'd never met him before—and I would probably never ever see him again—but he told me exactly what I'd needed to hear. It was like he was talking just to me the whole time.

The insurance industry was going to be, appropriately enough, my own little personal insurance policy. I couldn't have cared less about achieving the Kingdom; I didn't believe in that heaven-and-hell crap anyway. But the idea of an insurance policy that could, if nothing else, keep me financially stable and relatively happy was enough to make me focus even stronger on my new career plans. He could keep his fire and brimstone. I just wanted to make a living as something other than a fledgling con artist.

I snuck out the back during the closing hymn. The congregation was singing along with the choir, some song about finding a new life in Christ. It was a pretty moving spectacle, actually, with so many people singing with such passion and volume. My hope was that everyone was so into singing the hymn that they wouldn't catch the honky leaving early. I don't know if anybody noticed; I didn't turn around to find out. I just didn't care.

It reminded me of how I'd left Eden.

CHAPTER FOUR

The next day, bright and early, I set out on my new crusade. I was a changed man. An easy buck was an easy buck, but there was something to be said for a legitimate job that would pay me for doing actual work that was actually also legal. That seemed like a hell of a combination at the time, you know, given what I'd been doing before. I had this whole new sense of direction that morning. I was going to prove to myself and the rest of the world that I could get and do a real job, one that I could actually talk about.

I took as hot a shower as I could stand. I was trying to make enough steam in the bathroom to iron out at least some of the wrinkles in the only dress clothes I owned. It wasn't much, let me tell you. A pair of khaki pants, an oxford shirt, and a navy-blue blazer I'd bought at a thrift shop somewhere along the way. Not really sure why I bought the stuff, to tell you truth. I guess it was just something I figured I might need one day, you now, just in case I decided to go legit. They looked like hell and didn't fit worth a damn, but they were all I had to offer. Part of me thought that if I looked hungry enough, it might actually work in my favor that I was wearing secondhand—not to mention second-rate—dress clothes to an interview.

While I got dressed, I rehearsed my spiel. I had just moved down from Vermont, where there just wasn't any work that I could get. The fact that I hadn't gone to college was because my parents couldn't afford to send me. They were farmers, you know, and money was tight. But from them I'd learned the value of hard work for an honest day's pay, and I'd also learned that I would only be rewarded inasmuch as I earned. I was ready to work hard to provide for myself. I hoped it sounded both genuine and professional.

Driving through the crowded streets of Hartford, I was suddenly, painfully aware of how much of a small-town kid I really was. We definitely weren't in Eden anymore, Toto. Cars whizzed by me on either side, people on their way to work. Part of me was completely intimidated by all these professional types surrounding me on every side. I could see them looking at me, and I started imagining what they were thinking. But it was kind of a cool feeling, too, to know that I was right there with them. As far as they knew, I was just like them. I was just another ant in the hill, making my way to the nine-to-five job that paid my mortgage.

The first place I went had seemed like the best option on paper. It was a big firm with national offices all over the place. Their ad said that the position had room for advancement, and that they often promoted from within. If I worked hard, they claimed, I could be making six figures inside of a few years. That sounded good to me. My parents had never made any real money in their lives, so the thought of that many zeros in my bank account was exciting to me.

The thoughts of those zeros pretty much disappeared as soon as I walked in the place. When I got there, the receptionist looked at me like I had three heads when I told her I was there about the help-wanted ad. She asked if I had an appointment. "No," I admitted. "I just moved here, and wanted to hit the ground running. Is it a bad time?"

She shot me a look that I couldn't quite tell you what it was. Maybe it was anger that I'd bothered her. Maybe it was just her thinking she was better than me. Then she looked down at a desk calendar in front of her. "Can you come back at two? We can fit you in then." She hissed it almost, you know? Like a snake trying to warn you. There wasn't any hint of optimism in her voice. Nothing to indicate that she thought that I had a snowball's chance in hell of ever getting past her desk as a genuine insurance agent for this company.

I thought for a minute, trying to make her think I was in demand, and that my schedule was so crazy I'd have to move some things around if I was going to stoop so low as to come back at two and fit her into my day. "I think I can make that work," I said after a couple of seconds. "I'll see you at two." I turned to go, but stopped. "Thanks for fitting me in," I said to her over my shoulder. I gave her my best poor-puppy-dog look.

She almost cracked a smile. Almost. Did she appreciate my attempt at looking pitiful, and was now going to give me a chance? "You're welcome."

I turned to go again. I didn't feel much better about my chances, but at least there was a little light of hope there.

She cleared her throat. "Um, sir? You might as well fill out this application while you're here. That'll save you some time when you come back," she said. Her voice sounded a little bit friendlier all of a sudden. Maybe my pitiful look had worked, and now she was going to finally take me seriously. Or was she just going through the motions that she had to go through? Something her boss had told her to do?

Whatever it was, I took it as a positive sign. I took the application she was holding out to me and sat down to fill it out. Name, address, all the usual stuff. Because I didn't have a mailing address yet, I left that blank. For a contact phone number, I listed my cell number. Then I came to the question of criminal background.

Have you ever been convicted of a crime? If yes, please explain.

If you've never been in the position of having to answer that question with a yes, you'll never be able to appreciate the heartbeat-skipping moment that comes with lying. Trust me when I tell you, though, it sucks. Especially when it comes on right after you've had what you thought was a divinely inspired moment of life-turning-around action.

Like I told you before, I'm not a religious man. My parents thought organized religion was a ridiculous charade, so I was pretty much baptized into the world of agnosticism. Atheism, apparently, required too much devotion to a cause for my parents to follow. They weren't real big on all-or-nothing kinds of belief systems. After all, believing in nothing itself constituted a united and organized stand against something, which meant its own kind of odd dogma. So my parents instead chose to believe in nothing. They figured everything would sort itself out in the end, no matter what they did.

Despite growing up in what was pretty much a religious vacuum and not having any real religion I claimed as mine, I said a small prayer at that moment of truth, when it came time to answer the question about my experiences with the legal system. Silently I said in my mind, "God, if you're out there, let me get past this. I promise to turn the corner. But I've got to get this job before I can do that. Please. Just this one time, then no more lying." I checked the "no" box and moved on. If God listened and I got the job, I really hoped I could hold up my end of the bargain. I mean, I fully intended to. That much I was sure of. But I needed God to hold up His end of the bargain in this thing.

For my job history, I listed my father's farm as my only work experience. I figured that, if nothing else, it would be a good conversation piece. Kid from a farm in Vermont wants to sell insurance. The American success story come true, you know? Yeah, it was an exaggeration. But it wasn't a total lie. I'd helped my parents on the farm for many years. I hadn't gotten paid anything, outside of them giving me a place to live. But it was still a job, and I kind of hoped they'd skip calling them to make sure I'd worked there. They'd pretty much disowned me by then, and I didn't think they'd be real happy about giving me a job reference. But I'd worked there, damn it, and that counted as work experience, as far as I could see. So God and I were still straight.

It took me about twenty minutes to get the application filled out. I handed it back to the receptionist, who had gone back to her earlier bitchy attitude. She looked at the piece of paper I handed her like it was a snake. She didn't even look up as she muttered, "Thank you. See you at two."

I pretty much lost any hope I'd managed to build up in my mind about getting this job. My spirits sank immediately. If she was the one who passed the applications on to her boss, there's no telling what she might tell him about me. I would be known as the Vermont hick with no mailing address who showed up without an appointment. The hayseed hick who thought he could sell insurance. I was going to be the butt of a bunch of jokes around the old water cooler.

I wanted to disappear as I walked out of the office. It was the first time in my life I'd felt totally like I wasn't a part of this world. I hadn't been born into it, and working my way into it wasn't going to be quite so easy as just showing up in a ratty blazer and announcing my presence. It reminded me again of those Connecticut tourists that invaded Vermont in the fall. They had it all—money, cars, houses. But they'd been born with parents that already had it, so they were just continuing that cycle, you know? I didn't know how I was going to break into it.

Outside, those feelings of not belonging got even stronger. People walked by me, talking importantly on their cell phones. Their conversations, I imagined, were high-level business deals involving millions of dollars changing hands. The longer I stood there watching the world go by me, the worse I felt about myself and my position in it. I couldn't understand some of the words these people were using, and I felt hopeless about my prospects for ever entering their world.

I walked slowly back to the truck, looking at the ground and feeling totally dejected. My mind began to race, and when I get to thinking, it's usually a bad thing. The ideas my twisted thinking is able to come up with usually take the path of least resistance, no matter the subject. And in the case of my own survival—which would mean I'd have to be able to make a living—that path of least resistance meant they went straight to thinking about how to scam some poor bastard out of money. It would be the easiest way to live, and it was a job I was at least qualified for. I had to physically stop walking and take a minute to clear my mind. I didn't want to go back to those days, and I just had to keep plugging away until I found something.

Back at my truck, I looked again at my list of job prospects. Clearly this was going to involve a lot more luck than I'd first imagined, and I decided on a different strategy. Where I'd first thought that bigger was better, it occurred to me that bigger might also mean harder to get. So I looked for ads for smaller companies. I figured those might be the ones that had less of a formal application process. I kind of thought it would be possible to start small, you know, and get some experience. Then I'd show up and tell that bitch what's what.

The first one to catch my eye said it had an "immediate need," and that little golden rainbow that I wanted to see, the phrase involving a willingness to "train the right person." I hadn't noticed it the first time, I guess, but I was now really happy to see that it also said, "No phone calls." No phone calls meant no appointment necessary, or at least that's what I told myself. That was my next target.

Driving to the address listed in the ad, I kept looking at the buildings around me. I was expecting to see a high-rise building appear, but all I saw were run-down, squatty little buildings with bars on the windows. Broken windows and graffiti. A man sleeping on the street with an empty malt liquor bottle lying next to him. I parked on the side of the street outside a windowless brick building. I was a little confused as I got out of the truck. This couldn't be an insurance agency. It looked more like a one-story prison.

But the address above the door matched the address in the classified ad, so I assumed that I was at the right place. And you can bet that I wasn't in the position to be judging a book by its cover, given that I was hoping for a little bit of temporary blindness on the part of my would-be employers. If it was a small-time operation that I was looking for, then I guess you could say that I'd certainly found that. If nothing else, it would be an income. And like I said, it was just a place to get experience.

By that time, I had already planned the speech I was going to give that receptionist from the first place when I got a job there and had the chance to fire her. I can hold a grudge, you know, and I don't miss a chance to get back at somebody that does something to me. But what's more is that I wasn't trying to impress anybody by telling them where I worked. Hell, I didn't even know anybody to try and impress. So I really didn't care what the outside looked like. Or the inside, for that matter. I just wanted a job.

The door was solid metal, with a small peephole at eye level. There was no doorbell, no knocker. I made a fist and banged; the hollow noise echoed through my ears and the vibration from the door rattled my arm. I stepped back from the door, waiting for it to open. I thought of that scene in *The Wizard of Oz*. The one where they knock on the door at Emerald City. It was kind of like that.

I shot a quick glance down the sidewalk to my left, where an old woman wearing an old, ripped dress with flowers on it and an umbrella hat shuffled along on her bare feet as she pushed a grocery shopping cart filled with a bunch of random stuff she'd salvaged from trash cans.

"What?"

My head snapped around, back to facing the door. The tough-sounding voice that had barked the question came from behind it.

"Uh, hi," I said. I felt a little strange standing there talking to a door, but whoever it was that was talking to me hadn't decided to open it yet. "I'm here about the insurance job?"

The sound of multiple deadbolts sliding back. A chain being unhooked. Might have even been a bar releasing the tension it had had when it was pushing against the closed door to keep other people out. The door cracked open a few inches, and all I could see was a single pair of eyes staring at me questioningly. Brown eyes, a little bit bloodshot.

"You're serious?" the voice asked after a second's worth of looking at me.

The question surprised me. "Of course," I said.

"You from the NAIC?"

I had no idea what that meant, so I answered honestly. "No. I'm here about the job, sir."

The door opened more, and all of a sudden there was a towering black man wearing a poor-fitting brown suit and yellow shirt that didn't hide the bulging muscles in his arms. His tie had a shiny look, almost like it was metallic. It kind of looked like it had been sprayed with lacquer. It was the second time in as many days that I'd felt immediately uncomfortable in the presence of a person of another race.

I pretty much felt ashamed of myself for that. I had never actually considered the idea that I might be working for a black man. Whenever I thought of business owners, for whatever reason, the image was always of white guys in suits. But then I thought about the exterior of the building, I realized that the thoughts I'd had a second ago about appearances were happening again. I was in no position to be worried about what I thought my boss was supposed to look like. I needed a job; this guy apparently needed an employee. I quickly decided that I didn't care about what he or his office looked like. If has was black, big deal.

He motioned me in and I entered.

CHAPTER FIVE

The inside of the office, even to my small-town, farmer-kid mind, looked like anything but a professional setting. Fluorescent lighting, manila folders in a stack on the floor next to a desk, brown shag carpeting, two desks. It was a far cry from the place I'd been earlier, where a cute receptionist had at least been behind a desk, even though she was kind of a bitch to me. This guy was sitting on the other end of that spectrum.

He sat at one of the desks and motioned for me to have a seat in the chair next to the other desk. It was one of those discount office store chairs, black fake leather that was cracking in places. As I sat, somewhere beneath me there was a loud squeak that sounded like the chair was in physical pain. But both it and I managed to keep from tumbling to the floor. Somewhere there was music playing just loudly enough to be heard. I couldn't tell where it was coming from, but it was some old R&B tune.

And the smell. The whole office smelled like those cheap cigars you get in the foil packaging at a convenience store. It was like the smell was just coming up out of the carpet and filling the whole room.

I sat there for about two minutes, waiting for the guy to say something. Anything. But he just sat there, sizing me up, trying to figure out if this white kid in the wrinkled clothes was for real. Finally he coughed, cleared his throat, and introduced himself. "I'm Victor Baines," he said. "And you are?"

"Billy Faulkner."

He nodded and chewed on the inside of his bottom lip. "You're new in town, I'm going to guess," he said after a second.

"Yes, sir," I said. "I just moved down from Vermont. Looking for a fresh start."

More lip chewing. "Figured you weren't from around here. Anybody white who knows Hartford would have seen the address in that classified ad and stayed the fuck away." He laughed. "I've owned this little outfit for fifteen years, and you're the first white guy who's ever shown up for a job."

I didn't quite know how to take that. I didn't want to admit to myself that it made me feel uncomfortable. I wanted to say it didn't bother me, and that a job was a job. But it kind of did bother me, you know?

But more than that, I needed a job. That thought was at the front of my mind, and I was willing to push any uncomfortable feelings somewhere down deep inside if it meant I'd make enough money to eat. Before I had a chance to say anything, though, he beat me to the punch. It was almost like he was reading my mind.

"Listen, kid. I don't give a rat's ass if you're white, black, yellow, or plaid. We're not going to be friends. If you get this job, I'm your boss, and that's it. If you can do what I need you to do, I'll hire you." He turned in his chair to face his desk, then grabbed a yellow pad of paper from his desk, yanked open a drawer, and took out a pen. He wrote something on the paper, then looked back up at me. "You ever sold insurance, kid?"

I thought briefly about lying, but remembered my promise. Honesty. New leaf. All that. "No, sir," I admitted. "But I'm a quick learner. You show me what to do, and I'll promise you I can do it. I'm organized, I'm depen—"

"Shut up, kid." He laughed. "You know how many half-assed unemployed fucks walk in here and tell me that they're quick learners that are dependable and organized? How many people that can't read a book are good at multitasking? Hell, half of them can't read better than a second grader, and most of 'em are drunk. I don't want to hear that. I want to hear about you." He coughed again, then spat into a nearby trash can. "You said you're looking to make a new start. What's that about? Tell me about it."

I don't know what got me started, but I just started talking. Maybe it was the fact that he didn't mind cussing around me, even though I was interviewing for a job. Maybe it was the smell of the cigar smoke that was giving me a contact buzz. Maybe it was that ball of phlegm he'd coughed up from somewhere down in the deepest part of his charred lungs. Whatever it was, I unloaded. I told him about Eden. I told him about my parents. I told him about wanting to get the hell out of Anytown, USA, and do something with my life. And I told him about the maple syrup scam.

That's when he started laughing. "You telling me you sold those people the same crap they can buy in the grocery store?"

"Yes, sir," I said. And then I was laughing along with him. "Dumb motherfuckers didn't know the difference." As soon as I'd said it, I stopped laughing. I couldn't believe I'd just busted out with that in the middle of a job interview. "Oh, God," I finally managed to say. "I'm sorry. I usually don't swear like that. It's just, you know, I guess –"

He cut me off again. "Bullshit, kid. A little curse word here and there, it's good for the soul." He laughed again. "White boy scamming rich white people," he said to himself. "What a concept." More scribbling on the notepad.

Then he turned his attention back to me. He scratched his chin, looked at me like he was looking at a painting somewhere behind my head. Studying me. "You know, people say that you can't teach an old dog new tricks. Once a scam artist, always a scam artist." He let that last shot hang in the air, like a smoke ring he'd blown after pulling on one of his Swisher Sweets.

I was silent, my pulse banging in my wrist. Did this guy just call me a scam artist? Yeah, I'd run something of a shady business, but look around you, dude. You call this an insurance office? You've got a hell of a lot of nerve throwing insults around like that, you know what I mean? But I swallowed hard and resisted the urge to let him have what I thought he actually deserved. "Like I said, sir. That's behind me. I'm here to make a new start," I finally managed to say.

He had this way of positioning his left hand, his thumb under his chin with his index finger lying flat against his cheek and his middle finger right under his nose. The other three fingers were curled around, like he was hiding something in them. He worked his bottom lip with his teeth and kept studying me, silent the whole time. "New start, same shit," he said finally.

Just like that, I was back down in that hopeless feeling. Just a second before, I'd been rolling along. Four words later, I'm done. Reality was creeping in. My past was not going to be an easy thing for me to deal with, and I was going to have to develop a better story. If I couldn't get a job in this place, there was no way I was going to get a job anywhere respectable. I was already thinking ahead, thinking about packing up the truck and moving on. I started to stand up, because I figured this interview was over.

"Where you going, kid? I'm not done yet."

It kind of scared me, the way he said it, because I'd been all wrapped up in my own thoughts. But I did what he'd told me to do and sat back in the chair. Maybe there was more insulting left to be done. He leaned back in his chair and dug a thin, black cigar out of the inside of his suit jacket. He lit it and blew out a stream of blue-gray smoke. He was smacking his lips while he blew, savoring the taste of that smoke. It smelled a little bit like cherry pie. The way he kept running his tongue across his teeth and moving his mouth around, it looked like he was eating cherry pie, too.

"Look, kid. Billy. Billy. Billy Faulkner. Listen here, Billy Faulkner. Selling insurance? It's just like selling that bullshit syrup you were hawking out of your truck. Same goddamn thing, just a different name. All this," he waved his hand around, pointing at the inside of the office, "is just a big con game. The shit I sell? People don't need it. They don't want it. Hell, they don't even know what they're buying. But they think they do. They think they need it, they think they want it, and they think they know what it is."

He took a deep drag off his cigar and blew the smoke out violently. "I need somebody who can sell rat shit to a housewife and make her think she's getting filet mignon to serve her husband for dinner." He paused for a second and looked at me, dead serious. "I need somebody who can sell Aunt Jemima syrup and convince people they're getting something special."

He tossed the pad of paper back onto his desk, and then turned to face me again. "You were straight with me, kid, so I'm going to be straight with you. I'm not what you might call a regular insurance agent. Most of my clients don't drive Mercedes, and they don't spend their summers in Newport or Block Island or wherever the fuck else those rich white folks go. But they scrape some money together and hand it over to me, because I make them trust me. That's all there is to it. If you can sell fake maple syrup, you can sell my insurance. Simple as that."

I was stunned, to say the least. "Are you offering me a job?"

His entire face all of a sudden turned to stone. He looked at me, almost like he was accusing me of something. His eyes narrowed. "What? You got an issue with working for a nigger?"

My heart flew into my throat. The word hit me like a brick being thrown at my head. He'd said it with so much violence, so much anger in his voice. Those were emotions that hadn't been there just a few seconds before. I was scared speechless, to tell you the truth. Then he burst out laughing. "Billy Faulkner, you're going to have to get a sense of humor if you're going to make it in here," he said. "Dumbass cracker."

He stood, and I did too. He extended his hand, I took it in mine. "You be here tomorrow morning at nine. We'll talk about money and all that shit then." He looked me up and down, and the expression on his face told me he wasn't impressed with what he saw. He reached into his pants pocket and pulled out a wad of bills. He peeled off a pair of hundreds and handed them to me. "Get yourself some pants and a couple of shirts. Call that your signing bonus." He looked at me again, then pulled out another hundred. "And for chrissake, eat something."

I put the money in my pocket and smiled, kind of devilish-like. "I didn't accept the job yet," I said. I looked him up and down like he'd done to me. "I'm still trying to figure out if I want to work for a nigger."

He burst into another laugh , this one bigger than the last, and slapped me on the back. "Billy Faulkner, you're all right, kid. For a white boy, that is. Now get the fuck out of my office and don't let anybody out there catch sight of that money, or you'll be back to being your old broke self in no time at all. I'll see you tomorrow. You're gonna be all right here, kid."

He pushed me out the door and shut it, leaving me standing on the sidewalk. I'd done it. I'd gotten a job. Granted, it wasn't necessarily the be-all and end-all. But it was a job, and I'd come by it honestly. Things were looking up all of a sudden. I could hear the deadbolt being locked behind me, and Victor's laughter still coming through the thick door.

CHAPTER SIX

I started to head back to my room. I felt great about the fact that I'd landed an honest job. And it seemed like it had been so easy to do, you know? I'd spent so long doing illegal work that it kind of became normal for me, you know, to be worried about getting caught. I didn't realize how much it had become part of my daily life. So when I was in this new place all of a sudden, with a job that was a real job that wasn't going to get me arrested, it was like I felt totally free. And since I'd never really felt it before, it was really, really amazing. I don't have any other way to describe. It's one of those things that if you've never felt it before, you can't quite understand how good it feels. And it was all happening so fast around me. It was a fun ride to be on, I can tell you that much.

Victor seemed like a good guy. Good sense of humor, easygoing. I figured he'd be easy to work for. He didn't strike me as the type to be on my ass about getting work done. It bothered me a little bit that we hadn't talked about how much he was planning to pay me, but my father told me once that something was better than nothing. And since I had nothing just then, anything Victor wanted to pay me was better than that. And if that wad of bills he was carrying around in his pocket was any kind of sign, I thought there was a good chance that he might actually pay me enough to make it worth my while to get out of bed in the morning. So I let my worries about payday slide, and I tried to count my blessings.

I hadn't driven too far when I saw a men's clothing store that was advertising a big sale. One of those folding signs with the neon letters stuck to it standing outside the door. It wasn't any sort of upscale place, that much was pretty obvious from the look of the outside. No mannequins wearing the latest styles standing in the window, no rich-sounding name written in expensive-looking letters above the door.

Instead they had clothes hung up on a metal rod outside, and that sign telling men that they could save up to 50 percent off anything in the store. I figured the two hundred bucks Victor had given me for clothes would be enough to at least get me some new work clothes.

I parked the truck on the street and stopped for a second outside the place, checking out the suits hanging on the rack on the sidewalk. I didn't know a lot about business suits, but even I could tell these were cheap. I pulled one of the jackets off its hanger and slid it on. Before I could even start to tell you what I thought about it, a voice from inside yelled at me.

"You try that on inside, boy!"

The sudden noise startled me. I looked into the dark entryway, and I could barely make out the frame of what I guessed was a man standing in the doorway. Looked more like a five-foot-tall, black, shapeless thing standing there. But that deep voice told me it was a man.

"Yeah, you. You want to try on the clothes, you do it inside."

I slid the coat off and returned it to the hanger. "Sorry about that," I said. "I didn't realize that was how things worked."

I slowly walked towards the doorway, leaving the suits on their hangers. As I got close to the entrance, the figure blocking my way came more into focus. His body wasn't quite as menacing as his voice suggested. He was about my height and build. In other words, he wasn't any kind of awesome specimen of humanity, you know? The kind of guy that if you were an eyewitness to a crime, you'd describe him as having an average build.

He stepped back to let me come in, and as my eyes adjusted to the lower light inside, I could make out his features. He was black—no surprise there, given the neighborhood. But he was *really* black. Midnight-black skin. Short-cropped hair. Plus that whole average build thing.

The inside of the place had a stench of bad cologne, and a whole lot of it. Something spicy and not totally disgusting, just too much of it. A stereo speaker sitting on the floor in the back corner of the place crackled from too much bass being pushed through it, and under the crackle a singer crooned something about "you got, you got it bad." The man who'd been blocking the doorway now stood behind me, no doubt trying to figure out why this white kid was coming into his store.

"Help you find something?" he grunted.

I cleared my throat as I turned around to face him. "Actually, I just got a job working down the street, and my new boss told me I needed some new clothes to go with the new job. I saw your sign outside, and thought I'd see what you had." It felt really good to say that. I needed a new uniform to go with my new life. A businessman's uniform, at that.

He looked at me. "Damn straight you need some new clothes." He laughed under his breath as he took in the full picture of the clothes I was wearing. "Tell me. Who's a white boy like you workin' for down this part of town?"

"Victor Baines."

What had started as kind of a polite chuckle all of a sudden turned into a full-blown belly laugh. "You workin' for that hustler? Goddamn! Went and hired himself a white boy, tryin' to get hisself some cred with the money folks, huh?"

I didn't know what to say, so I just smiled, like I was part of the joke. "Yeah, I guess." I turned away and began to look at the selection of shirts folded and stacked on a table in the middle of the store. "How much?" I asked. "For the shirts?"

"Twenty bucks each," he said. "Three for fifty. Those are some good shirts, too. Worth twice that."

I ran my fingers along the front of a shirt. The cloth felt rough to the touch, and the tag on the inside collar was the name of a brand I'd never heard of. But for fifty bucks for three of them, I wasn't too worried about it. I picked out three shirts—one blue, one white, and one with blue and pink stripes. I turned and put them on the counter behind me—I didn't want to get accused of trying to steal anything in this place—and turned back to look at the rack of folded pants hanging along the back wall.

"Those slacks are fifty bucks apiece. Best deal in town," he assured me. "Don't have to iron 'em. Just put 'em on when you wake up, and you ready to go straight to work lookin' good."

They felt almost like they had a thin layer of plastic on them, sort of like they'd been stiffened with some kind of heavy starch. I found two pairs of khakis in my size, figuring they'd serve the purpose for the time being. I took them to the counter and put them next to the shirts.

The store owner made his way around the counter to the register. "One-fifty," he said with as much of an authoritative tone as he could. "Tax is included in the price."

I knew that was a lie as soon as he'd said it, but I wasn't going to open my mouth. I handed him the $200 Victor had given me, and he pressed a button on the cash register. The cash drawer came flying out as the register made a series of beeps. I couldn't help but notice that there was no receipt printing.

"Victor give you these?" he said, eyeing the bills. I nodded. The salesman took a marker and drew a line across each bill. "Counterfeit pen," he explained. "I don't trust that son of a bitch any further'n I can throw him." After he held the bills up to the light and looked at them, he was satisfied that they were real. He put them in the cash drawer. He took out two wrinkled twenties and a ten and handed them back to me, then reached under the counter and brought out a brown paper bag, like one you'd get at the grocery store. He took the pants off the hangers and folded them, sticking them in the bottom of the bag. He put the shirts on top of the pants and handed me the bag. "You want the hangers, it's an extra ten bucks," he said.

"Must be nice hangers," I said. "I'm good." I pocketed my change, took the bag, and turned to go. "Thanks," I offered over my shoulder.

"You're welcome." He coughed loudly. "Hey, white boy. Let me tell you something. You gettin' mixed up with Victor, you watch your ass. You best know he's got a lot of enemies around here. You tell him that Big Boy told you that. You tell him. Big Boy."

I said I would be sure to let him know, and I headed out the door. I went to my truck, satisfied that I had the clothes to at least look kind of professional in my new job. It was weird. I felt a lot like a little kid who'd just gotten his back-to-school clothes. Kids get so excited about that stuff, you know. The whole first day of school when things are new and exciting. Before that long, harsh reality of the school year sets in. And what's funny is that those kids fall for it every year, you know? They get excited every year, because I guess maybe they think that this year's going to be different. But it never is. It always turns ugly.

CHAPTER SEVEN

All those feeling of excitement about being like a kid on the first day of school ready to show up in my cool new clothes pretty much disappeared immediately. The next morning, I showed up at the office at ten minutes before nine o'clock, feeling like an idiot. The clothes I'd spent a cool hundred and fifty bucks on hung on my frame like I was a scarecrow. Actually, that's a pretty good description, because the shirt felt like it was made out of straw. The damn thing itched everywhere, and the arms were two inches too long. I'd rolled the sleeves up, but then it looked like I had some kind of oversized wristbands on my forearms.

And the pants didn't look any better. That whole story he'd given me about the creases staying in them was because the creases were pretty much sewed into the pants themselves, so there was no way to get rid of them, even if you wanted to. The visual effect was that I had a pretty nice little ridge running down each leg, from waist to ankle. It looked a little like one of those pictures you see on TV, one they take from space of a mountain range. Those damn creases looked like mountains from space. I cursed Big Boy aloud when I got to work.

Victor hadn't given me a key to the front door, so I had to knock. The door opened a crack and, when it was clear that I wasn't an enemy who was going to come in and destroy everything inside of the office, it opened fully, allowing me to enter. Victor took one look at me and started laughing harder than I'd heard a man laugh in a long time.

"Who in the hell dressed you, cracker?" he cackled at me.

"Some guy a couple of blocks away," I said, trying to sound like I was from this world, raised on the streets. Trying to play it off like I knew I'd gotten screwed and was just pissed off enough about it to take care of things they way they should be taken care of. "Son of a bitch named Big Boy."

When he heard the name, he started laughing even harder, which I didn't think was possible. Victor was doubled over, holding his stomach, coughing like he had emphysema. "Big Boy sold you that crap? Oh, cracker, you got some learning to do. But we'll go ahead and call that lesson one."

He coughed some more, then all of a sudden the laughter stopped, and Victor suddenly turned serious.

"Sit your ass down in that chair," he said. He sat down at his own desk and looked at me. "You listen to me and you listen good. The first lesson I'm going to teach you is that you don't trust anybody. Not me, not your friends, not some half-assed salesman named Big Boy." He laughed again for a second at the last mention of Big Boy's name. "They're all in this game to get when they can, and they couldn't care less about you at the end of the day."

My brain sparked a little bit when he included himself in the list of people I shouldn't trust. The old con artist in me, the one that I had thought was dead and buried, suddenly came back to life. That was language that that part of my brain could understand. Trust nobody. Everybody is out to screw you, and it's just a question of who screws who first and last. The goal is to be the one on both ends; what happens in between is a kind of give-and-take. All that matters is that you're the one who goes in on top and comes out on top.

I thought for a second about Big Boy's words from yesterday, about how Victor was going to get what he had coming to him. "He didn't have a lot of nice stuff to say about you, actually," I said. I tried to make it sound like I'd been doing research, like I'd found out something Victor needed to know. Like I was his spy out there in the world reporting back.

Victor didn't even seem to care. "Big Boy's a pain in my ass," he said out of the corner of his mouth. "Motherfucker owes me some money and he doesn't want to pay it. Not my fault he's so damn broke."

That made sense, I guess. If anybody knew about owing other people money, it was me, so I could see how that might make Big Boy think Victor was a bad guy, especially if Victor was hounding him for money the way I'd seen bill collectors do it. So I put it out of my mind.

Victor took a deep breath. "What I'm about to tell you falls under what we people in the business world like to call 'proprietary information.' That means you tell anybody about it, and I can sue you," he said. "More importantly, though, it's what I like to call information that if you tell anybody, I'll not only deny I ever said any of it, I'll make sure you beat me to hell. That means I'll kill you, just so there's no misunderstanding. Clear enough, cracker?'"

The look in his eye was enough to tell me exactly how serious he was. He wasn't making a threat; he was making a promise. I nodded silently. I tried to put on my best poker face. No expression that would tell him I was getting a little scared all of a sudden. I understood what he was saying. I just wasn't quite sure yet why he was saying it.

"Good. Look, cracker. There's plenty of insurance agents out there who sell what you might call real insurance products. Car insurance, life insurance, health insurance. All that. Hell, they'll let you insure anything you can put a value on if you're willing to pay the money." He paused for a second, letting that sink in as he leaned back in his chair and lit one of his sticky-sweet cigars. As he exhaled, the blue-gray smoke came drifting out of his mouth in a perfumed cloud. "To those people, I wish them luck. They're working with what you might call a different client base than what I've got around here," he said as he waved his hand, talking about that big world out there in the surrounding neighborhood.

"I've made a lot of enemies in this business, and I'm not just talking about other people in the business. I'm talking about clients," he said. He paused again, again letting what he was saying register in my brain. "If you stick this out with me, you're not going to have a lot of friends, cracker," he added, "so if you want friends, get out now. I'm the wrong guy for you to be working for."

I didn't move. I sat totally still in my chair, staring straight at Victor's forehead, not making eye contact, but not shifting my line of sight. This was not what I'd expected. I had kind of seen myself shooting the breeze with other businessmen at the bar, talking about how clients were a pain in the ass, and the vacation I was going to be taking soon.

We sat there together in silence for what seemed like five minutes. I was waiting for him to talk. To tell me about how it was all part of the business world, something I didn't know anything about. I was a student in this game, you know, trying to learn from my teacher. I kept hoping he'd say something, but he just kept on staying quiet. I was starting to feel really uncomfortable. I don't like just sitting in total quiet. Finally, though, Victor decided that it was time to go on teaching me some more.

"Good. Then let's talk about the next thing you need to know, which is that you don't actually work for me in the way that most people think about when they're talking about a boss. You're not going to sign a contract, you're not going to be on any kind of official payroll."

I moved uncomfortably in my chair. From what he had just said, it sounded a lot like he expected me to work for free. I was all about doing the job, but I'd be damned if I was going to do it for no money. Wasn't that the point of having a job? You work, you get paid. Pretty simple equation.

Victor must have known what I was thinking, because he didn't wait too long before he started talking again. "You're going to get paid, cracker, don't worry. You're just not going to get some payroll check with all the tax deductions. You're what I call an independent contractor. I'll write you a check every Friday for the week. Seven hundred bucks to start. Once you bring in some clients, you'll get more because of commissions. You get a percentage of whatever your clients pay. Make sense?" He raised his eyebrows and looked at me, silently wondering if these terms met with my approval.

Yeah, that made sense. And to tell you the truth, $700 a week seemed like a small fortune to me. That was more money than I could have thought about making in my old life. I didn't know if it was what every other new insurance salesman was making, but I didn't care. It would totally be enough to make me happy. But since I didn't know if that was a lot or a little compared to other people, I didn't want to seem unprofessional, so I nodded thoughtfully, like I was thinking it over. Like I had a choice in the matter, you know?

After a few seconds, I said, "Sounds good to me." Nothing too over the top, nothing too gushy. Just the facts. Sounds good to me. And that was very true. It sounded incredibly good to me.

"Then we're good," Victor said. "Now comes the part where I tell you things that you tell anybody about, and I kick your lily-white ass so bad you'll wish your mama had never met your daddy in the first place."

*   *   *

It didn't take me long to figure out why Victor had managed to make, as he'd said himself, so many enemies in the world, and why he told me I wouldn't have any friends if I worked for him. At his core, Victor was really just like me. He was nothing more than a dyed-in-the-wool con artist. He talked to me about a lot of different ways he had for what he called "up-selling" products to clients, specifically older people.

What it all boiled down to was that he was running a series of bait-and-switch scams, where people thought they were buying one product but getting another. And in every case, the product that they were actually getting was a whole lot more expensive than what they'd originally signed up for, which meant that Victor got a lot more money for his services. While he was telling me about it, he actually admitted that my own maple syrup business had actually been a selling point for me as he saw it, because I clearly had the mindset to sell insurance the same way he wanted it sold. I apparently didn't have any hang-ups about lying right to people's faces about what it was I was selling them. Just the way he wanted it. A convincing liar, he told me, was his perfect employee.

It was nothing very complex, really. Victor wasn't interested in explaining the specifics of products to his clients, so he didn't do any business in things like annuities or investments. You know, the kind of things real insurance agents sold to their clients in addition to life insurance or whatever else. He was strictly insurance. Multi-policy bundles were where he lived, and that was what made up the bread and butter of his usual scam. He'd talk you into a policy.

For example, maybe you needed to make sure you had coverage in case you had to go to the doctor. So he'd find something that seemed like a pretty good, pretty cheap health insurance policy. He'd come to you—that was another of his rules, never have client meetings in the office—and bring all the paperwork. He'd tell you all about it. It was a great policy, he'd say. Best one out there for the money. He'd done all the research.

Then he'd pretty much hot-box you into signing the papers, and get you to write him a check right then and there. If you wanted to think about it, he'd tell you it was a limited-time deal, and if you didn't sign it right now, it probably wouldn't be around when you finally decided you did want it. And then you'd get stuck paying a lot more for what would probably not be as good a policy.

The first time he took me along on one of his "house calls," as he called them, it was like I was with a different person. He put on this whole act of being an educated, well-respected businessman who had nothing but the highest levels of respect and concern for his clients' well-being. The first one he took me to see was an old woman that was recently widowed, whose children had told her that she needed to get some kind of supplemental health insurance to cover expenses that her Medicare wouldn't pay.

That was the perfect target for Vincent, I found out pretty quick. He targeted people just like this poor woman with his advertising. He'd make promises that there was no way any agent could have possibly kept, but average people didn't know that. They trusted him. He was slick, I'll give him that much. He had this way of putting those old people at ease. They trusted him almost immediately. They didn't have any reason not to, after all, at least not when they first met him. And he didn't give them a reason to think there was anything wrong until it was too late for them to do anything about it.

This poor woman invited us into her home, offered us coffee and little sugar cookies from a round blue can in her kitchen. It was a simple, one-story house. Lots of photos and a few pieces of artwork. Nothing glamorous; nothing that even struck me as being that nice, in fact. It was just an average, old-woman's house, minus the cats that you always think of old women who live alone having.

He introduced me as a new associate working for his firm whom he'd taken under his wing. After we'd gotten all the hellos and the how-are-you-doings out of the way, Victor unloaded a stack of paperwork six inches thick from the briefcase that he carried with him just because it made him look more professional. The woman's eyes about bugged out of her head when she saw it, which was exactly what Victor was gunning for.

"I know it's a lot of paperwork," he said in a way that made even me think he was sorry to have so much stuff for her to read through. "You know, if you want me to, I can just summarize all of this for you so you don't have to bother reading through it all. It's mostly just a bunch of insurance language that you probably wouldn't be able to understand. Insurance people are as bad as lawyers when it comes to writing these things out," he added, with a good-natured laugh. It was all part of his act. And he was good at it.

Of course the woman was grateful to be given the chance to have all that information explained to her, because there was no way she was going to be able to read all of that. In all honesty, though, if she'd actually taken the time to read it all the way through, she'd realize that about 95 percent of the papers weren't in any way related to her. A lot of them weren't even related to insurance at all. He'd printed out about a hundred pages of some legal papers he'd found on the Internet. But she didn't take that time. And that's exactly how Victor wanted it.

He explained it to her, throwing in references every once in a while to a whole-life policy, which he told her was included in the premium. He never actually said what that premium was; he left it up to her to ask, which she didn't, because it didn't occur to her that the premium had changed from the first time they'd met in this same kitchen, where Victor had sworn up one side and down the other that he would get her the health insurance policy that she was looking for, at a price she could afford. As long as she didn't ask, he didn't see as how he needed to tell her anything about how much it had actually gone up.

"The thing about this policy, ma'am, is that the offer is only available for a little while. I only heard about it through somebody at the actual insurance company. A friend of mine let it slip that they were basically giving this policy away. So you've got to get in on it now if you want to avoid paying a lot more money."

"Oh, you kind man," she said. "I can't tell you how nice it is to know that you're looking out for me so much."

He flipped through the paperwork, guiding the unsuspecting widow through all of the complex information about what she was getting, and pointing to lines where she needed to sign and date. She did as she was told. She kept telling him how kind he was to take the time to explain this all to her, and to help her out like this. She was like a little lamb getting led to the slaughter, and she had no idea what was coming.

Victor just beamed at her, saying, "This is how my own mama raised me, and my mama wouldn't hear of me doing anything less for a person in need." He hadn't prepared me for that little line of crap, so when I heard it, I almost laughed out loud. I managed to turn it into a cough, and Victor gave me a look that told me to shut the hell up. Then he changed in a second, like he was putting on a different mask. He looked back at her with this look of caring, this poor woman that he was about to rob blind.

Once it was all signed and she'd written a check for the first installment on the policy, he took the stack of papers and her check and put them all carefully back in his briefcase, then looked at his watch. "If I get this paperwork back to the office now, I can get it filed today, and you'll be fully insured before you go to bed tonight," he said as a way of getting out of there.

She told us good-bye and couldn't stop telling us how much she appreciated our work as we left; she actually told me how lucky I was to be working with such a fine man as Victor, and that he would be an excellent professional role model for me. I just smiled and told her how I knew that already.

On the ride back to the office, Victor was really proud of himself. "That, cracker, is how it's done. I just made about fifty grand off that woman."

While that was definitely a lot of money for the time we'd spent working on it, I couldn't help but think that there was no way the woman would be able to pay that, judging by the contents of her small house. There was nothing in that house that said she had any kind of money sitting around. It was all well and good that she owed him that much, but if she couldn't pay, what was the use?

When I mentioned that to Victor, he smiled at me. "Due diligence, cracker," he said. "That's your next lesson. You always do your due diligence before you approach a client. Her husband had a life insurance policy worth about half a million dollars, and besides that, she's got two sons who are both financial guys in Manhattan. And she just signed, on their behalf, a contract that lists them as co-guarantors of the premium payment. We'll get the money. Don't you worry about that." The self-satisfaction in his voice was obvious.

"Don't you ever worry about getting sued?" I asked. "I mean, if you're getting these people to sign stuff that they don't understand, what keeps them from coming after you?"

"For what? You heard me in there. I explained everything to that woman. I told her that she was getting the health insurance we'd talked about, plus a whole-life policy that was included in the premium. She said that sounded great, and signed on the dotted line."

And he was right. Victor had never lied to her. He'd been anything but honest about telling her about some of the specifics— things like the actual premium she'd be responsible for paying—but he'd never outright lied to her. He'd covered himself as far as that was concerned.

The whole thing made me a little uncomfortable, but I justified it in my own mind with the fact that it wasn't so much the old lady that was going to get screwed out of money, because it was her sons that were on the hook for the premium. If they had all the money I figured they did, then it was pocket change for them. Those guys on Wall Street made a fortune. And when I really thought about it, what I'd just watched Victor do was about the same as selling fake maple syrup to tourists in Vermont. So I tried to forget about how it made me feel. I figured I could do this if I just focused on the whole as being a job, and if I didn't look at the people I'd be stealing from as actual people.

CHAPTER EIGHT

I picked up the techniques pretty quickly, actually. A little too quickly, actually. It felt too natural, and it bothered me, if only for a second, that it was such second nature for me to be screwing little old ladies out of their life savings. But I came back to the fact that we never went after people who didn't have some kind of financial backing to support them, whether it was an investment banker child, or a hefty life insurance payout, or some other source of extra income. That was a rule we stuck to. It helped me sleep at night, at least.

After a couple of months of working with Victor, I'd managed to settle into my new life. I had an apartment—nothing to write home about, but it was a place to sleep, at least—and I'd managed to get some new work clothes that were a little nicer than my first try. I'd gotten a new cell phone with a Hartford number, which cut the last ties I'd had to Vermont. I took the stuff I'd bought that day from Big Boy and threw them in the dumpster at my apartment. I didn't want to be reminded of the fact that I'd actually spent good money on that crap. And even though I wasn't making what you'd totally call an honest living, I was making a living as a professional, and it felt good.

I spent the first part of my time with Victor following him around, learning what to say and what not to say. Finally one day, Victor let me off my leash to see what I could do on my own. I had learned a lot from him, both about life insurance and about human nature, what made people trust you. That was the most important part of this whole game, he'd explained to me. "Get people to trust you and you'll have them eating bird shit out of your hand," he used to tell me.

When I started trolling for my own new clients, the technique I quickly started to rely on was to scan the obituaries in the newspaper to find who had recently been separated by death from the one they'd married. The nice thing about the obits was that they told me everything I needed to know: who had died, what they'd done for a living, whom they'd left behind, all that. From there, it was a pretty simple matter of doing a background check on the survivors to see who qualified under our requirements of having that financial security to fall back on when the bait-and-switch premium took effect.

One of my most memorable clients was a woman named Doris MacMillan. I'll never forget Doris. It felt almost like losing my virginity, I guess. In fact, I wooed that woman like I was trying to get her in bed for the first time. Her husband of fifty-six years had died of a stroke at the age of eighty-seven, leaving her and their three children. One of those children happened to be a successful venture capitalist in Chicago, I learned. It was fortunate for Doris that he'd chosen such a moneymaking profession; the other two kids—a son and a daughter— were both public school teachers, and her husband had been a house builder who'd never really made it that big. So that venture capitalist was the golden ticket who was going to make sure she had all the money she needed. As it turned out, he was mine, too.

Even though it wasn't my first time at bat, I was still a little nervous about the act I was about to put on. It was kind of like being onstage; no matter how many times you did it, you still got butterflies in your stomach before you actually went on.

In the months I'd been practicing and fine-tuning on smaller clients, Victor had taught me to make my style and my act my own, because that would make it more genuine, more believable. If I tried to pull the same act as Victor, it would come across as shallow and fake. The client would see through it, and the whole game would be over before it had even really started. That story about being a poor black child raised by a single mom who worked eight jobs wouldn't quite fit my own life, for a lot of reasons. But if I made up my own story, it would be a lot easier to earn the widow's trust.

I took that advice to heart, and tried to come up with a story to fit the specific case I was going after. That was how I operated on all my marks. I'd build up some lie to jive with what I'd read in the obituary. It usually involved a relative who'd known someone who had put me in touch with the person. In my experience, mentioning family relations who had similar acquaintances put people at ease, even if I didn't offer a shred of proof that I'd ever even heard of the person.

So for this Doris, I came up with a story about my grandfather having worked with Walter—her late husband—many years ago, and when I'd seen the name in the obituaries, the memories came flooding back about the man my grandfather had always talked about as being the best builder in the business, and a man he'd always looked up to. I practiced it over and over until I was confident that I could pull it off, and I went to the calling hours at the funeral home. I was standing in that receiving line feeling like a kid about to meet his prom date's father for the first time. My palms were sweating, my heart was racing; I wanted to bolt out of there. I'm not sure if it was an attack of conscience or just nerves. But whatever it was, I was scared as hell. The moment of truth was about to be there, you know, and I was all of a sudden getting cold feet.

I was the next in line to tell poor Doris how sad I was to have heard about Walter, and I took a deep breath as I took her hand and looked her in the eye. From that point on, the old Billy Faulkner did his thing, just like he was peddling jars of fake maple syrup to leaf peepers on the side of the highway in Vermont.

"Hi, Doris. I was so very sorry to hear of Walt's passing."

She looked at me with a blank stare. It was a questioning look she gave me. "I'm sorry, young man, I'm all out of sorts. I can't place your face."

I smiled sympathetically and said, "No apologies necessary. We've never actually met. I'm Billy Faulkner. My grandfather worked with your husband many years ago, and he always spoke so highly of him. I felt like I knew him myself, and I know my grandfather would want to be here if he could be. But I think the two of them are probably playing poker together up in heaven."

I pretended to wipe away a tear for effect, and watched the change come over her face. It couldn't be this easy. The look in her eye and the smile she gave me told me that she'd swallowed the whole thing, and I was in just like that. She and I would soon be doing business together.

I gave it a few days, and then called the widow at home. I told her I'd been thinking about her, and said that I didn't think my grandfather would ever forgive me if I didn't look after her in any way I could. And it was because of that that I wanted to talk to her—just friend to friend, of course—about her existing health insurance policies, so that we could make sure that she'd be covered in the event anything happened. Of course there was nothing to worry about; I'd make absolutely sure that she was completely taken care of. My grandfather wouldn't have had it any other way. In fact, I'd come to her house as soon as it was convenient for her. That way, I'd be able to spare her the trouble of coming all the way to my office.

It went like clockwork, like I'd written a script for her to follow and she was playing the part perfectly. I went to her house with a bunch of official-looking documents and pamphlets that showed how much she could be forced to spend if she so much as got the flu. God help her if she had something major happen, like if she happened to slip on a patch of ice in the winter and broke a hip. It would bankrupt her for sure.

Victor had taught me to lay it out to the client as a worst-case scenario, never saying anything that might make them think that there was any hope for Medicare to cover everything. In fact, I needed to tell her that Medicare specifically wouldn't cover everything, and that she absolutely needed this supplemental insurance, because it was the only way that she'd be fully covered. And given that it only cost her twenty dollars a month, it was $240 worth of yearly peace of mind that she wouldn't even notice in her bank account.

She couldn't have been nicer to me. And she couldn't have been more appreciative. "For the first time since Walter's passing, I feel like my luck has finally changed," she told me. She said that my coming into her life was a gift from God—she actually used those words—and that I must have been sent by Walter himself to take care of her. It always surprises me that people can be as trusting as they are, especially when they're talking about money.

I went back to the office and started filling out the paperwork for what was basically a needless health insurance policy, as it sure as hell wasn't going to cover anything beyond what her Medicare policy already paid for. Then I started to get the paperwork together for the curveball that I was about to throw at her, a whole-life insurance policy that was going to commit this woman to a forty-five-grand-per-year premium.

All I needed was one year, which she would be obligated to pay for, and I'd clear more in one shot than I did in a year's worth of selling fake maple syrup.

*   *   *

The insurance industry is, I found out pretty quickly, a big con game, even for the ones who are playing by the rules. Think about auto insurance. That's the insurance product most people are pretty familiar with. You pay your premium, you get your form telling you about your coverage, and you put the proof of insurance card in your car. You don't think about it. All you know is that you're insured, and that's that.

But then you have a wreck. Maybe it's not your fault, but that doesn't matter. The fact of the matter is that you're suddenly what they like to call an "insurance risk," meaning that you might actually cost the insurance provider money. Mind you, they're not going to be losing any money on account of you, so it's more accurate to say that the insurance company isn't going to make as much off you as they would if you weren't such a high-risk driver.

So they either jack your premium up to cover the possibility that you might have another wreck and cost them a little cash, which would mean less money for them, or they just cut their losses right then and there and cancel you altogether. And why did they do this to you? Because you actually had the need to use the product they're selling you for the exact purpose they sold it to you for in the first place. Like I said, one big con game.

And what's more, the insurance people are in good with the lawyers, so you have to buy this stuff in order to legally drive. If you get caught driving without it, you get a pretty hefty fine thrown at you. So it's a product you have to buy and pray that you never have to use. And then if you do, you have to pay more. And it's pretty much the same basic idea for any insurance product. As long as you pay for it and don't use it, the insurance company loves you. But once you actually use the service they've sold you, you're in trouble. It's just about as close to legal stealing as anything I know of.

That thought made what I was doing seem pretty much just the way things were, at least in my mind. Victor had a policy that was his standard add-on to the rinky-dink health insurance policy we were talking these people into buying from us. It was what is known as a whole-life policy. In a perfect world, a whole-life policy does two things: it pays cash to the beneficiaries on the death of the policyholder, and it provides an investment product that allows the policyholder to borrow money, assuming the investment itself makes money. That's the perfect-world setting.

But the reality is that there's almost never a perfect-world setting, unfortunately, and whole-life policies pretty much don't ever make financial sense. But when you're in your eighties and your husband has just died and some long-lost family friend appears at your doorstep, you're not worried about what makes financial sense. Especially when you don't even know that you're about to be buying it.

Because of her age—and this was another reason we targeted elderly people—the premium for life insurance was a lot higher, which gets back to the scam these companies are running. You see, when you're older, it's a lot more likely that you, as the insured person, are going to die sooner rather than later, and that means that the insurance company is going to have less time to make up the cost of the payout plus their profit. So they've got to get more up front to cover the payout in the end.

Now, if we were still operating in that whole perfect-world setting, Victor and I would have been serving as go-betweens between the insured and an actual insurance company. But like I said, that perfect-world setting isn't a reality too often. In our case, instead of sending money to the insurance provider, we were funneling money into an LLC that Victor had created as a holding company, The Principal Hartford Life Insurance Corporation of New York.

It was a ridiculously long name that Victor had chosen for exactly that reason. It sounded totally official. Plus, it had enough references to real insurance companies to make it sound like a real company, at least to his mind. All that life insurance money went into PHLICNY, as it was referred to on paper, and from there, it was split up between a few bank accounts with names that didn't really mean anything to anybody except Victor. At the end of the day, though, it was Victor's way of hiding the money he was stealing money from his clients.

With a whole-life policy, though, the life insurance part of the thing was only half of the premium. The other half was that investment part I mentioned. Again, in a perfect world, we'd be investing that money in worthwhile stocks or mutual funds or whatever else would theoretically make money for the clients. Stuff I didn't understand at all. And Victor didn't know the first thing about investing money, and he figured out that it was just easier to deposit that part of the premium in his own bank account.

"An investment in Victor," he called it. "They're investing in this company, started by a black entrepreneur in a low-income neighborhood. They're investing in America's future." I had to laugh when he said it. The man was as good a con artist as I'd ever seen, myself included.

Things did get a little dicey, though, when our would-be clients got the premium notice. We didn't offer installment plans or payment options. We weren't running a charity, after all. You paid in full, by check, when you got your bill. That check we made you write when you signed the policy was only a down payment on the premium. And yeah, it was a real small down payment.

If you didn't pay your bill on time, you got one warning after that, mailed twenty days after the first notice. After thirty days, as stated in the contract, the premium began to accrue interest at the annual rate of 28 percent, compounded daily. After the first notice, the phone calls usually started to come in. People would tell us that there must be some kind of mistake. We'd sound as concerned as we could, and we'd promise to get back to them.

If we did actually call back, it was only to tell them that there had been no mistake, that the premium due shown on the bill was, in fact, the amount due. It's in your contract that you signed, thank you very much. Please make payment in full. Have a nice day.

Then came the lawyers. They'd argue and they'd yell and they'd threaten. But Victor was always cool, always calm. He'd explain that the client had signed a legally binding contract, and that there was nothing he could do. Unless, of course, the client wanted to work out an alternative arrangement whereby Victor would be fairly compensated for his services in exchange for allowing the client to get out of the contract without further penalty. It was usually about this time that he'd mention the automatic annual renewal, just to make it sound like he really was looking out for the client's financial interests, now that it was pretty much obvious to everyone that the client was in over his or her head, financially speaking. That automatic renewal meant that without ninety days' advance written notice, the policy would automatically renew at a 6-percent increase of the previous year's premium.

He was a scumbag, but his contract was airtight. He'd made sure of that. No lawyer could get past it, no matter how hard they tried, or what acts of God they threatened to send his way. He never gave in to any of them. He also never had a client renew their policy after a year. Some times it took longer to get his money than he would have liked, but he always got it in the end.

That was the beauty of his game. There was always a source of money that would get the premium paid, and then they'd decide to cut their losses. And the really beautiful thing about the lawyers' involvement is that they usually ended up costing the clients even more money, so a lot of times the client would just cut the lawyer out of the equation, pay the premium, and tell Victor to go to hell. He'd just go to the bank instead.

It worked perfectly, I have to admit. The whole system seemed pretty foolproof. It was work, to be sure, because you had to convince these people they wanted what you were selling. And then you had to fight to get your money. But once you got the money and they'd cut you out of their lives—which they always did, once they realized how badly you'd screwed them—you laughed all the way to the bank. And then you started it all over again.

*   *   *

I put together about two hundred pages worth of random text, with the required legal forms thrown in, the ones that required her to pay the premium. Most of the pages were actually copies of the same online article; it was something I'd read that morning about the buildup of nuclear weapons in some country that I couldn't pronounce in the Middle East. It didn't matter, of course, because I had no intention of letting her read any of it. It was strictly for show. I made sure to put little, taped-on "Sign Here" flags so that Doris would know exactly where she needed to put her name to make this whole thing official.

I headed over to her house, ready to get the whole thing signed and done. She welcomed me in, just like always, and led me into the kitchen, where she poured me a cup of coffee. A few minutes talking about the good old days when Howard and my imaginary grandfather worked together, and then it was down to business. I reached into my briefcase and pulled out the huge stack of papers, watching her face out of the corner of my eye. Sure enough, there was the deer-in-the-headlights look I was hoping for. I made an extra show of having to really work to lift the stack up to the table, making it look like I'd had to use all my strength to get that much weight up that high.

"Now, I know this looks like a lot of paper," I began, "but it's the specifics of your policy that we talked about. I managed to add a whole-life policy, which means that you'll have some extra money to live on, plus money for your kids when that unfortunate time comes."

"I already have life insurance, Billy," she said. "So I don't think I'll be needing that."

I assured her that she did, though. "You can never have too much life insurance, Doris. Plus, like I said, this gives you some extra money for now, just a little running-around cash in your pocket. And I'm not supposed to tell you this," I said in a quieter voice, "but I got this deal from a friend of mine at the company. He's not really supposed to give me this much coverage for so little." I gave her a little wink and a smile. I was her partner in crime, who was helping her to get out there and have one last run at painting the town red. "And it's all included in your premium," I added.

She smiled and tilted her head a little. Her eyes got a little glassy. "I'm so lucky that you came into my life," she said. "You really are a guardian angel."

I put my hand over hers. "My grandfather wouldn't have had it any other way," I said. I shifted gears a little bit, changing my tone to sound more professional. It was time to get this thing signed. "We've got two choices here, Doris. I can leave this mountain of paperwork with you to read. But I have to warn you that it's all lawyer and insurance agent language, so it's not going to make for very interesting reading. And it's probably not going to make much sense. Or I can just explain it to you in a quick, nickel tour of the highlights, get you to sign it, and have you insured by the end of the day."

"Oh, I think I'll let you explain it to me," she said. "I could never make it through all of that reading."

Candy from a baby. I told her the basics of a whole-life insurance policy, leaving out the fact that it was actually a less-than-great investment opportunity in the best of circumstances. I kept assuring her that it was all included in her premium, and that she'd be covered for her other health concerns, like we'd talked about. Over and over again, she told me how fortunate she felt to have had the good luck to meet me, how it was a heaven-sent miracle, how God Himself must have made this meeting possible.

I didn't give a rat's ass, to be totally frank with you, what cosmic force she wanted to give credit to for putting us together. I just wanted her to sign the papers and let me get my money. Besides, before she was done with me, I was pretty sure she'd be cursing my name to her God and any other supernatural being that happened to be listening at the time.

She finally signed the papers and cut me a check for that pesky little down payment, and we said good-bye to each other. I promised her that I'd get back to the office immediately and file the paperwork, so that she'd officially be insured "before the sun set in the west." That was one of my little lines that I used every time. Old people seemed like they got a kick out of it.

On my way back to the office, I was mentally patting myself on the back for a job well done. The irony of the fact that I was congratulating myself for running what was just another con game wasn't lost on me, especially since I'd taken this job as a way to get into a more legitimate line of work. At least I was legally covered, although I knew I was operating in what was a gray area at best. I'd get over it, though. Doris and her son's money would help make me feel a lot better about what I'd done.

CHAPTER NINE

It was about six weeks after old Walt's funeral that my phone started blowing up with calls from Doris. At first, the calls were nice enough. She'd leave messages telling me about how she was a little confused, and that there must be some kind of mistake in our billing department, because the premium she'd gotten billed for was significantly more than what she'd been told she'd be paying. I'd already been taught how to deal with those calls, and following Victor's instructions, I ignored them. But she kept calling back, God bless her. She was not going to be ignored. The messages started to get more and more frustrated. They even started to sound a little angry. And then came the call from her lawyer.

His first message was friendly enough, but there was a definite feeling of seriousness to what he was saying that told me he wasn't someone who took kindly to being jerked around by an insurance company. Especially not by an insurance company that was scamming his client out of tens of thousands of dollars.

I gave it a few days, then waited until about eight o'clock one night to return his call. I figured he'd be out of the office by then, and I'd get some kind of answering service, which I did. I left what I thought was a very polite message, saying that I was returning his call after having investigated the matter. All I wanted was to "make this whole thing right," but I'd found that there was no error in billing. Doris had signed on for a whole-life policy, in addition to her supplemental health insurance, and the bill she'd received in the mail was accurate, and due in full. I left it at that, knowing all too well that I'd be hearing back from him again.

It didn't take him long to get back to me, either. The next morning, there was yet another message from her attorney. He wanted to meet in person to discuss the bill, because he was pretty sure there was a mistake. He offered to come to my office, and asked me to call him to set up a time.

Victor had emergency plans for just about every situation that might come up, and visits from lawyers were no exception. He was absolutely not going to budge on his rule that no client, no lawyer, no person not working for his company—and that meant everybody except for him and me—would be allowed inside the office. In the case of lawyers, the first response was to say that it would be more convenient to meet at the attorney's office, because I'd be in the neighborhood on another sales call, and it just made sense.

That was usually enough to change the venue. The lawyer could run his own billing scam and get paid for the time he would have spent driving down to our office when he was actually just sitting at his desk. If that didn't work, then it was on me to sound as sorry as I could, and tell him that the office was actually being repainted at the moment, and it wasn't a good time to be hosting anyone. In the event the would-be meeting attendee was still dead set on coming to the office, the last option was to say that the office was actually being renovated completely, and that I was working from home. If that didn't work, well, then, just don't call back anymore.

I got with Victor for a few minutes to work out our strategy before returning the call. Step one would be to get the meeting moved to the lawyer's office. Once I'd managed to get that far, we'd go from there. Victor told me not to sweat it. He'd dealt with this sort of thing before. When I called the attorney back, he picked up on the first ring. Sure enough, he was willing to come by that morning.

"I'm actually on my way out to a sales call right now," I said, "so it probably makes more sense for me to come by your office instead. Say sometime around eleven?"

The voice on the other end of the phone sounded like a man who knew when he was being played for a fool. The lawyer sighed heavily before agreeing to meet me at eleven at his office. He gave me the address—somewhere down on Trumbull Street—and told me to be on time, because he had an appointment at eleven thirty and he didn't "want to waste more time on this mess" than was absolutely necessary.

After assuring him I'd be there, I hung up and turned to Victor. "What now?" I asked, expecting some sort of fatherly advice from the man whom I always thought of as my mentor in this business. He just looked at me blankly.

"What do you mean?" he finally said. "You got yourself in this mess, you're getting yourself out. I'm pushing your white ass out of the nest, baby bird. Time to either fly or die."

My stomach jumped into my throat as I remembered something Victor had told me long ago, something about how everyone was looking out for themselves, and that the sooner I learned that, the better off I'd be. At that exact moment, I knew without question that Victor would throw me under a bus without a second thought. And that's exactly what he was about to do, as he left me on my own to dangle in the wind while this lawyer beat me like a piñata.

I turned to face him, looking him straight in the eye. "You mean to tell me, Victor, that you're going to just cut me loose and let me take the fall for this alone? I have to tell you, that pretty much sucks, man."

He gave me a little laugh. "You're damn right, cracker. You're on your own in this one." He turned away and began to walk back towards his desk, then he stopped and turned back to me. "You fucked up, kid. You better make it right. That's all I got to say about that." He pulled out his desk chair and sat, pretending to focus on a paper sitting in front of him.

"Victor," I said with a tone of desperation in my voice, "what do you suggest I do?"

"That's all I got to say about that," he said again. That was his way of telling me that there wasn't a damn thing he was going to do to help me out of this one. I had to figure out what to do to save my own ass.

So this was how it was going to end. My mind started racing to those worst-case scenarios again. I had these visions of a trial that was going to end with me spending years in prison. I looked at my watch. It was nine thirty, which meant I had an hour and a half to figure out what I was going to tell Doris's attorney. How I was going to explain a stack of missing documents that I should have been able to show the lawyer. How I was going to explain the premium that was so much higher than what we'd talked about during our first meetings. I had no idea at all how I was going to explain any of it. And without any kind of guidance or support. This wasn't going to end well for any of us. That much was for sure.

I sat down at my desk, my mind still going over all the ways I'd be tortured in prison. I kept trying to focus on the conversation I was going to have to have very soon, but I couldn't calm my thoughts long enough to even form an idea about what I would say.

But then I had a moment of clear thinking. As I sat there worrying, I realized that I was going to go down for this. There was no way out of it. And if that was going to happen, I was sure as hell not going to go down alone. I wanted to punish Victor, to hang him out to dry and let him take the fall for all of this along with me. I mean, it had been his idea and his coaching that had gotten me into this situation in the first place. And then I realized that there was no reason why I couldn't do exactly that.

I packed up the papers that were relevant to Doris's case and stuffed them into a folder. I tried to move slowly, casually even. I didn't want to give Victor any idea about what was going on inside my head.

Victor looked over at me. "What's your plan, cracker?" he asked as he lit another one of those cigars.

"I'm not totally sure yet," I lied. "I think I'm going to get out of here and get a little fresh air to try to clear my head." I jerked my chin in his direction as I said, "Those Goddamn cigars are giving me a headache."

He just laughed at me. "You're so white it hurts me." He turned his back. "Do whatever you gotta do, cracker. Just make sure you cover your own ass."

I grabbed the folder and stood up. It was a much more dramatic action than I'd meant for it to be, one that seemed so final and absolute. It felt to me like I was giving the guy about to shoot me the finger.

Victor didn't pick up on it, though. He just sat there and continued to look at the same spreadsheet he'd been studying so hard for the last five minutes, all as a way to show me the fact that he had no interest in helping me with this situation, and didn't plan to lift a finger.

I scratched the back of my head as I stood there, trying to think of something to say. I finally managed, "Okay, Victor. Wish me luck. I'll let you know how it goes."

He grunted without looking up at me.

I walked out the door for the last time. I'd never see Victor again.

CHAPTER TEN

I went back to my apartment and immediately got to work. I knew I didn't have a lot of time to get it cleaned out, so I mentally wrote off ever getting back my security deposit. To tell you the truth, that was going to be the least of my worries. I needed to get the hell out of town in a hurry. It would have been nice to have that $600 back, but I didn't have the time to worry about it just then. I stuffed my clothes into my duffel bag, and the ones that wouldn't fit got thrown into a plastic garbage bag. A quick run through the bathroom, and I had everything I needed. I looked at my watch. It was now after ten, which meant that I wouldn't have quite as much of a head start as I'd hoped for. But it was what I had, so it was what I had to deal with.

I took the door key off my keychain and left it on the coffee table. I'd call the management office once I was clear of Hartford to tell them I'd be breaking my lease. They'd hit me with threats to collect the money I'd committed to pay, but that was another thing I just couldn't worry about. I took one last look at the place, turned, and shut the door behind me. It was another one of those overly dramatic moments in my life that had started out so great but that ended up so being so horrible. The life I'd had dreams of living once upon a time had turned out to be an impossible fairy tale.

I got in my truck and headed north, out of town. It was just like how I'd gotten there. I had no idea where I was going. I was leaving Hartford the same way as I'd arrived, with no actual plan and no real destination. I was just running away. Again. I was headed north, for no reason that made any real sense. It just happened to be the direction of the first exit for Interstate 91 that I saw.

At exactly three minutes after eleven, according to my watch, my phone rang. The sudden noise scared me; my nerves were tense as I fled the scene. I felt like the criminal that I was and always had been. The difference now as opposed to when I left Vermont was that now I really felt like I was a criminal, and I also felt some sense of remorse and even shame about that. Maybe it was a sign I was growing up.

"Hello?" I said into the phone.

"Billy, it's Steven Lindsay. You almost here?"

I shook my head a little, and allowed myself just the hint of a vindictive smile. Yeah, counselor. Be there in no time at all. "Steven, right. Hi. Sorry, yeah. I'm running a little late. I tell you what. I'm probably going to be tied up here at this sales call for another ten or fifteen minutes. Do you want to come by my office this afternoon so we can clear up this whole mess?"

There was a pause on the other end. "Yeah, I can move some things here. We need to get this cleared up, because you're fleecing this poor woman for everything she's got. I'll come by at one thirty."

"Perfect," I said with a degree of satisfaction. "You know the address, right?"

"Yes, I do," came the reply. Was that fear I heard in his voice? Maybe he didn't want to bring his $5,000 suit down to the poor part of town. Afraid he might get his clothes stolen. Or he might get shot. "I will see you at one. Do not make me wait for you." And with that, the attorney hung up the phone.

I put my phone back down on the seat next to me and pushed a little harder on the accelerator. I needed to get as much distance between me and Victor's office as I could before one o'clock. I still had no idea where I was going, I just knew I had to go.

I kept the speedometer needle steady at seventy miles an hour as I drove up I-91. It all felt strangely familiar, the further north I got. It felt like I was going home, even though I knew that was impossible. Going back to Vermont—especially back to Eden—was out of the question. Not only was there no professional future for me there, I figured my parole officer would be anxious to get his hands on me so I could explain why I hadn't been checking in with him the way I was supposed to be doing.

I hadn't eaten all day, and I was starting to get hungry as I drove into Massachusetts. Northampton was the next exit, according to the signs, and though I'd never been to the town before, I had some memory in the back of my head about it being a college town. And college towns usually had pretty good, pretty cheap restaurants. That fit my need at that point, so I decided to give it a shot.

I eased off the accelerator and took the exit ramp, then followed the signs that led me up Mount Tom Road towards downtown Northampton. It was just about one o'clock when I found a parking spot on Main Street; I figured that right about now, Steven Lindsay, attorney at law, would be knocking on Victor's office door, looking for me. I'd like to say I felt badly about doing what I did to Victor, but the son of a bitch put me in that position, and I was not going to be his fall guy. He was much guiltier of any crime than I was; it had all been his idea, after all. He'd get exactly what he deserved, as far as I was concerned.

I parked my truck on the street and pumped a couple of quarters into the meter. I looked around for somewhere that might be a decent place to eat lunch. Main Street reminded me of what I thought a town's Main Street ought to look like. Lots of brick buildings, mostly local businesses, with plenty of trees. A tall clock tower dominated the skyline, if you could call it that.

There was a café near where I'd parked that looked like it could work, and I scanned the menu that was positioned right outside the entrance. It looked like a pretty average, burger-and-fries kind of place, and that fit my mood just fine. I was more interested in filling up my stomach and figuring out my next move than I was in having some sort of gourmet experience. And I figured a burger wouldn't set me back too much cash. I pulled my phone out of my pocket just to give it a quick look; no missed calls. Not yet. I silenced the ringer and returned it to my pocket. I knew that I didn't want to answer any phone calls I was about to get.

The first thing I noticed when I walked in was that the place was practically deserted. A female voice called out as I walked through the door, telling me to sit anywhere, so I chose a table in the corner. The woman with that voice walked over after a couple of minutes and gave me a menu identical to the one I'd been reading outside.

"Welcome to the Pioneer Café," she said. "I'll give you a minute to read over the menu. Can I get you a drink while you're reading?"

I looked around the restaurant. "You sure you can handle bringing me a beer with this crowd?"

She gave me a sarcastic smile. "Yeah, thanks. I think I can handle it."

I immediately felt badly for having said it. This was, after all, how this poor girl was trying to pay her rent, and if there were no customers, that meant no tips. And that meant no rent payment. "Sorry," I said. "Can I get a beer? Whatever you've got on draft is fine."

She spun on her heels without saying anything, and walked away. I looked back at the menu. The standard kind of food you'd expect to get in a place like this. A burger would do for now. Nothing too fancy. Just something to fill up my stomach. I put the menu down, leaned my head back, and closed my eyes. I realized how exhausted I really was.

My phone buzzed in my pocket. Right on time. It was either Victor or Lindsay; I didn't have any intention of talking to either one of them ever again, so it didn't really matter to me which one of them it was. I let it go on vibrating until the voice-mail system kicked in to answer, and then closed my eyes again.

I really believe in the idea that every situation we find ourselves in is actually the result of a lot of other events that came before, events that happened in order, you know, with every one of them leading to the next. If I hadn't been conning tourists with fake maple syrup in Vermont—an idea that came to be simply because I lived in Vermont—I wouldn't have ended up in Hartford. And that event had set into motion a whole other sequence of events that led me to this seat in this restaurant in this town, alone with a waitress who no doubt hated my guts.

Where was I going? That was the question. What was the next stop in this crazy path that had started so long ago? My decision to head north out of Hartford had been just because that was the turn that had come first, you know? I could just as easily have gone south, east, or west. But I was here right now, and it dawned on me that there was nothing holding me anywhere. No job, no girlfriend, no family, nothing. I was free to go wherever my truck could take me, to go whatever direction the wind might blow me. I was totally free to do whatever I wanted, wherever I wanted to do it.

"You must be having one amazing dream."

I snapped my head forward and opened my eyes, looking up at the waitress, who was now standing next to the table, pad of paper and pen in hand. "What?"

"That smile on your face. It looked like you were enjoying whatever it was you were thinking about," she said with a wink.

And was that a smile I saw? Just maybe she didn't hate me as much as I'd thought. "Here's your beer," she said, putting a pint glass of liquid that could very easily have been chilled urine on the table in front of me.

"Yeah," I said. "I guess I was. I was just thinking about where I'm heading."

"Really? And where's that?"

I laughed softly and gave her kind of a crooked smile. "I have no idea."

"Okay," she said, now her voice sounding a little unsure about the nut job that was the only person in the café. "What about food? Any idea there?"

"Cheeseburger and fries. Burger medium," I said.

"Glad to see you've at least got that one decided on."

She wrote down the order and was gone again as quickly as she'd appeared. I took a slow sip of the beer. It wasn't very good, but at least it was beer. My phone buzzed again. The angry rattle in my pocket made me laugh a little. I could picture the scene. Victor was probably throwing me to the wolves, telling Doris's attorney how I'd gone rogue on him, and done all of this bait-and-switch work on my own. He, of course, was all on the up-and-up. Nothing illegal about Victor, no sir. Whether or not Lindsay would believe his line of bullshit was another matter. Even though I'd never met Lindsay, I was pretty sure he'd seen through my own cock-and-bull story, and I was confident he'd know that I'd learned it somewhere. And that somewhere was Victor.

I was sick of thinking about Victor, and Steven Lindsay, Esq., and Doris, and all of the crap associated with that whole chapter of my life. Even though I'd only left that morning, that chapter had ended. I wanted to move on, to leave it in the past. I closed my eyes again and tried to imagine pure blackness. I hoped that if I could do that, it would push the other thoughts out of my head.

I don't know if I fell asleep, or if I was just incredibly focused on the blackness in my mind, but I didn't hear the waitress return until I heard the loud rattle of a plate being put on the table in front of me. I opened my eyes to see her sitting across the table, a sandwich on a white plate in front of her. "Sorry to wake up you up again," she said, "and I'm sorry to intrude. But I was hoping I could eat lunch with you, since my shift is officially over."

I made a gesture with my right hand, waving at the seat across from me. "Glad to have the company," I said. I took a bite of my burger and as I chewed, I introduced myself. "I'm Billy. Billy Faulkner."

"Billy Faulkner? Let me guess. You're a tortured writer? Me too. I'm Molly Richardson. Pleasure to make your acquaintance, Mr. Faulkner."

"I'm not really a writer," I said matter-of-factly. "It's just my name. But everybody says something about it, so you're in good company."

"That's okay. I really am a tortured writer. Emphasis on the tortured. We can still be friends though, right?"

I laughed. "Yeah." I nodded. "I think we can be friends."

She smiled. She had a cute smile. The more I looked at her, actually, the more I realized she was a really attractive girl. Dark brunette hair to her shoulders, pulled back in a ponytail, really blue eyes that sparkled when she smiled, and a totally sweet voice. Having her sitting across from me made me realize that I'd been on my own for a long time. Way too long a time.

"So tell me about Billy Faulkner," she said.

Give the girl credit. She didn't waste any time.

"There's not much to tell," I said. I explained that I'd grown up in Vermont, but left out the unpleasant circumstances that had led up to my departure from that fine state. I told her I'd been selling insurance in Connecticut, but that I'd just gotten burnt out by that whole scene. "It's so corporate, you know," I said, trying to make it sound like I'd been some kind of high-powered businessman. "I just couldn't handle it anymore, so I had to get away."

She nodded like she understood. "I totally get it. I was doing the whole college thing here. Smith College, to make my mother happy. She went to Smith, back when I guess it was actually cool to go to an all-women's college. But I wasn't getting anything out of it." She paused, like she was waiting for me to say something.

I took another bite of my burger before saying anything. "I totally know what you mean." I waited to see if that was the appropriate interjection.

"Yeah," was all she said in reply. We ate in silence for a few minutes, then she asked, "So you really have no idea where you're going?"

I shook my head and smiled. "None at all. I didn't even know I was coming here until I got off the highway."

Molly just stared at me for a minute. Finally she broke her silence. "That is so cool. I mean, that's just cool!"

I looked at her. "What do you mean?"

"You're so Kerouac," she said. "You're like a guy who who's just out there on the open road, headed towards some awesome future."

I had to agree with her. It was really cool. I was a man with a mysterious past and no definite destination. I was just going where fate took me; my body was along for the ride.

"Where do you think you might go?" she asked me.

"I honestly haven't given it a thought yet. You have any ideas for me?"

She giggled softly, like a little girl. "You ought to go to Nantucket," she said. "Like Ishmael."

I had no idea what she was talking about, and I told her so.

"*Moby-Dick*, silly. The book about the whale?"

I'd heard of it, but hadn't ever read it. Molly seemed to think that a guy in the big-time world of insurance should have read it, though, so I played off my ignorance as a lack of sleep. "Of course," I said. "I knew that. My brain just isn't quite working so well right now. I'm going on about three hours of sleep. Another reason I had to get out of the insurance business." My phone started buzzing in my pocket again. I ignored it.

She looked across the table at me. "You need a place to crash tonight? You're welcome to sleep on my sofa."

She really was working fast. I couldn't tell if she was coming on to me or just trying to talk. I thought about the invitation. Once I walked out the door of this place, I was back in the world of no plans. What she was offering was, at least, an option for tonight. I could get some rest—something I really needed—and make a new plan.

"That is actually the best invitation I've gotten in a long time," I said. "You sure you wouldn't mind?"

"Of course I don't mind. But I should warn you ahead of time. It's just a sofa. You don't need to get too excited about it." She stood up from the table. "Let's go, if you're done. I got your lunch."

I looked up at her, standing next to the table. She looked the same way that she had at our first meeting, when she'd given me the menu and I'd commented about the fact that she didn't have any customers in the place. "Why are you being so nice to me?" I asked.

"We're friends. You said so yourself," she said. "And besides, you seem like a nice guy." She gave me a wink and extended her hand. I took it in mine, and she pulled me up to my feet. "Come on, Billy Faulkner. My car's out back. I'll bring you back in the morning to get yours. Don't worry about the meter. They don't check them this time of year."

She led me through the back of the café, through the kitchen, and out into a back alleyway, where an ancient, white Volvo station wagon was parked. "It's not much, but it's paid for," she said, like she was apologizing. "Kind of like the rest of my life," she added.

I nodded silently. I knew exactly what she meant.

CHAPTER ELEVEN

Driving through the winding, narrow streets of Northampton, Molly talked constantly. She was a writer—she was adamant that I think of her as a professional writer, not a waitress—who'd become "profoundly disillusioned with the state of academia," as she put it. I wasn't entirely sure what that meant, but I understood the end result, which was her dropping out of college. "I wasn't learning a damn thing about how to be a better writer," she said of her time at Smith. "I was wasting years of my life, years I could have been dedicating to writing a truly great novel."

Her decision to drop out of school had been a tough one for her, financially speaking, as her parents had refused to support her if she wasn't going to be in school. She decided to say screw it, and just latched on to her inner bohemian. She decided to take a job waiting tables to make the rent while she finished writing what she was convinced in her mind was the next great literary masterpiece of the Western world. After ten minutes or so of listening to her talk about what she kept calling her tortured existence, I began to zone out, and stared out at the window at the scenery. I'd lost interest.

Northampton, from what I could tell from the passenger seat, was a lot like every other small town in New England. It felt really familiar to me. Lots of brick buildings, lots of trees. It's funny, because so many people think that's all there is to these towns. Brick buildings, a university or two, a house where George Washington is rumored to have slept during the Revolutionary War. And in all honesty, the people who run those towns like it that way. They show the tourists what they want them to see. And they don't want the tourists seeing how the working class lives. It took us about twenty minutes to cross the interstate and get to Molly's apartment, which was exactly the kind of place where a working-class girl would live, and one of those places they don't show you on the tour. It makes the whole place seem just a little too normal, a little too real.

The complex itself was totally ordinary. There was a central courtyard, with apartments on two levels in an angled, horseshoe kind of layout around the courtyard. The exterior was blue-gray siding and brick painted to match, with white-painted trim. Metal railings stood along a cement walkway on both floors of the apartments, and fake brass numbers on the doors were the only way you could tell the difference between the individual apartments. It reminded me way too much of a cheap motel you might find on the side of a highway somewhere.

As she pulled into her designated parking spot, Molly read my face, and knew what I was thinking. "It's like the car," she said. "I can afford it."

She didn't say it like she was being defensive or apologizing for how the place looked. It was just matter-of-fact. The reality was that she was living her life the best way she could, paying the rent with tips made off six-dollar cheeseburgers eaten by people who usually wouldn't even bother to leave 10 percent on a bill, let alone 20 percent.

Molly led me into her apartment—she lived on the first floor of the complex—and turned on the light. She had an amazing amount of stuff crammed into what was really a tiny space. It had one big room, plus a tiny kitchen and an even tinier bathroom. A futon did double duty as both a couch for watching the television that was all there was in one corner of the room, and a bed. A metal rack on wheels that looked like something a hotel bellhop would use to transport luggage had all kinds of clothes hanging on it. There was nothing that really qualified as artwork on the walls. A few prints of abstract paintings, plus a poster advertising a Ramones concert from the seventies.

And books. There were books everywhere. Stacked on the floor, sitting on the table in the middle of the room, sitting on makeshift shelves she'd built herself from cinder blocks and scrap wood. I didn't recognize many of the titles, but I figured they were what you would call literature, since she thought so highly of herself as a writer. Almost all of them were paperback—cheaper than hardback, I figured—and a lot of the covers were torn. Many of the spines had bright yellow stickers that said "USED" in black block lettering.

Molly grabbed some clothes out of a small chest of drawers that sat against the far wall, and disappeared into the bathroom. "Make yourself at home," she called from behind the closed door. "The TV remote should be on the floor near the futon. Or you can read a book," she added. "You probably noticed I've got a few."

"Yeah, I noticed that," I said.

I took a seat on the futon and found the remote control on the floor underneath it. I pressed the power button, and after a couple of beeps from the TV, the screen lit up. Some cop show where a kid had been murdered and the detectives were putting together the evidence to see if they could figure out who'd done the deed. I couldn't have been less interested in the story if I'd tried, but it was background noise. And a distraction. It kept me from thinking about the reality that my life had turned into.

My phone buzzed again in my pocket. Persistent bastards. I pressed the button to ignore the call, then immediately took advantage of the fact that Molly wasn't in the room, and powered off the phone altogether. That would solve that problem, at least.

When Molly came out of the bathroom, she had changed into a pair of cutoff shorts and a tank top. She had a tattoo on the back of her shoulder that I hadn't seen before. No crazy pictures or anything, just black script writing. It was hard to make out, but the longer I looked at it, the clearer it became. It was the words "BAD ASS" in all capital letters.

Molly saw me staring, and offered an explanation. "It's in honor of my brother," she said. "He committed suicide when he was seventeen. He used to tell me that when he grew up, all he wanted to be was a badass." She laughed softly. "Never actually told me how he was going to become this badass. He just knew that he wanted to be a badass."

I wasn't sure how to react to this news. Other people's misery and suffering always made me uncomfortable, and I never knew how to handle a situation that involved someone else telling me their problems. The problem was, I didn't want to sound like I knew what she was going through, because I didn't. I didn't even have siblings, so I couldn't possibly relate to someone who'd had a sibling kill themselves. Hell, I'd never known anybody that killed themselves at all, so I really had no idea what it felt like. But I needed to say something. I couldn't just sit there silently after she'd dropped that bomb. I decided to keep it simple. I told her I was sorry to hear about her brother.

"He wanted to be a badass and he wanted a Viking's funeral," she said. "That was his other thing. He always said that he wanted a Viking's funeral."

"What's a Viking's funeral?" I asked. I hoped I didn't sound ignorant, but I'd never heard of anything like that before.

Instead of just telling me what it meant, Molly began looking at the bookshelves. She mumbled to herself as she ran her fingers across the beat-up spines. She eventually stopped at one of the few hardbacks she had in her overflowing collection. It was, I noticed, covered in clear plastic. Some sort of protection against time and age, I guess.

She tossed the book to me. "*Beau Geste*," she said, as a way of both introducing me to the book and explaining what a Viking's funeral was. "It was his favorite book. He bought it at a garage sale one day, went home, and read it cover to cover. Wouldn't put it down."

It was pretty hefty, at least compared to the books I usually read—392 pages. No pictures. This was a serious book. "He read the whole thing in one day?" I had never read any book in a single day, let alone one that was four hundred pages long. "That's a lot of reading."

"Yeah. He got totally into it. You should try it. You might actually like it," she said with a wink.

"I'll see about that," I said as I put the book on the floor underneath me. Molly sat down next to me on the futon, and as I pretended to pay attention to the action on the television screen, I was trying my best to get a better look at her out of the corner of my eye. She was really attractive. Beautiful, even. Maybe it was just because I'd been surrounded by such bottom-feeders for so long, but I couldn't stop thinking about how pretty she was.

The skin on her face was perfect, and it wasn't because of makeup. It was completely smooth, except for one little scar, right below her chin. And that was nearly impossible to see. It couldn't have been more than half an inch long, and because of where it was, it was pretty much invisible when you looked at her from the front. The only reason I could see it was because I happened to be looking at her mouth when she turned her head, and the light caught it just right.

"What's that?" I asked, pointing towards the scar.

"What's what?"

I gently put my finger on her chin. "This."

She blushed a little, like she'd been caught telling a lie. "Ah, yes. My hideous scar," she began. "It was a bike accident when I was a kid. Same old story. Kid rides bike, kid goes over handlebars, kid cuts chin. I was eight. It didn't hurt that bad at the time," she said, "but when I put my hand up and felt all the blood? Oh God. I lost it!" She laughed a little at the memory. "And today I have this ugly scar to remind me of that horrible day."

"It's not ugly," I said, with what I thought might have sounded like hope in my voice. I wasn't sure where my brain was taking me at that moment; it was a sort of out-of-body experience, where I was just along for the ride. "I think it's cute. Just like the rest of you."

As soon as I'd said it, I wanted to rewind and take it back. I have no idea what part of my brain had taken over and caused me to say that, but it wasn't the part I was used to dealing with on a daily basis. I fully expected a look of horror and disgust to come from Molly as she sat next to me.

"So you think I'm cute?" she asked coyly.

I felt something fire in my brain, like the spark you get when you bang two pieces of steel together. "Beautiful," was all I managed to say.

"You're sweet, Billy Faulkner," she said, as she turned her head to face me directly. I felt her hand go behind my neck and pull me towards her. I literally didn't have any power to resist. I felt myself being drawn towards her, our eyes meeting briefly before mine closed and our lips met. It was the first time I'd kissed a woman in as long as I could remember. When I felt her tongue slide into my mouth, heat began to come up into my chest, and then flowed to my arms and down into my stomach. My legs went numb. Thank God I was sitting at the time, or I would have collapsed on the floor.

She pulled away after what seemed like way too short a time and looked at me. I could see a smile on her face and a brightness in her eyes, and I knew she was feeling the same thing I was. "I think we're going to get along just fine, Billy Faulkner," she said, just before she pulled me closer for another kiss.

CHAPTER TWELVE

I'm not one to kiss and tell, sorry to disappoint you, but let's just go ahead and say that the time we spent together that evening was some of the most intense moments of my life. Even though I'd only known her for a few hours, I felt more connected to Molly than I had to any other human being that I could I ever remember being with. It was like we shared some kind of bond that was just pulling us together, binding us tighter and tighter. It was amazing, and that's all I'm going to say. You can fill in the blanks, I'm sure.

We fell asleep in each other's arms, wrapped up in a tangle of sweaty sheets on top of her futon. When I woke up, I had no idea what time it was. I could see that it was dark outside, but beyond that, I had no clue. And I didn't really care what time it was; I would have been happy to lie in that moment for the rest of my life. I looked over at Molly, who was still asleep. Her head was resting on a pillow, my right arm stretched out beneath her neck. With my left hand, I stroked her hair as I watched her sleeping. She looked gorgeous lying there. There was a glow around her face. I just wanted to stay right there forever.

That bond I felt with her—I knew it was going too fast to last. If I'd really stopped to think about it, I would have known then that this was going to be one of those things where, after she woke up and we exchanged a few uncomfortable comments back and forth, I'd leave with promises to call her, both of us knowing we'd never speak to or see each other ever again in our lives. But that was the rational part of my brain thinking, and the part that was so ridiculously taken by this woman was in charge of my thinking. I was a different man than the one who'd fled Connecticut the day before.

The longer I looked at her, the stronger the feelings I had, and the more my non-rational thinking began to dominate. I began to think about the possibility of a future together with her, thoughts that I knew were both out of character for me, and incredibly premature. We'd shared an intense sexual experience, to be sure, but we'd known each other for a few hours. How could I possibly be thinking like this already? I didn't know this girl at all.

For just a second, my old thinking crowded out this new, optimistic, romantic side. I began to look at the situation like the old Billy, the guy who took what he wanted and ran. I could slide my arm out from under her if I really tried. If she woke up, I could say something about having to go to the bathroom, and that I'd be right back. Wait for her to go back to sleep, slip out the front door, and never look back. Just like old times.

I knew in my gut that it was the right thing to do. I didn't need to get involved with this woman, who had such a bright future. She was smart, she was creative, she had her shit together. I was a con man with no professional experience that I could mention in polite company, because I'd been breaking the law since I entered the grown-up world. It wasn't fair to her.

So I took a few deep breaths and started to slowly pull my arm out from under her. As my hand slid by her neck, I felt something in my stomach. I really liked the way I felt with my arm under her. She mumbled softly in her sleep and rolled over, facing away from me. I stayed motionless until her breathing went back to the steady rhythm of deep sleep again. When I was sure she was totally asleep again, I pulled my arm slowly out from beneath her.

I got off the futon as quietly and gently as I could, afraid that any sudden movement would be like shooting off a flare announcing my escape attempt. I found my clothes and got dressed slowly, never taking my eyes off Molly. I told myself I was watching to see if she woke up; I wasn't sure what I'd say to say to explain myself if she did actually open her eyes. But that's what I told myself I was doing. On a deeper level, though, I knew I was trying to keep that vision of her, that picture of beauty asleep, a slight smile on her face as she dreamed peacefully, so that I could remember it later when I was gone, and needed a happy memory. My stomach did a somersault at the thought.

When I'd finished getting dressed, I had worked up enough courage to leave. It was the right thing to do. I knew that, even though it felt wrong in my heart. I couldn't destroy this girl's future by attaching myself to her. I took a last look, then turned to go. I had my hand on the doorknob when I remembered that my truck was back near the restaurant where I'd first met Molly. I had no idea how to get back to where it was, and no way to get there. I was stuck.

I had to smile. It seemed like fate, which had brought me to this point through the insane route I'd taken, had a few more tricks up its sleeve to get me to do whatever it was that I was destined to do. And apparently that destiny involved me staying right where I was, instead of sneaking out like a thief. Maybe I was talking myself into staying because I really liked this girl. Maybe I was being unfair by staying. Maybe I was being selfish. I didn't care. The reality was that I had no way of getting back to my truck. That was a fact. So I was staying put for now.

I wasn't going to try to get back in bed with Molly. For one thing, I wasn't tired anymore; but I also didn't want to risk waking her up by getting back in bed. That would require explanations, and at this point, what she didn't know wouldn't hurt her. My self-doubt and over-analysis of the situation were things I didn't want to have her find out about just yet.

I saw the book she'd given me earlier, *Beau Geste*, and I figured that right now was as good a time as any to start reading. I didn't have anything else to do. So I grabbed the book from the floor, then took a seat in the room's only chair. It was an old, upholstered thing that looked like it had come from a thrift store, with a beat up-looking small table next to it with a cheap lamp balancing on top. I turned on the light, opened the book, and settled in to read. I wasn't expecting to be able to pull off the cover-to-cover reading that Molly had said her brother had managed, but I figured it would give me something to do, at least. And clearly somebody had thought it was a pretty good story, so maybe it would be some entertainment for me, too.

*   *   *

I don't know how long I'd been reading when Molly came up behind me and kissed the back of my neck. The Geste brothers had all admitted their individual guilt in the theft of the Blue Water sapphire, and had all joined the French Foreign Legion. I'd learned, too, what a Viking's funeral was. It was basically a floating funeral pyre. The dead Viking was laid out on a ship, which was floated out into the water after having been set on fire. The body of the dead Viking was consumed, along with the ship, by the flames. All things considered, it seemed like a pretty cool way to go out. But my attention and focus were both shot as soon as I felt her lips touch my skin.

"You're really getting into it, huh?" she asked, seeing how much I'd read.

"Yeah," I admitted. "It's a really good story. I can see why your brother liked the idea of a Viking's funeral," I added. "It sounds pretty awesome."

She nodded. "I totally agree. If you've got to have a funeral, might as well make it one with fire, right?" She walked over to the blinds and opened them, letting the morning light come in. "What time did you wake up?"

I shook my head. "No idea. I woke up and couldn't get back to sleep, so I started reading. My watch is in my truck."

"Did you sleep okay?"

"Yeah, I did. You?"

She just smiled without saying anything, then made her way into the kitchen and began making coffee. "I'm assuming a big-time insurance salesman who's cashing it all in and running away still likes his morning coffee," she said. And then, without waiting for an answer, "Do you take it with cream and sugar?"

I smiled at her, enjoying the fact that we already seemed to be building an actual relationship. Those earlier thoughts about running away from her were gone. I was here, now, and I liked it. "Black," I said. "I drink it big, black, and strong."

"Just like your women?" she asked with a wink.

It felt good to laugh. Just for a minute, I allowed myself to lounge in the moment, enjoying the feeling of whatever this was that we were having, a feeling I hadn't experienced in a very long time. Molly looked gorgeous standing in the kitchen, even though she was doing something as ordinary and everyday as making coffee. It was a sight that I thought—even though it was my first time ever seeing it—that I could get used to seeing a lot in the future.

I guess you could say it really was love at first sight. Every logical thought in my brain flew out, replaced by a lot of completely ridiculous thoughts of love, marriage, and being together forever with this woman. This woman, I reminded myself, that I hadn't known existed twenty-four hours earlier.

I was lost in thought when she walked up with a cup of steaming coffee and offered it to me. I could feel the heat from the first sip go all the way down my throat, burning as it passed. It tasted awful, but I didn't care. I loved the fact that she had made it for me. It felt like a grown-up relationship, the kind of thing I'd been hoping to find to complete my grown-up life. But since my professional goal had pretty much blown up in my face, maybe, I thought to myself, I could do an end-around and start with the wife first, then find the job. "Thank you," I finally managed to say to her.

"My pleasure," she replied from the kitchen with a smile. She poured herself a cup of coffee. And then, as if she were reading my every thought through some sort of ESP, she said, "Isn't this amazing? I mean, I really haven't known you for that long, but I feel like we've got this connection, you know?"

She had basically lobbed the ball into my court, and now it was up to me to either let it go by or to smash it right back to her by saying what I was really feeling. "I totally agree," I heard myself say. "It is amazing." Overhead slam, right back at you, Molly.

She didn't say a word. Instead, she walked over to the chair where I was sitting, and put her coffee on the table next to it. Then she wrapped her hands around my neck, and brought her mouth down to mine. Without ending the kiss, she pulled me up to my feet. Before I knew what was happening, she was leading me back to the futon, unbuttoning my shirt while she kissed me. As I fell onto the futon mattress, I looked up into her eyes and felt again that connection she'd talked about just a minute ago. At that moment I remembered, too, that the blinds were open; I didn't care, though. I ripped her clothes off and pulled myself to her, trying to join our bodies into one.

CHAPTER THIRTEEN

Molly and I spent the next two weeks together living like a happily married couple. Or at least the next best thing. We did all the things you do when you're first in love. We went on walks together, holding hands as we passed by all the stores and art galleries in Northampton. We went to the grocery store together, we cooked together, we hated to be apart when she had to go to work. More than once I went with her and sat in a corner booth sipping on coffee or eating a sandwich as I watched her work. I knew on some level that this excitement was just the honeymoon stage of the romance; if this relationship progressed to the point I was now definitely hoping it would, the infatuation would wear off. But at the same time, I was enjoying riding the wave, and I planned to stay on it for as long as it wanted to carry me.

We told each other about our lives. I told her about growing up in Vermont, and she gave me the rundown on her own childhood. She'd been born in a small town in Western Massachusetts. Her father worked for a paper company out there as a salesman, her mother was an old-fashioned housewife. Her brother had been her only sibling, and when he'd killed himself, the whole family went into kind of a tailspin. Nothing was ever the same for her. Then, after she'd dropped out of college, she pretty much cut off all contact with them. That was something we had in common. Families can be an absolute pain in the ass, you know? You can pick your friends, but you can't pick your family.

Every once in a while, more or less just out of habit, I'd check my phone messages, which had started to die down in number. On the day I had taken off from Connecticut, I'd had fourteen messages. I didn't listen to any of them; instead, I just kept hitting the number-seven button to delete them as soon the next one came on. None of those people had anything nice to say to me. I could guess what specific words they were using, but instead I just chose to live in blissful ignorance. After two weeks, the calls had all but stopped entirely.

They were still calling me every once in a while, but those calls all went straight to voice mail. And more often than not, the caller didn't bother leaving a message. They figured I'd gotten the message already, and there was nothing more they could threaten me with to get me to call them back. So I didn't.

It was getting to be a little bit of a pain with them calling me, so I figured I'd solve the problem by getting a new phone number. I talked to Molly about it, and we figured out that we could add me to her existing account, and get me a new phone and a new phone number for a lot less money than it would cost me to get a whole new phone contract. And since it was in her name, those people in Connecticut had no way of finding me. Problem solved.

After her shift on the fourteenth day of our life together, Molly finally asked the big question. She was wondering what it was that I planned to do with myself. We couldn't live on the money she made at the café, at least not if we wanted to eat more than once a day. She barely made ends meet when she was just trying to feed herself; when I'd become part of the mix, I was another mouth that her budget couldn't feed.

"There are plenty of businesses in this area, you know," she said to me that night. "With your experience, I'm sure you'd have absolutely no problem finding something great."

"Yeah," I said, halfheartedly. I wasn't ready yet to tell her about how much I'd exaggerated my business accomplishments. I'd let her think I was some kind of business tycoon for a little longer.

"And just think," she added with a tone of happiness, "we could move out of this rathole and get a place with a yard. And even a dog." She looked at me and smiled. "Do you have any idea how long I've wanted a bigger place?"

I nodded. I understood. I'd grown up in the land of open spaces and endless views. So yeah, I understood. Better than she knew. But I also had a whole lot of baggage I needed to unload on her. But there'd be time for that. I would just have to fake it for a little while longer.

As the days went by and I pretended to look for a job, I began to think about what it had been like when I got to Hartford. And even though that part of my life hadn't ended exactly the way I'd hoped it would, it did make think about the fact that I'd been able to pick up my life, move to a new place, and find a job, despite the fact that I had a police record and no verifiable experience. What was to say I couldn't do it again if I put my mind to it? That gave me some confidence and a little motivation to give the whole job-search thing a little more effort. So the next day I decided to actually put my mind to it and see what I could find.

I got up early the next morning, went out, and got the newspaper. I sat in the chair sipping coffee while I read through the want ads. Both my confidence and my motivation were immediately destroyed, though, because there was nothing that sounded even remotely promising. Everything that would fit with my image as an experienced insurance salesman required a college degree and professional references. I had neither.

When Molly asked me about the prospects, I told her that nothing looked like a match for my skill set. I didn't tell her that my "skill set" involved conning people out of their hard-earned money.

She picked up the paper and looked over the ads. "Billy, there are four or five jobs here that sound like perfect matches for you," she said, putting the paper down on the table next to me.

I took a deep breath. Now was the time to tell her. If we were going to have a future together, she deserved to know what she was getting herself into. "Molly," I began, "let's sit and talk."

I followed her over to the futon and sat next to her. This was the moment of truth, God help me. I fully expected her to tell me to never call her again right after she kicked me out. I looked at her face; there was no sign that she knew what was coming.

"What's wrong, Billy?" she asked.

I took another deep breath as I chewed on my bottom lip. "Here's the thing," I said. "I'm not sure how to tell you this, so I figure I'll just tell you the truth and whatever you decide you want to do is fine." My heart was racing and my palms were sweating. I wouldn't have been more nervous if I had been about to ask her to marry me. "I'm not . . ." And then I lost it. I lost my nerve. I couldn't do it.

"You're not what?" she asked.

My brain raced through a series of possible answers to that question. I settled on what seemed like a safe course. "I'm not . . . I'm not sure I can keep doing the insurance game," I said. I exhaled heavily for dramatic effect. I wanted her to think this was something I'd been thinking about for a long time. "I just can't see myself doing it anymore. I'm burned out on that whole corporate scene." I tried to look pathetic.

Molly was silent for what seemed like a long time. Then she started laughing. "Honey," she said, "seriously? You thought I was going to get mad at you for wanting to change careers? Please! I want you to be happy, and I want you to do something that makes you happy." She put her arms around me, and kissed me lightly.

I heaved a quiet sigh of relief. That had been easy. Too easy, in fact. Lying was more than second nature for me. I hadn't really noticed it before, but there it was. Lying was apparently my go-to reaction for any situation.

I managed to push that thought out of my mind, though, and said, "Thank you, honey. I can't tell you how much your support means to me." That, at least, was the truth. I was more than grateful for her support, both financial and emotional, and for her willingness to stick by me as I changed careers.

"You don't need to thank me," she said. "It's what you do for someone you care about." She smiled, then looked down towards the floor for a moment. Then made eye contact with me again as her hand crept across the futon and took mine. Her fingers wrapped around mine. "Someone you . . ." She paused for a second. "Someone you love."

My stomach began to do flips as my heart pounded out of my chest. I looked at Molly, maintaining eye contact. She was blushing, almost like she was embarrassed to have admitted that she was in love with me. I squeezed her hand. "I love you, too," I said.

It was one of those moments that couples always remember, the moment the "L word" makes its first appearance.

*　　　*　　　*

It wasn't a lie. I told myself that repeatedly. I hadn't lied to her about my job search. The truth was, I really couldn't see myself working in the insurance industry any longer. For starters, I was pretty sure that any office I applied to would get wind of the scams I'd been running, and that could mean a few things, none of them good. It could mean I wouldn't get the job, but that was no big deal in the overall scheme of things. More importantly, it could result in me getting arrested, if there was any sort of legal authority chasing after me—because they'd know where I was. So the business world was a part of my past that I would not be revisiting in my future. That much was for sure.

But that left me with few options. I was still on my own little kick about making a fresh start—another fresh start, I guess you'd say—and making an honest dollar for an honest day's work. But the problem was, I didn't think I'd ever actually performed an honest day's work in my life. Doing that just once would, in reality, be its own version of a fresh start for me.

But at least it was out there. I'd admitted that I didn't want to work for any business-oriented outfit. Molly had taken that news so much better than I could have ever hoped. And when she told me that she loved me, I got all the symptoms of a lovesick teenager. My heart raced, my palms sweated, I got butterflies in my stomach. I really was in love with this girl, and that came with a whole other realization, and that was that I did, in fact, need to find some sort of gainful employment, so that I could at least provide a little bit of financial support for her. She deserved better than what she was getting, but I made a pact with myself that I'd do my best to at least be half the man she thought I was.

So back to the want ads I went, looking for I didn't know what. Telemarketing didn't appeal to me at all, because I knew how I felt every time those jackasses called me. I wanted to reach through the phone and strangle the life out of them, and I didn't want to be that guy on the other end of the phone.

For some reason, though, and I truly can't tell you what it was that caught my eye, I stopped on a help-wanted ad that started with the requirements of being able to speak fluent English and being in possession of a valid driver's license. I didn't read the details. I skipped over the actual job description to the last two sentences. It said that the pay was "competitive," whatever that meant, and ended with the magic words that I always loved to see: "Willing to train the right person." This could be my golden ticket, I thought to myself. Of course, I still didn't know what it was that they'd be training me to do.

I went back and read the description. Landscaping. How hard could that be? Pull a few weeds, plant a few flowers, work outside. Hell, I was a farmer's kid. Landscaping was what I was born to do. I grabbed my phone and dialed the number without really thinking about what I'd say. The guy on the other end picked up after the first ring.

"Homestead Organic Landscaping."

Organic. I'd heard the word like the guy had shouted it at me. I had a quick flashback to my maple-syrup-on-the-side-of-the-highway days in Vermont. "Uh, yeah. Hi. My name is Billy Faulkner, and I was calling about the job you've got advertised."

"Oh, hi. Stewart Goodsen. I own the business. Have you landscaped before?"

I tried to sound a little like this was below me. "Oh, yeah," I said with a tone of what I hoped was extreme confidence. "I grew up on a farm in Vermont."

"Okay," he said doubtfully. "You realize we're not farming, right? This is mowing lawns and weeding flower beds to start."

I nodded my head involuntarily, as if he were sitting right across from me. "Totally cool with me. I can do that."

"So you're obviously fluent in English," Stewart continued without sounding like he was even trying to be funny. "But do you have a driver's license?"

"Yep." I'd actually just the week before gotten my official Massachusetts driver's license, so I was even a registered voter in the state.

"No driving offenses I'm going to find out about? No DUIs or anything like that?"

I thought for a quick second. No DUIs to speak of. Just don't ask about my arrest record, and we're all set. "Nope, all clear," I said.

"Okay, look," he said after a pause, "I'm on my way to a job site right now. And I'm in need of somebody pretty quick. Our season is getting busy, and the fucking wetback I had running the mower ran off with his little señorita to God only knows what horrible place he came from. But I want to meet you before I offer you anything. You free to come over to the house where I'm working today?"

All of a sudden, this guy reminded me a little of Victor. He was clearly a no-holds-barred kind of guy who didn't take any grief from anybody, and didn't have a problem saying exactly what was on his mind. I figured he and I would get along pretty well.

"Yeah," I said to him. "I'm free. What's the address?"

He gave me the street number of the house, and told me he'd be there for the whole day. It was, he said, a really big house with a huge lawn and garden that he maintained, and it would be an all-day affair today. I said I'd be there as quick as I could, and hung up. I immediately called Molly to tell her the news, but got her voice mail. I left a message, saying only that I thought I'd figured out what I wanted to do, at least for the time being, and I was going off to talk to the owner of the company. I left out the fact that it was a landscaping job, just in case it didn't work out the way I was hoping. Once I had the job, then I could tell her. I'd probably have to exaggerate a little, maybe tell her I was in charge of a crew or something. Something manager-level. Just so she wouldn't think I was taking something too menial.

I might just become a landscaper, I said to myself. That sounds like a respectable profession. Granted, it wasn't glamorous work, and I wasn't going to crack the Fortune 500 list, but what the hell. It would be an income, a paying job that I could at least admit to doing. Yeah. Landscaping was an honest man's profession. Things were starting to look up in old Billy Faulkner's world.

CHAPTER FOURTEEN

As much as I sat there and thought about it after I'd hung up, I could not figure out what I was supposed to wear to a job interview for a landscaping position. I didn't want to wear a suit. That just seemed ridiculous on every possible level. But I didn't want to look like a scumbag that ate out of a dumpster, either. I felt like a girl trying to figure out what to wear for a first date. I tried on six or seven different outfits before I finally just settled on a pair of jeans that were relatively clean and a knit polo shirt. That seemed like it told people I was conscious of the fact that I needed to look slightly better than the average homeless man, but wasn't so uptight that I was afraid to get a little dirt on my hands and grass stains on my clothes.

I followed the directions Stewart had given me to the house, and when I pulled up, my jaw felt like it dropped six inches. To say this house was huge didn't do it justice. It looked like a hotel from the street. It was a gargantuan, brick thing, with enormous white pillars in front and black shutters on the windows. It went off in several different directions, and looked from the outside like it could have comfortably slept twenty people.

I parked the truck on the street and got out, and as I walked through the front gate, I could see what he'd meant about this job taking all day. The lawn looked like something you'd see on a golf course, and the flower beds were perfectly manicured. I could hear the roar of a lawn mower coming from the back of the house, so I made my way around to find Stewart.

I saw a guy who looked like he was in his early twenties. He was about six feet tall, blonde hair, sunburned, wearing a white knit polo shirt with the word Homestead embroidered on it. He was directing four kids who looked like they'd just gotten out of seventh grade as they did various tasks around the yard. He looked my direction and waved. "Billy?"

I nodded my head and waved back. I walked over and extended my hand. "Billy Faulkner," I offered. "Nice to meet you."

He smiled. "Nice to meet you too," he said as he looked me up and down. "Stewart Goodsen." He pointed at the kids who were now busy pulling weeds out of a flower bed as he continued, "This is my little merry band of incompetents." He turned back to face me, studying me. His mouth was furiously chomping on a piece of gum as he looked me over. "You sure you want to mow lawns?" he asked with a slight smile.

I nodded my head. "Beats the hell out of sitting on the couch."

He nodded in agreement. After a lengthy pause during which I grew increasingly self-conscious and concerned that he was going to tell me I didn't get the job, he finally let out a sigh. It almost sounded like he had resigned himself to say what he was about to say. "Like I said, it's ugly work. But I need somebody. And you're standing here. You meet all my requirements." He laughed sarcastically. "So as long as you've got a Social Security number, I guess you get the job."

I promised him I did and that I was a fully legal citizen of the United States. He took me at my word and led me back through the gate in the front yard to his own truck that was parked near where I'd left mine. He rummaged around in the cab and came out holding a T-shirt that looked like it had spent a long time crumpled up on the floor of the truck. "Extra-large," Stewart said as he tossed the shirt to me. "I'll give you the first one. Every one after that is ten bucks."

I stood there, holding the shirt in one hand. Stewart popped his head out of the truck. "What are you waiting for? There's no dressing room."

I snapped out of the daydream I'd been in long enough to ask him what he meant.

"Change your shirt. That T-shirt's your new work uniform. Jeans might be a little hot, but that's your problem. You want the job, you start now," he said.

I nodded vigorously. "I want the job. Totally fine. Ten bucks a shirt," I rattled off. I quickly slipped off the polo shirt I'd worn and replaced it with the T-shirt. I looked at the loafers I was wearing on my feet. They were totally not appropriate for the work I was about to be doing, but I didn't have anything else to wear at the time. So loafers it was going to be.

Stewart noticed. "I'm not trying to be an asshole here, but I have got to get this lawn cut pronto. If you can give me two hours pushing a mower in those, I can let you go home and change after that," he said, pointing at my feet.

They had certainly seen better days, and I was pretty sure that walking through this lawn wasn't going to do any more damage to them. I laughed as I said, "No sweat. I've worked in worse." He started to lead me back through the gate when I stopped him. "You never mentioned money," I said, "outside of the fact that shirts are ten dollars each."

"Oh, yeah," he said flatly. "That." He scratched his head and looked at me again before replying. "How's twelve to start grab you? You show me some skills, we'll talk about bumping you up."

Twelve dollars an hour was pretty much what I considered a financial insult. I was overqualified for the job. He'd said that much. Hell, if I wanted to buy another shirt to wear to work—don't even get me started on the fact that I was going to be wearing a T-shirt—it was going to cost me damn near an hour's worth of work. I was having second thoughts all of a sudden. Maybe I'd made a horrible mistake. Was I really at that low a point that I was willing to accept a job that required I be able to speak English as the major requirement?

The argument I had with myself didn't last long. The answer, of course, was that yes, I had sunk to that level. My own decisions, my own actions, my own choices I'd made to this point in my life led me here, and I needed to accept that fact. The sooner I got over whatever issues I might have had with doing a little menial labor for pay, the sooner I'd be able to get on with my life. And now that I had Molly, my life had a future that I'd never really thought was possible.

"Twelve bucks sounds great," I finally said. "What say we get started right now?" We shook hands. It was official. I was now a landscaper.

In the backyard, the four kids were still pulling weeds out of the same bed they'd been working in when I saw them the last time. Stewart pointed at them as he said, "College kids out here for the summer. You might have to yell at them a little to get them to work, once you get comfortable with the job. You know what they say, summer help, summer not."

I laughed at his joke, but wondered what he meant by my having to yell at the kids. The comment gave me a little hope that maybe he was thinking of me as more than the guy who was going to be mowing lawns. Maybe he planned to put me in some kind of overseer role, which I hoped might pay slightly better than twelve dollars an hour. But I didn't press the issue just then. I figured what I needed to know right now was that I was mowing lawns in a T-shirt and loafers, and that's all that I needed to really think about. It was a job. I'd get paid to do it. And for that, I was grateful. Everything else would take care of itself. But before I got started, I had to call Molly and tell her the great news.

*   *   *

Stewart, I learned pretty quick, was a man of his word. He'd been absolutely correct when he'd told me that the job wouldn't be glamorous. I came home from work every evening covered in dirt and grass stains. My hands had a semipermanent stain of black, and trying to keep my fingernails clean was something I gave up on after two days. But it was easy work, and I really felt a sense of accomplishment every time I cashed my paycheck, because I knew it was an honest income.

After a couple of weeks on the job, I'd graduated from running the lawn mower to managing the crew of four kids I'd worked with on my first day. I was making more money now—sixteen dollars an hour, with the promise of both a potential raise in the future and an end-of-year bonus—and the kids and I got along pretty well.

They were college buddies from the University of Massachusetts down the highway in Amherst. They were working to make a little extra cash for the fall semester, with the added benefit that Northampton was "full of chicks," as one of them said.

As summer hit its peak, we were busy seven days a week. The houses we were working at were all huge, and the owners were demanding like I never knew was humanly possible. The grass had to be cut in specific patterns, and each homeowner had their own preferred style. Beds had to be mulched and lawns had to be fertilized and flowers had to be fed. And all of it—every single product we put into the ground—had to be organic.

These people were paying big bucks to have their consciences eased by using overpriced organic products on their lawns, and that need for personal redemption had made Stewart and the Homestead Organic Landscaping Company a fortune. It was a brilliant business model that had capitalized perfectly on the whole organic movement. Stewart played the part of concerned environmentalist, and his clients ate it up. All he had to do was throw out a few statistics and talk about ground water toxicity that resulted from too many chemical fertilizers, and he had them eating out of his hand.

One day in early August, I was walking by one of the kids on my crew fertilizing a rose bush. He had the bag of rose food next to him, and was sprinkling it along the base of the stems. I noticed that the bag looked different than the one I remembered him using, and asked about it. He looked around, almost like he was scared, before answering.

"Dude, it's not the organic stuff," he said quietly. "I spilled the bag and didn't want to tell you or Stewart, so I grabbed a bag of stuff at the store on my way to work this morning. Don't tell on me, man," he said. "I really need to keep this job for as long as I can, and Stewart'll kick my ass if he hears I'm using the real stuff."

I told the kid to relax. "Just don't let these people see you using that on their flowers," I warned him, pointing at the house. "Do it quick and get the bag out of here."

He was right, though. Stewart took the organic part of his business very seriously. He'd told me that from the first day he put me in charge of the crew. "Billy, our reputation is all we've got," he said. "We screw up one house, and word gets around fast with these people. So don't screw up."

And in Stewart's mind, there were a lot of ways one could screw up. There were, of course, the standard ways. You could show up late— or not at all—or just slack off while you were on the clock.

A lot of stuff I turned a blind eye to, like milking the clock. The kids on my crew were bad about that. You'd have thought they were putting a nuclear bomb together because they were working so slowly. They'd tell me they were just being thorough; but the truth is that they were just trying to get as much money as they could.

The thing with our work was that it had to be done in a day if we were doing standard maintenance. We'd show up and mow and edge the lawn, plus do all the weeding and fertilizing and pruning and whatever else needed to be done. And all of it had to be done in a single visit. If it took us five hours to finish a yard, that was fine. If it took us twice that long, well, that's how long it took. And with hourly employees, it's a pretty simple math problem to see that the longer they took to do a job, the more money they made.

But the one thing I was told had to be maintained above everything else was "the integrity of the process." That's how Stewart always phrased it. "The integrity of the process is essential to our brand," he'd tell me. It was a bunch of college-boy talk, but what it boiled down to was that the customers were paying for organic treatment, and our reputation was really based on the fact that we used the products we were saying we used. We didn't take shortcuts with commercially produced chemicals; we were true to our name, and used only natural fertilizers.

So this breach of trust by this kid was pretty major. But it was getting close to the end of the summer, and pretty soon he'd be back at school. And really, who was ever going to know that he'd used something he'd bought at a hardware store instead of from some hippie at a greenhouse? These people sure as hell wouldn't know. All they cared about was their image, being able to say they were doing good things for the environment by overpaying for landscaping services that used only organic methods.

It was just a different version of my own old maple syrup trip. These people didn't know the difference, so what harm was there? And really, it was only time. It wasn't like we were constantly using non-organic stuff and charging for the more expensive organic fertilizers. One time was not going to ruin our reputation. I figured we were safe.

And Stewart never did find out, as best as I could figure out. He never brought it up to me, anyway. The leaves changed when fall came, and our work slowed down, and then the leaves all fell off the trees. Now that college was back in session, it was pretty much just Stewart and me to do the work, so we'd end up raking leaves during the week. I didn't mind it, because it meant a paycheck. I'd gotten used to telling other people what to do, so when it came my turn to do the work, it took a little getting used to. But I actually like raking. It gives me time to think, time to daydream about things I want.

One day I was raking and thinking about how I wanted something more out of my life than what I had. I was happy, don't get me wrong. I knew that given my past, the fact that I was making any money at all—not to mention the fact that I wasn't sitting in jail for my insurance scams—should have been enough to keep me content. But by this point, Molly and I had started talking about our future together, which included getting married, having kids, buying a house, all that. And even though I knew I was lucky to have what I did, I knew, too, that I couldn't support a family raking leaves and pulling weeds. I needed to be my own boss. I needed what Stewart had.

I remember that night, sitting at the dinner table talking to Molly. I told her about how I wanted more so that I could give her the life she deserved. She told me I was being silly—that I was a great provider, and she couldn't ask for anything more. Basically all the stuff she felt like she had to say to make me feel better.

But I wasn't listening to her. I'd already made up my mind. I knew enough about landscaping at this point to be able to do whatever needed to be done. It's not like we were talking about rocket science, after all. Make it look pretty and everybody's happy. Throw in the organic element, and everybody's even happier. Hire a couple of kids who'll work for cheap, and pocket the profits. Easy as being a pimp in Las Vegas.

The only real question was where to set up shop. I couldn't compete with Stewart, and I didn't really want to, so Northampton was out. But the rest of the country was basically open to me. The more I thought about the whole thing, the more I realized the value in being the only game in town, so to speak. Not necessarily the only landscaper, but the only organic landscaper. That way, no matter who came after me, I'd always be the first. And as long as I could build that almighty reputation—and preserve the integrity of it—I'd have it made. So it was just a matter of where to go.

That night, as I drifted off to sleep, I was thinking about that exact thing. Where Molly and I could go to start our new lives together. Some small town that didn't already have somebody who'd cashed in on the organic craze in landscaping, but where there were people who could afford to pay for it. I dreamt that night about whaling, of all things. I can't remember ever dreaming about it before. I can't even remember talking about it, even. What I knew about the history of killing whales you could fit in a coffee cup. I'd watched a special on cable one night, but that was about the extent of it. Basically, from what I'd seen, it involved huge ships sailing around the world, chasing whales. And when they'd filled up with whale oil, they'd return home, where they'd cash in their cargo and watch the money roll in.

I woke up in the middle of the dream and immediately knew where I wanted to go. Nantucket. Molly had mentioned it once, when we'd first met. And living in Northampton, I'd heard other people talk about it. It had once been the whaling capital of the world, back when that was a business. Today it was an island full of opportunity. God only knows there was plenty of money out there. Even as a kid from Vermont I'd heard the stories about the rich and famous people who spent their summers out there. And now that I was living in Massachusetts, I'd actually seen some of those people firsthand. They had to have lawns and gardens that needed taking care of out there. And surely they'd be willing to pay a little more for organic gardening services.

I fell back asleep and dreamed about Nantucket.

CHAPTER FIFTEEN

The next morning, I was back at work raking leaves. But now I had a new energy, as I mentally went through the process of how I saw my new business venture taking shape. There was all of the start-up costs to consider, but I figured that it wouldn't take too much money to get some flyers printed, and deliver them to houses. That didn't include the fact that it was going to cost us a little bit to move, of course, but we could figure that out. It would be an adventure, just like the guys who went out on those whaleships back in the day. I'd heard those trips made a lot of money for the guys who went on them. I was hoping that my little adventure would have the same kind of ending.

I hadn't talked to Molly about the idea yet. I wanted to have the whole thing figured out in my own head before I dropped that on her. It wasn't so much that I was worried she'd totally hate the idea. I just didn't want her to have to worry about details. I was afraid it would be enough of a shock to her system as it was. I didn't have any idea what she was thinking about what our future involved.

I spent the next several days with my secret plans, calculating how much I thought it might cost, researching landscaping companies on Nantucket on the Internet, and thinking about the best ways to market myself. I already had a name for the business—Faulkner Organic Landscaping—so it was really just a matter of deciding on how to advertise. I liked the name, actually. It was right to the point, you know? It was no-nonsense, not cute, just exactly what it claimed to be.

Day-to-day living was going to be a challenge. I'd figured that much out from reading what I could find about life on Nantucket. Rents were really high, food prices were more than we were paying now. Basically the whole cost of living in general was higher. But at the same time, the amount of money I could charge for landscaping services was also higher, so I was pretty sure that we'd be just fine once the summer rolled around. And there were plenty of restaurants that no doubt employed waitresses, so Molly could get a job until my own business started to grow. And she could write too. Maybe for the newspaper. Or she could write the book she kept mentioning.

It wasn't a foolproof plan. Far from it, actually. I found an online blog written by a year-round Nantucket resident. The way he described it, life on Nantucket—especially in the winter—was pretty tough. But those challenges didn't seem too bad, especially when you thought about the fact that there was so much money to be made. It was the kind of place where a guy like me—a guy with no real education and no real experience—could make a lot of money, so long as I was willing to work hard at it. I knew I had a good idea, and I knew I had the work ethic to make it work. So the tough part that went along with living on an island thirty miles out in the ocean didn't bother me. We'd be making enough money to leave during the winter if we wanted to. Nothing to worry about.

I had most of the specifics worked out, at least in my own mind, and I finally decided that the time was as right as it was ever going to be to let Molly know about my idea. I was nervous when we sat down to eat dinner, because I had no idea about what to expect. There was no telling how she was going to react.

My heart was racing as I worked up the courage to make my grand announcement. I'd rehearsed it multiple times that afternoon, playing around with my delivery, and deciding on the best way to explain my points. But when the moment of truth came, everything I'd prepared left my brain as soon as I started talking. "What would you think about us moving to Nantucket so I could open my own landscaping business?" I blurted out.

And it hung there in the air like a balloon, just waiting to be popped. My original thoughts about this discussion—the ones I'd been rehearsing all day—had been to ease my way into it by first talking about how nice it would be to own my own business, then sliding in the idea of Nantucket. But now I'd just gotten it all out there at once, and the only thing I could do now was wait for Molly's reaction.

Sitting across from me, she looked a little confused at first. "Your own landscaping business?" she asked. "Do you really know enough about it to start your own business?"

That gave me the chance to talk more about the business idea, which I'd originally wanted to do in my opening in the first place. I explained the idea of doing organic lawn care to start, and building the business as I went along. I told her I'd done the research, and that there wasn't anyone on Nantucket doing organic landscaping, so it would be a way for me to get in on the ground floor and build up a business, like Stewart had done. I had the experience. I just needed the chance to do it myself.

She sat quietly for a few minutes, probably thinking of all the things that could possibly go wrong and why this was such a horrible idea. Finally she broke the silence. "I've got a confession to make," she said softly, her eyes looking down towards the floor. "I don't know how to tell you this, so I'm just going to say it. I quit my job."

No matter how many guesses you gave me, that was not something I would have ever guessed her to say. "Today?" I asked.

She shook her head. "A week ago. I just couldn't take it any more. I'm sorry I didn't tell you, Billy," she said, tears beginning to well up in her eyes. "I'm so sorry."

I stood up and walked to her side of the table, wrapping my arms around her. "You don't need to apologize," I told her. "It's okay. I understand." I kissed the top of her head gently. "But if you quit your job, what have you been doing for the last week?" I asked.

She gave me her best attempt at a laugh. "I've been going downtown and hanging out," she said. "I've drank more tea in the last week than I did in the last year." She smiled up at me. "You're sure you can forgive me?"

I nodded my head. "Positive." I smiled and stroked the side of her face. I'm sure you know how easy it was for me to forgive her, especially since she still thought I was this former badass insurance guy. I still hadn't told her my own confessions.

"Nantucket, huh?" she asked after a second. She smiled and winked at me. "When do we leave?"

The nervous tension that had built up in me finally flooded out, and I started laughing. It was laughter made up of total and complete relief more than anything else. "I hadn't gotten quite that far just yet," I said. "I was too worried that you'd tell me you wouldn't go."

"Billy Faulkner, I'd follow you into hell," she said as she kissed the back of my hand. She stood up and led me over to the futon, then pushed me down into it. "Wait right there," she ordered.

She went to the bookshelf and looked at the collection of books on a particular shelf, stopping at a specific paperback. Apparently satisfied that she'd chosen the right one, she pulled it out and brought it over to the futon, where she sat down next to me. I looked over at the book. It was a travel guide for Nantucket.

"I've always wanted to go to Nantucket," she said, her voice sounding more and more excited. "Ever since I read *Moby-Dick* when I was twelve, I've wanted to go." She started flipping through the book, reading out loud parts that caught her eye. The pages were dog-eared and old, like she'd read it a bunch of times. She clearly knew the contents pretty well.

As we sat on the futon planning our next move, any tension that either of us might have been carrying through the day as we hauled our secrets around with us had disappeared with both of our revelations. We were both noticeably happier, even though it hadn't dawned on me that neither of us had seemed nervous or tense before. I guess I hadn't noticed that Molly was tense because I was too wrapped up in my own little secret plan.

But now that the dam had burst and the waters had come pouring out, I started to think back. I had actually noticed that Molly hadn't been herself for the last week, but it just hadn't registered. Obviously she'd been keeping all of her own fears about the future inside, the same way I had been. But now that it was all out in the open, there was nothing but happiness to go around.

She kept flipping through the book, pointing out historic sites and museums we could go visit, and restaurants that all sounded good. Good and expensive. It was going to take some effort from me to keep her thinking realistic. I'd have to explain to her that we'd be able to do all of those things once we got settled and started making some money. But at first, things were going to be a little hard. We might not get to eat out and we might not get to do a lot of fun things. But we'd be able to do those things soon enough. Once the business got going, we'd be able to do all of them and more. It was just going to take some time.

I really didn't want to be a buzzkill for her, because I was excited that she was so happy about the prospect of moving to Nantucket. I was afraid that if I burst her bubble about it, she might come to her senses and realize that we weren't going on a vacation. It was more like we were relocating to a place where other people went on vacation so people like us could wait on them. So I kept quiet and let her have the moment. There would be time enough for reality to set in. Things were going to work out. I could feel it.

*   *   *

Once we'd made the decision to go, time went by fast. We spent the next week packing up the apartment. I turned in my two-weeks' notice at work; Stewart said he wasn't totally surprised, but I didn't tell him what my plans were. I just said it was time for me to move on, and wished him the best. He offered to serve as a reference for my next job if I needed it, and I thanked him and told him I'd let him know. I did want to work those last two weeks—both so I could stay in Stewart's good graces in case I did end up needing him down the road, and also to get as much extra money as I could before we left.

And that meant that I couldn't spend as much time as I would have liked helping Molly pack. But she really seemed to enjoy doing it herself. She kept telling me how excited she was for the next phase.

She took on the job of trying to find us a place to live, a job she took very seriously. The more she looked into the housing that was available, the more she figured out that it was going to be an expensive deal. She quit talking so much about the fabulous restaurants, and instead began to look at how far it was to the grocery store from addresses of different rental houses. After days of searching and a lot of phone calls back and forth, she finally decided on a place that was the top floor of a two-story duplex.

A married couple—both teachers without kids—lived in the downstairs part; Molly and I would live upstairs. We would have two bedrooms, a large living room, and a kitchen. It wasn't a lot—and it certainly wasn't cheap—but it was, as far as we could see from the maps, centrally located. It also had a parking place for the truck, and we could afford it. Barely.

There was one catch about the lease that bothered me. It was only good through the thirtieth of April. On May first, the rent went way up, and we were welcome to keep on living there as long as we agreed to pay the new rate. It would go back down October first, the owner had told Molly, back to the amount we would be paying when we arrived.

Staying would mean spending an additional $10,000 on top of what we were already paying just for those five months, if we decided to stay. I was sure we could find something else cheaper by then, so I told Molly not to worry about it. We'd solve one problem at a time, and it would be easier to solve that one after we'd gotten to the island and spent some time there. Once we knew some people, we'd find somebody who could help us out.

On my last day of work with Stewart, he handed me an envelope. It was my last paycheck, he told me, plus a little something for sticking out the year with him. Three hundred little somethings, to be exact, which was a very nice little surprise to get. I thanked him a ton, told him I'd really loved working with him, and gave him a friendly hug good-bye.

I was really kind of sad to be leaving him. He'd given me my first legitimate job ever, and I'd learned a lot from him. And now I was going to take that knowledge and start my own business. At least that was the plan.

We decided that we'd survive with one car to start out with on Nantucket, so we sold Molly's Volvo. We were able to find a girl at Smith who needed something to get her through her senior year, and her father had finally agreed to give us $1,000 for it.

Our worldly possessions, if you want to call them that, fit pretty well into the bed of my truck. Molly's apartment had been what she described as "mostly furnished," so the only piece of furniture that she took with her was her futon. Other than that, we had Molly's books and our clothes. We left the front door key inside the apartment on the kitchen counter, as the complex manager had asked us to do, and shut the door. We were on our way.

It was a Thursday, exactly two weeks before Thanksgiving, at about ten o'clock in the morning, when we left Northampton. We headed south on Interstate 91, and I had one of those weird déjà vu moments as we drove back towards the world that first started this whole trip I was on. But once we turned east on I-90, I started to relax. And I relaxed even more when we got to the exit for I-495 heading towards Cape Cod.

We were going to drive to Hyannis, where there were ferries that went over to Nantucket. At this time of year, they didn't go quite as frequently as they do during the summer, but there was a ferry that took cars leaving at two forty-five in the afternoon, which would put us in Nantucket around five o'clock. I'd called and made a reservation, paying what I thought was an insane amount of money to take my truck twenty-six miles across the ocean. We'd also arranged with our new landlord to meet him at the house we were renting at six thirty. That should give us enough time to get off the boat, get something for dinner, and find the house where we were going to be living, I thought. It was all incredibly exciting to think about.

A couple of hours later, we were crossing the Bourne Bridge over the Cape Cod Canal. It felt like a new beginning. There wasn't very much traffic on the highway, and we zipped around the rotary at the bottom of the bridge, heading towards Hyannis.

I'm not totally sure what I was expecting from the town of Hyannis, but whatever it was, the reality of the place didn't come anywhere close to living up to what I had imagined. I guess I'd pictured yet another quaint little New England town, especially since the Kennedy family seemed to love the place so much. But what I got was strip malls and fast-food places strung along the road like soldiers lined up in formation.

Molly looked out the window as I drove and pretty much said exactly what I was thinking: "Looks disgusting," she said.

We made our way through the streets down to the dock where the ferry would be leaving from, and got there at about one forty-five. There was a man outside who motioned for us to stop, and I rolled down the window. "You folks taking your truck over to Nantucket?" he asked good-naturedly.

I told him we were, and he checked us in. He gave me the boarding passes for both us and the truck, and told me to pull up to the waiting area. I parked the truck and we went inside the building that was both the place where passengers bought tickets and where they could also hang out while they waited for their boat. There was a big-screen TV on one wall—it was tuned to a twenty-four-hour news station—and long rows of wooden benches all over the inside. A few people were scattered around the room, sitting in small groups. The ones I could hear were speaking in what sounded like some kind of Caribbean pidgin; I guessed they were Jamaicans. I'd heard there were a lot of Jamaicans who worked on the island.

We took a seat together, talking quietly about the whole adventure that was unfolding in front of us. Things were going well so far. We'd found a place to live that we could afford, even if not comfortably. We'd gotten out of Northampton and to Hyannis without any problems. We had our reservations to get the truck over to the island. And here we were, waiting for the boat. I looked at Molly and kissed her. We were both feeling the same sense of gratitude for the way things had worked out for us. And there was this feeling in the air that things were going to keep on getting better, the further ahead we went.

CHAPTER SIXTEEN

When it was time to drive the truck onto the ferry, I was a little scared when I saw what it involved. It was like driving into a cave, and I couldn't see very well because the cargo hold was so dark. A kid who might have been eighteen was motioning me forward, and I kept inching ahead, terrified I was going to slam into the back of the car in front of me. He finally held up both hands, telling me to stop. I put the emergency brake on and exhaled. I didn't realize I'd been holding my breath the whole time I was pulling on.

After a second, I asked Molly if she wanted to go up and sit inside. It was almost a three-hour ride across, and I thought the truck might get a little uncomfortable. So we got out and made our way up a narrow flight of metal steps, through a door, and into one of the main passenger seating areas.

We took a seat and looked around. There weren't a lot of people on the ferry, and sitting in one of the plastic chairs that was bolted to the floor wasn't any more comfortable than it would have been sitting in the truck. As the boat pulled away from the dock, I suggested we go outside. "They say salt air is good for the soul," I added with a smile.

She took my hand and we went out a side door. The air was chilly, and the wind felt like it was blowing tiny drops of water in to our faces. There were a few boats in the harbor. Most of them looked like they were pretty beat up. They were working boats, I guessed. Boats that people took out to make their livings. There weren't too many boats that looked like pleasure crafts. I could smell the exhaust fumes from the ferry mixing with fuel. But the further we got from the harbor and the faster the boat moved, the more the air smelled like the ocean.

We walked as far forward as we could, looking over the side. As the boat picked up speed, the mist of spray coming off the side of the ferry grew larger. It made me realize how truly small we were, looking down at the Atlantic. I thought about the whalers who had probably left that same harbor on ships, knowing that they might be gone from home for years at a time. And some of them would never come home again at all. I wondered if they had any idea how huge the world really was at the time, and whether or not they felt like I did at that moment, as the boats they were on left their homes.

We stood there for a long time. I can't tell you exactly how long it was, because I was totally lost in my romantic thoughts about old-time sailors. But when I looked back again, land was out of sight. Ahead of us there was nothing but open ocean. We were officially at sea.

I felt Molly's hand shivering in mine, and suddenly felt the chill of the ocean breeze, like I was feeling it for the first time. We went back inside and got a cup of coffee, then took a seat, this time at a booth-style table with benches on either side. She stretched out on the bench across from me and was asleep within minutes. I looked up and saw a rack of tourist brochures on the wall nearby, so I grabbed a few. I went back to my seat with my reading material, and started to read through the one on top of the stack.

The one on top happened to be one from the Nantucket Historical Association, advertising its whaling museum. It was interesting to me, you know, because history was always a subject I thought was cool back when I was in high school. The brochure had a lot of photos of some actual whalers, plus some of the inside of the museum itself. The main attraction, it seemed like, was a huge whale skeleton that was hanging in a large room. I made a mental note that I wanted to make sure we went there soon.

The next thing I started to read was a free newspaper that had been in a rack next to the brochures. It was obviously aimed at the tourists, despite the fact that there weren't nearly as many of them at this time of year as during the peak of the summer season. A couple of restaurant reviews, a few human interest stories about people and organizations on Nantucket, a lot of advertisements for local businesses. Bike rentals seemed to be a hot business. So did antique shops and art galleries. There was also a map of the downtown area. I studied it, even though none of the street names or landmarks meant anything to me. There'd be time to figure all that out. I stuffed the map into the back pocket of my jeans, then put down the paper and looked out the window.

I could see the outline of land starting to come into view on the horizon. I watched as the island that was to become my new home slowly started to take shape. After a few minutes, I could see the shoreline. We were coming in from the north, which was the protected side of the island. So there were no rolling waves crashing, just calm water all the way in. We glided slowly between two long, stone jetties that marked the entrance to Nantucket Harbor.

"Is that it? Is that Nantucket?" Molly asked, her voice a mixture of sleepiness and excitement.

I smiled at her. "Yep. That's it. We're here."

We stood up and started to walk back to the truck. Inside the belly of the ferry, there was a lot of activity as the different crew members got ready for the boat's arrival in Nantucket. We found the truck and got in, and my adrenaline started pumping from the anticipation. We could feel the boat slowing down, then bumping gently against the dock. We had arrived.

After what seemed like a long time, daylight flooded into the interior of the ferry as they opened up the door for vehicles to exit. All around us we could hear the sound of engines turning over and coming to life. I started the truck and waited to be told it was my turn to go. When our time finally came, I followed the car in front of me off the ferry and out onto Nantucket Island.

We didn't have any real immediate agenda, but my stomach was definitely announcing that it was time for me to eat. I turned to Molly and asked, "You as hungry as I am?"

"Starving," she said.

As we idled forward, we passed a strip of take-out food places, but there was nowhere to park. I didn't have any idea where I was going, and I didn't want to be that guy who stopped in the middle of the street because he was lost, you know, so I just followed the car in front of me. I hoped he knew where he was going. The driver made a left turn at the corner, and I stayed right behind him. We were passing more storefronts—restaurants and T-shirt shops, mostly—and I saw a long space of open curb that seemed to be a legal parking area. I swerved over and parked the truck. "Let's get out and see what we can find," I said.

I locked up the truck and we started walking without any sense of where we were going, or even what direction we were walking. Molly was like a kid in a candy store, taking it all in. "I've dreamed about this place for so long," she said as we walked along. "I can't believe I'm actually here. I'm really walking on Nantucket."

After a couple of blocks, we found a restaurant that advertised hot soup on a sign hanging inside the front door, and that sounded perfect. We went in, took a seat, and a waitress appeared, anxious to make something resembling a tip. The place was nearly empty, which explained her eagerness to serve.

She went through the day's specials as she handed us menus and asked us what we'd like to drink. I had a cup of coffee; Molly just wanted water. The waitress's eagerness was gone as soon as we'd ordered our drinks. Coffee and water didn't add up to a big tip.

We looked over the menus, pointing out things that sounded good. But we both ended up ordering the same thing, a bowl of clam chowder. "It just sounds Nantuckety," Molly said, laughing.

I had to agree, and when the waitress returned with our drinks, we gave her our order. Two bowls of chowder, one water, one coffee. She might make a couple of dollars if I decided to tip her 40 percent of our final tab. You could totally feel the disappointment dripping off her.

Within minutes, she was back with our chowder. Steam was coming up off the bowls, and we went at it like we hadn't eaten in a month. When we'd finished, I pushed the empty bowls aside and pulled the map out of my pocket. I spread it on the table and tried to figure out where we were. It took me a second to figure out where the ferry had come in, but once I'd gotten that, it was just a matter of tracing the line we'd driven. "We're on South Water Street," I announced with a tone of authority, "a couple of blocks away from Main Street."

Molly giggled. "So what do we do with that information?"

I shrugged. "I don't know. I just thought you might like to know where we were on this little island."

But Molly was right. I knew where we were according to the map, but it only covered downtown. And that wasn't going to help much, especially since we'd been told that our new house was a few miles outside of town. I needed a better map.

Our waitress came back to clear the bowls, scowling at us as we sat looking at our pathetic map. We looked like the lost tourists that we basically were, and she didn't feel like giving us any help. Maybe she would have changed her tune if we'd spent a little money, but that wasn't going to happen.

"Do you guys need anything else?" she asked. She knew the answer, I think, because she already had the check written out and in her hand, ready to slam it on the table.

"No, thanks," I said, trying to sound friendly. It came out more as an apology than anything else.

She dropped the ticket on the table in front of us. "Pay at the register," she said offhandedly as she walked away.

I glanced down at the total. Twelve dollars was a lot of money for what we'd ordered, but there it was, circled in black ink. Twelve bucks. No smiley face, no "thank you" scribbled in girlish handwriting. Just twelve dollars. I fished two dollars out of my wallet and put them on the table. That was going to have to be enough for her tip. We walked up to the register and paid.

As we were leaving, I said to Molly, "That was an expensive bowl of soup. We need to be careful."

I had no idea where we would find a map, but I assumed it couldn't be all that hard. This was a tourist town, after all. So we started walking towards Main Street. Even though there was no street sign, it was pretty obvious when we'd hit it. It was a lot wider, and covered in cobblestones. There were lots of stores on both sides, and there was a fountain in the middle of the street. It was decorated with Christmas-themed greens.

We took a right and kept on going up Main Street. Most of the stores we passed were high-end boutiques, you know. Most of them sold clothes and jewelry. I looked in the windows at some of the displays, but I wasn't about to go in and ask how much anything cost. I was sure I couldn't afford it anyway. We eventually came to a less-glamorous-looking store that sold newspapers and magazines, and I thought it was a good bet that they'd have a map.

Inside, I asked the young woman behind the counter if they sold maps, and she pointed to a wooden shelf with several different ones. I looked them over, and finally decided on the one that looked like it had the most detail for destinations outside of the downtown area. Four dollars and change. The meter was running, and I could feel my cash running out like blood from an open cut. Everything really was a lot more expensive out here.

CHAPTER SEVENTEEN

Time went by, and we gradually grew more and more used to living on an island. Our rental house was small for two people, to say the least. It had sounded a lot nicer and a lot bigger in the online advertisement, but at least the downstairs people were nice enough. Chris and Judy taught at the local high school, and they'd moved to the island four years ago together. We were really lucky to have them so close, because they gave us a lot of information that we needed in order to be able to survive. I'd had no idea moving to Nantucket was going to take so much getting used to.

One of the first things they told us about was what the locals referred to as the Nantucket Shuffle. It happened every year towards the end of spring, right before the summer crowds hit. Rents went sky-high as the demand for places went up, and a lot of the local people weren't lucky enough to have year-round rentals that they could afford. That left them in a sticky situation, because it meant that they had to find a new place to live that they could somehow afford. In other words, they had to move from where they were living for a couple of months—assuming they wanted to come back once the rents had gone back down—and that new place had to be cheap. Talk about a needle in a haystack.

In our case, we were going to be faced with that little problem on May first. Chris and Judy had been smart about it. They had played the teacher card with the landlord, explaining that they just couldn't possibly afford the rental increase and, since they were teachers, they should get a break. In the end, the landlord had agreed to a higher monthly rate in exchange for year-round housing.

But because we weren't quite so lucky in that way, we'd be moving out, bound for God only knew where. Chris told me stories about some of the past summers he'd been living there, when college students lived in the place we were currently staying. They came out to Nantucket for the summer and worked at odd jobs. They no doubt had their parents paying their rent, which meant they were free to spend all the money they made on booze. The parties he described were nothing short of epic. I'm talking parties that lasted until all hours of the night. And the fact that those parties were raging right above their bedroom made summer nights a rough time for them to get any sleep.

And then there was the money issue. Things weren't cheap on Nantucket, like I already told you. And it wasn't like the prices went down after the summer people left. No, gas still cost more than anywhere else in the world. About two dollars a gallon more. And our weekly grocery bill was huge. Plus it was hard for Molly to find a job, given that everything was pretty much closed down for the winter. She worked on some book she was writing. I'm not sure what it was about; she never told me. But she'd spend a couple of hours every day working on it. Nothing ever came of all that work, as far as I know.

After a month of looking without any luck, our money supply was just about at zero. We were getting desperate, but she finally lucked into a job at the local hardware store as a cashier. It wasn't much in terms of the money, but at least she had a paycheck. And the place was open all year. They sold lumber and supplies to the local builders who were working on projects while their wealthy clients were living the good life in places far away from Nantucket, you know, waiting for the temperatures to warm up before coming back to their summer homes. Another good thing about it was that it was close enough to the house so she could walk, which meant I could use the truck.

Watching our money run out so fast, I started to think that I'd made another huge mistake in my life by moving out to this Godforsaken place. The weather was horrible, for starters. The wind blew constantly, and when it came in off the ocean, that wind was colder than anything I could remember in Vermont. It was really easy to get depressed in that kind of weather. Cloudy, gray, and cold all the time.

But even though it was so cold, it never really snowed very often. That was weird to me. Even though it was snowing in places like Boston, Nantucket just got rain. Rain and that freezing cold wind. I found out later that it had something to do with ocean currents. The Gulf Stream apparently ran right by Nantucket, which meant that the water temperature around the island was warmer than other places. I don't know, exactly, because the first time I put my hand in it, the ocean felt like ice water to me. But anyway, because of those Gulf Stream currents, there was kind of a blanket around the whole island that ended up turning a snowstorm into a rainstorm.

But Molly's job made things a little easier for us, and she met a lot of builders. And those builders knew people who had gardens, which meant that I had a way of breaking into the landscaping business on my own. I ordered some business cards online for my new company, and she handed them out to anyone who was willing to take one. For my part, I went around putting them in mailboxes everywhere on the island. With any luck, I'd get a few fish to bite.

The first of April that year was a scary day for me. It was the beginning of our last month in the duplex, and I hadn't found anywhere for us to go once our lease expired. And I hadn't gotten any calls about my new business. I'd made a promise to myself that if I hadn't landed any clients by that day, I'd start looking for work on a landscaping crew. There were plenty of them around, which was kind of a mixed blessing in a way. It meant that there was plenty of work for somebody like me, but it also meant that there was a really good chance that my business idea was going to flop. With so much competition in the business, I wasn't sure I'd be able to make a living on my own.

But then it happened. The phone rang. It was one of Molly's builder friends who had gotten my card from her. Greg was a caretaker for a bunch of summer homes. He made sure that the house didn't get destroyed over the winter, and did any repairs they needed when the owners weren't around. A lot of his clients, it turned out, had pretty big gardens that they needed tended. And some of those people had said they were irritated by the lack of attention they were getting from their current landscapers. Apparently owning a multimillion-dollar summer home meant you were entitled to a little extra care from your hired help. That didn't bother me. I could stand that, if they were willing to pay me enough to do it.

So anyway, this guy asked me if I'd be interested in talking to him about being the landscaper for five of his clients. I told him absolutely I would, and we arranged to meet in town so he could take me around to the different houses and see if I was going to be a good fit. The houses weren't too far from each other—nothing was too far from anything else on that tiny island—so it wouldn't take us more than an hour for him to show me all of them and explain what they needed. I was all over it.

We met at a coffee place downtown. It was nothing more than an oversized closet, and there was no place to actually sit down inside. So we grabbed our coffees and sat outside on a bench. It wasn't so horribly cold anymore, and the sun was out. It was almost what you might call a nice day. Greg gave me the rundown on the clients who were looking for new landscapers. Two were related to each other—some kind of mother-daughter thing where the property had been in their family for generations and they had two houses next to each other up on the Cliff—two were gardens at houses in town, and one was out towards the western end of the island.

"You're organic, right? These people all like the idea of organic. It's all the rage these days, I'm sure you know," Greg said.

"I know the type," I said confidently. "And I'm totally organic. I grew up in Vermont, and you know how those people are about chemicals."

He laughed. "Yep. I've heard the rumors."

"In fact, I used to sell organic maple syrup from my own personal sources back when I lived in Vermont," I added. I had to laugh at my own little inside joke, given that my personal inside sources had actually been bottles I'd bought at a warehouse.

Luckily enough for me, he wasn't too interested in the finer points of raising organic maple trees, because he sort of sighed and stood up. "Let's get going," he said. "I'll drive."

We walked to his truck and got in. "We'll start out in Madaket," he said, referring to the western end of the island, "and work our way back down here."

As we drove, I looked out the window. What trees there were had begun getting green leaves again, and daffodils were sprouting up. Daffodils, it turned out, were a favorite flower of local gardeners, because the resident deer population wouldn't eat them. Apparently they're poisonous to deer. Who knew?

It struck me as weird that were deer out here, thirty miles out in the ocean. I couldn't figure out how in the hell deer would have gotten to the island in the first place. Chris had actually told me the story over dinner one night. Apparently a fishing boat had found a deer swimming out in the ocean one day, and rescued it. The boat was on its way to Nantucket, so they figured they'd let it out once they got there. That deer—the locals had named him "Old Buck"—lived out in the state forest, all by himself.

That summer, some guy felt sorry for him because poor Old Buck didn't have any women to satisfy his needs, so he decided he'd do the humane thing and import a few girlfriends to the island. Just to keep him company. From there, biology took over. Outside of a few hunters, there wasn't anything to kill the deer, so they eventually took over. Now they were considered a pain in the ass to anyone who tried to grow a garden, because the damn things would eat any plants that weren't protected from them. Or poisonous. Daffodils fit that description, so they were everywhere.

And then, in the whole make-lemonade-from-lemons idea, yet another summer person decided that it would be a nice idea to have a big festival to bring people to the island at the end of April to see all the daffodils in bloom. It was a slow time for businesses on the island, and any way to get people out there at that time was a good idea. So they started the Daffodil Festival, which had a parade of antique cars that started on Main Street and then went out to 'Sconset on the eastern end of the island. They had a big tailgate party out there while everybody walked around and looked at the cars and ate expensive food. Whatever floats your boat.

It took us about fifteen minutes to get to the first house. Like pretty much every other house on the island, it was covered in gray shingles. I'd figured out pretty quick that you could always tell the new construction from looking at the shingles. If they were new, they were almost yellow. But as they weathered, they turned gray. And the darker the shade of gray, the older the construction. In a way, it reminded me of one of those planned neighborhoods, where you have houses that all look alike. Sure, they might have different paint colors or flowers in the front yard, but at the end of the day, you could tell that all the houses were built more or less the same way. And they all looked the same. God help you if you ever got drunk and had to figure out which house was yours.

The house we stopped at was huge, with a wall of hedges around it. The front yard was gorgeous. The grass looked like it belonged on a golf course. And you could tell exactly where the property line ended, because everything on the other side of the borders was yellow or brown, waiting for warmer days to perk up and start growing. Obviously somebody had spent a lot of time and money keeping this lawn looking like this. And the neighbors obviously didn't care.

I whistled softly. "These people like their lawn, huh?"

Greg laughed. "Yep. They want it to look like this from the day they get here to the day they leave. And they don't care what it costs," he said.

That was good to know. Money, money, money. That's what I want. We walked around to the back of the house, where the lawn backed up to a large pond. More big houses were built around it. A pair of swans was floating around silently. There was a garden in the back, off to one side, but there were also bushes and various plants scattered around the place. This house by itself seemed like enough work to keep me busy for the whole summer.

Greg could tell I was impressed. "Big enough for you?" he asked.

I nodded. "Yeah, I think this might just do it," I said.

"But you can handle it, right? Your crew is big enough to do this? It's the biggest one of the five, but these people are the ones who are going to ride you like a rented mule if you screw it up."

"Totally fine," I replied. The thought of my own crew hadn't factored in to my plans just yet. That was something I'd need to take care of soon. But of course, that also required me to have money to pay a crew with, and that made me think about the most important part of this whole thing. "So how does it work with the money?" I asked.

"You mean getting paid?" He laughed. "That's always the big question. You bill me, I pay you," he said simply. "You'll be working as a subcontractor for me."

I didn't quite understand how that was going to work. I did the work for these people, then sent the bill to Greg, and he paid me. "How do you get your money back?" I asked.

"I bill them directly," he said. "They reimburse me for what I pay you."

Now it made sense. I was basically the landscaping version of a hooker, and Greg was my pimp. He'd no doubt be adding on to whatever amount he paid me, which meant he was making money off of me. Not a bad deal for him. But I didn't care. I needed the job, and this seemed like the best way to get my business going.

After a few more minutes of walking around the property, we left and headed back towards town. Greg veered off at a fork in the road, turning onto what I now recognized as Cliff Road. After a few minutes, he turned again and then again, and we pulled into another driveway.

"These are the family houses I was telling you about," he said. "Mother is here, daughter is next door. Both are pretty low-maintenance people, as long as you give them what they want."

He led me through a gate and into a garden that was small compared to the last house, but it felt really elegant. Like one of those gardens you see in an old movie, where some girl sneaks out of the house to kiss her boyfriend goodnight. The house was smaller, too. Just one story, with windows all the way around. Looking through the windows, I could see the ocean on the other side.

"So these people are right on the water?" I asked.

Greg nodded. "Yeah. High-dollar real estate up here," he said. "Even have their own beach in front of the house."

We walked around the side of the house so we could see the ocean. The lawn looked good enough, but it was pretty clear that it wasn't a big priority for these people. It was like just decided to let nature do what it wanted. Greg pointed to the house next door and said, "That's the other house. Same thing over there. Garden's about the same size and style. They like the grass mowed once a week at both houses, but the garden is the main thing. That has to look good all the time."

I nodded silently as I looked down at the beach. Off in the distance, I could see the ferry coming in, motoring slowly between the jetties. Somewhere out there was Hyannis, where Molly and I had started our trip. "That is one hell of a view," I said.

"Sure is," Greg said. "People pay a lot of money for houses up here. House a couple of doors down sold last year for something like twenty-five million," he said.

That was more money than I could even imagine ever having, not to mention paying for a summer house. But even though that price tag meant I'd never own one of those houses, it also meant that the people who did own them could afford to pay a lot of money to keep their gardens nice and tidy. I took one last look down at the beach before we left.

From there, we headed back into town to see the other two houses. They were close together and weren't going to need a whole lot of work in terms of landscaping, so they'd be easy to take care of in a single trip. When we'd seen the last one, Greg asked me what I thought.

"Works for me," I said. "I can get started as soon as you need me to."

"That's what I wanted to hear," he said. "The Madaket people are getting here in two weeks. He's got an old car that he puts in the Daffodil parade, and they come up for that. They'll want that garden looking like it's the middle of July, so that's your first priority."

I nodded. I was doing some mental calculations about what I'd need. I didn't have any equipment, but that was easy enough to get. Our landlord kept a mower in the garage at the house, so that was no problem. I could get the other things I'd need from the hardware store where Molly worked, where they had their own lawn and garden center. She got an employee discount, which would come in handy for that stuff. From there, I'd submit a bill and use that money to start hiring some kids to work for me. It was just a matter of getting that first paycheck from Greg.

We talked for a few minutes about how much I would charge, and we agreed on an hourly rate that I thought was way too high. "That doesn't include extra stuff," I said. "You know, fertilizer, mulch, plants, that stuff." I hated to sound like I was padding the bill, and I was a little scared that that was going to be a deal-breaker for me.

He nodded. "Yep. Just bill me for it and I'll get them to pay me back. No worries there."

No worries. What a nice thought that was. No money worries, no legal worries. Just counting money as fast as I could make it. I couldn't help but think I'd been crazy lucky to get to this point, but I wasn't about to start asking too many questions about how the universe was working just then. I was just happy to be where I was, and to have the opportunities that had suddenly been given to me, you know? All of a sudden, it was like I'd had a thousand-pound weight lifted off the back of my shoulders. I'd spent so much time worrying about how to pay for a new place to live, not to mention paying for our daily lives. And now, all of a sudden, those worries were gone.

"When should I get started?" I finally asked.

"You tell me," Greg said. "You're the one who needs to get that garden looking good in two weeks."

I smiled at the thought of having something to do immediately. "I'll get started tomorrow," I said.

"Sounds good." We shook hands, and I got out of the truck. I went and got myself another cup of coffee, feeling great about myself, my future, and my life in general. Finally I was a working man again.

CHAPTER EIGHTEEN

When I got home, I started working out the details of how I was going to get to work. I'd borrow the landlord's mower—what he didn't know wouldn't hurt him—but I needed a few other things, too. I drove down to Atlantic Home Goods to tell Molly the good news, and to see about getting myself the basic necessities. The parking lot was pretty empty when I got there since it was the middle of the day and most of the customers for that time of year would be eating lunch. Molly was sitting behind the counter inside, reading a magazine. She looked up when I walked in and smiled.

"Hey there, stranger," she said.

"Hey. I got some clients," I blurted out.

She jumped up and ran around the counter to give me a hug. "That's great, darling!" she yelled. Then she remembered that she was still at work, and she lowered her voice. "Did one of my builders call you?"

"Yep. Guy named Greg," I told her.

"Oh, Greg. I love him! He's so nice. You'll love working with him."

I told her the story about the morning's phone call, and my meeting with Greg. "So I need a few tools. Do you think you can hook me up with your discount?"

She nodded. "Totally. And I can put them on my account, so you don't even have to pay for them. They'll just deduct it from my paycheck."

That was better than I'd hoped. I'd already decided that I'd have to charge the stuff on my credit card. But this way, I could get the stuff I needed to get me going, and by the time it all showed up on Molly's check, I'd have enough money to offset the lost pay. Bonus to me.

I went to the garden center and started looking around. I'd need to put mulch in the flower beds, which was one of those things you can do to make it look like you've done more work than you really have. You know, it gives kind of a finished look to the landscaping. Plus most people think it smells good, even though I can't stand it. So it makes them think it looks better, I guess. And it doesn't take that long to put it down.

I'd also need a rake to spread the mulch around with, plus a trowel. Maybe a shovel, too. Then I looked up at one wall and saw hedge trimmers, which reminded me that the house had all of those bushes that would need to be cut. I could do it manually, but that was a lot of work. The gas-powered ones were way too expensive, and the electric ones weren't much cheaper. Those could wait. I'd just get the manual clippers—which weren't really all that much of a bargain, either—and suck it up. A few other things I needed, and I was in business. Literally.

I got my tools and a couple of bags of mulch, then piled everything up next to Molly's register. She recorded everything, writing it down in a little book they kept behind the counter to keep track of which employees had bought what stuff. Since I was the only customer she had, Molly helped me carry it all out to my truck, and we threw it all in the bed. When we were done, I wrapped her up in my arms and gave her a kiss. "We're going out to dinner tonight," I announced. "To celebrate."

She smiled. "Sounds good, Mr. Faulkner. I'll see you at home when I get done here."

She blew me a kiss as she walked back inside, and I was floating. I couldn't remember ever being as happy as I was at that moment. And then an idea hit me. I guess I was caught up in the excitement of all the great stuff that had happened that day. I don't know, exactly, but I got in my truck and drove back into town. I parked on a side street and walked into a little store that sold all kinds of kitschy hippie garbage. One of those places kids love.

It was kind of a cave, that place. You had to go down a few steps to actually walk in the front door. It was below some art gallery. Anyway, I walked in and started looking around. There were some incense burners on display, and the little place smelled horrible. At least I thought so. Some kind of purses made out of yarn were attached to a little pole, and a whole bunch of weird-looking clothes were hanging up against a back wall. Against another wall was the cash register, and a bored-looking Jamaican woman sat behind the counter. In front of her were a bunch of silver rings in a glass display case, and that's what I was looking for.

I looked at the rings. Nothing was more than twenty bucks, so obviously they were nothing spectacular. I found one I liked, and asked to see it. It had some little turquoise pieces set in it that I thought looked pretty. The woman sighed loudly and got up, then waddled over to take out the rings. There were a bunch of them together, sitting in a black velvet box, and she set the whole thing on the counter. I pulled the one I'd wanted to see out of its slot, and looked at it closely. I knew it was a cheap ring, but I didn't care. We weren't flashy people. It was perfect.

I paid for the ring, slipped it in my pocket, and went back to the house. When I got there, I went straight to the garage to check out the lawn mower. It looked good enough to me. It wasn't anything professional, but it would cut the grass, at least.

As an added bonus, there was a fertilizer spreader hanging from a hook in the corner, with a bag of fertilizer below it. I looked at the bag. It was standard fertilizer. Not organic, but I wasn't going to lose any sleep over that. The people who owned the house weren't going to be on the island for another two weeks, and by then, whatever I put on the lawn would have been long gone before they got there to see it. When they were in the house to see what I was doing, I'd make sure to use organic fertilizer. One time wouldn't be a big deal.

Once I was satisfied that I had everything I'd need to get to work tomorrow, I went inside. There was nothing left to do now but wait until Molly got home, so I sat down at her computer and started looking for a summer rental for us. We didn't need anything nice, especially since we were both going to be working. We just needed a place to sleep. And the less it cost, the more we could save. But the numbers that kept popping up for rentals were unbelievable. I had started my search with two-bedroom houses, and everything that was available was going for more than Molly made in a month. Even with the money I'd be making, it was going to be hard to pay rent and still manage to eat. There had to be something cheaper.

I heard Chris pull into the driveway. The car door slammed shut, and I waited a few minutes for him to get inside. Then I went out and down the stairs, and knocked on their door. He looked like he'd been through a war.

"Rough day with the kids?" I asked.

"You could say that," he replied. "I got into it with the superintendent. He doesn't like some of my teaching methods." He ran his fingers through his hair. He was definitely mad about something. "You can't teach these kids the way you used to be able to," he said philosophically. "You have to use different methods. It's just the way it goes. But that clown doesn't get it."

I tried to look like I felt bad for him, but I didn't really understand what he was dealing with. So I tried to change the subject to the reason that I was actually there. "Sorry to hear," I began. "I'm sure it's rough. And speaking of rough, I'm having a hard time finding a summer rental. I was wondering if you knew of anybody with something that we might be able to afford."

He exhaled heavily. "No," he said bluntly. "I don't know anybody. Sorry."

And that was that. He obviously wasn't in a mood to help. I apologized for bothering him, and told him that I hoped his day got better. I started to leave.

"Wait," he said. "I'm sorry. I'm just having one of those days. Not your fault. Let me think for a second."

I turned and walked back, hoping he knew somebody. Or at least that he knew somebody who might know somebody.

"I do know a guy. He's a cop. He has a little house on his property that he rents out. Likes to rent it out year-round, but the people he had there moved off-island, I think. I'm not sure if he's got tenants for the summer yet, but I can call him and ask."

I thanked him and turned to go. I went back upstairs, crossing my fingers that the house wasn't rented yet. Nantucket was one of those places where people who'd lived on the island forever—like the ones who'd been born there and never managed to move away—a lot of times had houses that had belonged to their parents, houses that had enough land to build a second little cottage. It was a great deal for them, really. They got the house for free, so the extra cottage was like a lottery ticket.

That cottage was usually built by another friend who'd also lived on the island forever, which meant that it was done for a lot less money than it would have cost otherwise. The homeowner would then rent it in order to make money to pay their own bills. And then, when the time came, they would let their own kids live in it. Everybody won.

A few minutes later, the phone rang. It was Chris, calling from downstairs. He'd talked to his friend the cop, and sure enough, the cottage was still available to rent. But I should go over there quick to see it, because there was no telling how much longer it would be available. He gave me the directions and told me his friend would be there all day. I thanked him again and hung up. It was almost three o'clock, which meant that Molly would be home in about two hours. I was starving, because I'd only had coffee for breakfast, and hadn't yet eaten lunch. But I decided it was more important to find a place to live than to eat. I could wait until our celebration dinner.

I drove over to the cottage. It wasn't more than five minutes away from our current place. I knocked on the door, and a middle-aged guy with a bushy moustache answered the door. I introduced myself, explaining that Chris had given me the address.

"How you doing?" he said in his thick northeastern accent. "Kevin Almodovar."

His last name was a common one on Nantucket, where a lot of natives had Portuguese relatives. "Billy Faulkner," I said, extending my hand.

"Cottage is around back," he said as he walked out and shut the door behind him. "Nothing much. One bedroom, one bathroom. But it's a roof over your head."

I followed him around to a small box of a house. He was right. It wasn't much. But it would be a roof over our heads. He unlocked the front door and let me in. Standard rental interior. The front door opened into a sitting area with a sofa, an upholstered chair, and a television set. Directly behind it was a small, round, wooden table, with the kitchen directly next to it. Off to one side was a bedroom, with a separate bathroom. The bare necessities. But it would work.

"How much is the rent?" I asked, somewhat nervously.

"That depends," he said. "I'm going to be honest with you here. I hate finding tenants for this goddamn thing. It's not hard, but I get stuck with these college kids in the summer who don't pay their damn bills and leave the place a mess. I'm sick of dealing with that crap." He shook his head dismissively. "You want a year-round lease?"

I hadn't thought about it, really, but it didn't seem like a bad idea. It would save us from having to go through the huge pain of moving back and forth again. But it was such a small place. Could we deal with that year-round? "How much would it be for a year-round lease?" I asked.

He scratched his head and thought for a minute. "Normally I'd say two grand a month," he said. My heart sank. That was more than we were paying now. A lot more. "But you seem like a pretty responsible guy who I'm not going to have to chase for rent. I'll let you have it for fifteen hundred a month. And that's a deal."

I looked around the inside of the cottage. Fifteen hundred dollars a month for this was a deal? We were paying that for an extra bedroom where we were now. But we also had to move in a month and, assuming we renewed our lease there after the summer, we'd be back in the same boat.

"Take it or leave it," he said, "but I'm doing you a favor here. Won't even make you pay first and last. Just a security deposit. And if you've got pets, I need a pet deposit, too."

I thought for a second. "No, we don't have pets."

"We?" he asked.

"Yeah. It's me and my . . ." I paused for a second. "My wife."

"Oh, okay. That's fine. Just wanted to make sure you didn't have ten friends you were planning on stashing in here. You'd be surprised how many times people have tried that one."

I'd heard stories about overcrowding in rentals. There'd been one newspaper article a few weeks earlier about the sheriff busting a place that had seventeen El Salvadorans—none of them legal residents of the country—living in a three-bedroom house. I couldn't imagine fitting more than two people in this shoebox, let alone ten. I thought about it a little longer, doing the math in my head.

Fifteen hundred dollars a month, when I thought about it, didn't seem too bad. With Molly's job, we could afford the rent and food. Any money I brought in—which I hoped would be a lot—would pay the bills, and let us build up a savings account. Somewhere in the back of my brain, a voice told me to pull the trigger now, without first talking to Molly about it.

"I'll take it," I blurted out. I nodded my head as if to indicate how serious I was about that. "Yeah. This'll be fine. When can we move in?"

Kevin said, "Well, it's the first of the month today. So if you want to move in now, you can do that. But I'll need a check from you first. One month's rent plus another fifteen hundred for a deposit."

We didn't have that much money in the bank. I wasn't sure how much we did have exactly, but I knew it was closer to three hundred than it was three thousand. "What if we said the middle of the month?" I asked. "Because, you know, I'm already paying for the place we live now, and I can't afford to pay for two places for a month."

He nodded his head. "Yeah, I know about that. It's an expensive island. I can pro-rate the rent for you. Just tell me when you want to move in."

We agreed on the last week of April as a move-in date, which meant that we'd only have to pay about $400 in rent, plus the security deposit. "I'll get the lease written up for you," he said. "You want me to list your wife on it, too, or just put your name?"

"Just me," I said.

"Sounds good. I'll figure out the exact amount you'll need to write a check for, and give you a call. What's the best number?"

I gave him the number for the house, and shook his hand. Our new landlord seemed like a good guy. I just hoped that Molly would agree with my decision.

*   *   *

That night, we went out to a restaurant that we'd never been to before. It was a big place out of town that wasn't too fancy. But this time of year, there still weren't too many places that had opened for the season yet. We didn't care, though. We were celebrating, and this would do fine.

We ordered a bottle of wine and some oysters. I hated the thought of slurping one of those things out of the shell, but Molly told me that she'd teach me to appreciate them. "Besides," she said with a grin, "they're an aphrodisiac. You might just get lucky tonight, Mr. Faulkner."

The waiter appeared with a dozen oysters sitting on a bed of crushed ice. He put the tray on the table between us, and Molly immediately started getting them ready to eat. Lemon juice, some kind of red cocktail sauce, a little horseradish. Then she picked up one of the shells and sucked in, smiling the whole time.

"Now it's your turn," she said. "Just close your eyes and let it slide down."

I looked at the tray in front of me. It looked like something that somebody had coughed up in the kitchen. Shiny little globs of phlegm sitting in shells. After studying them closely, I chose the one that I thought was the smallest. I picked it up. My hand was shaking, and I put it to my lips. I closed my eyes and tried to visualize how Molly had eaten hers. I exhaled through my nose and sucked the oyster into my mouth.

I tasted salt at first. Salt and cocktail sauce. Then the horseradish hit, stinging my tongue. And then it felt like the oyster grew to the size of a baseball and stuck in my throat. My eyes bugged out of my head and I grabbed my water glass, swallowing the thing like it was an oversized pill.

My eyes started to water, and I coughed. "Yuck," I finally managed to say.

"The first one's always the worst," she said with a laugh. "You'll get used to it."

I managed to force down two more over the next half hour. I let Molly enjoy the rest, since she at least seemed to actually like them. I didn't get what she was tasting. The thought of eating another one made me want to throw up. When she'd finally swallowed the last one, the waiter came and took the tray, and I swore that I'd never eat another oyster as long as I lived.

Before our dinner arrived, I took Molly's hands in mine and looked at her across the table. My heart started to beat faster, and I'm sure my palms were sweating. But she didn't say anything. Maybe she didn't notice.

"Molly," I said, "today has been the best day of my life. I can't tell you how much it means to me that you've been willing to follow me out here, to support me while I found a job, to stay by my side. And most of all, that you love me through all of this."

She just looked back at me and smiled. "Of course, Billy," she said. "I love you now and forever."

I took a quick breath. "Then I'm wondering if you'll do me a huge favor," I said softly.

"Darling, you know I'd do anything for you. Just ask it."

"Will you marry me?" I said.

She started crying immediately. Smiling, laughing, and crying, all at the same time. "Yes!" she finally said, almost as a yell.

I stood up out of my chair, and then got down on one knee as I pulled out the cheap silver ring I'd bought earlier. "This isn't much of an engagement ring," I said apologetically. "But . . ."

"Shut up," she interrupted. "Just put it on my finger and shut up. I love it. It's perfect. And I love you."

I slid the ring onto her finger, and we were officially engaged. I was still on my knee when the waiter reappeared with our dinner.

"Oh, I'm sorry," he said. "Am I interrupting?"

We both laughed. "No," I said. "I'm just finishing up here. Meet my new fiancée."

He put the plates down on the table. "Congratulations," he said with a smile. "We might have something behind the bar for you. To help you celebrate."

As he walked away, I sat back down and took Molly's hand again across the table. "You're sure you don't mind that it's not a diamond?" I asked.

"Positive," she said. "As long as it's from you, I don't care."

The waiter came back, carrying an ice bucket, a bottle of champagne, and two glasses. "Compliments of the house," he said. He popped the cork and put it on the table next to me, then filled two glasses. We toasted, then sipped.

"Yeah," I said after a few moments of silence. "This is now officially the best day of my life."

CHAPTER NINETEEN

By the time we left the restaurant, we were both fairly drunk. We managed to make it home, though. Thank God for no traffic, you know? We walked in the door, and Molly basically attacked me. She started kissing me, unbuttoning my shirt, grabbing at my belt. She pulled me into our bedroom, and literally threw me onto the bed.

"As my first order of business as your wife-to-be," she announced in a very official-sounding tone, "I'm going to make you forget every other woman on the planet."

She ripped her shirt off and threw it in the corner, then took off her pants. Before my alcohol-soaked brain could even process what she'd said, she'd taken off her bra and panties and straddled me. I will spare you the gory details, but let's just say that when we'd finished, I was exhausted, and I honestly didn't think that there was another woman anywhere who could make me as happy as Molly did.

We lay in bed together, her snuggled up next to me while she ran her finger up and down my chest. My breathing gradually returned to something resembling a normal rate, and my stomach stopped heaving from exertion. Nothing had ever felt so right in my life. I'd finally figured it out. I'd finally figured out how to be happy. The woman I loved had just agreed to marry me, I'd started the process of building up my own business, we had a place to live. For the first time I could ever remember, I truly had no worries, just like Greg had said.

"Molly," I said, "I wanted to tell you something."

"How much you love me?" she said with a giggle.

"Well, yeah, that, too. But something else. I found us a place to live."

She picked her head up. "Really? Where? When?"

"Today," I said. "It's not too far from here. Out towards the airport about a mile. It's a guy Chris told me about. He's a cop with a cottage on his property."

She looked at me. "Were you going to consult your fiancée about this?" she asked.

I laughed. "Yes, I was. But the guy is really nice and he offered me a really good deal on it," I said. "And I didn't want us to lose it."

She smiled at me. "Glad to see you're already looking out for our best interest."

"Of course, my darling," I said. "And the best part is, it's a year-round rental. We don't have to move in the summer."

Her eyes widened as she said, "That's great news, Billy! Can we go see it?"

I nodded. "Yep. I can't go tomorrow, though. Working, you know." I winked at her.

"Oh, I know," she said. "Trust me. I know." She poked me in the side playfully. "I'm so proud of you, Billy. I'm so excited."

I only half-heard her, because the champagne was hitting my brain full-steam now, and I was on the verge of deep sleep. "I love you," I mumbled.

I have no idea what she said back, because I was out right after I said it.

*   *   *

The sun shone through the window the next morning, and light flooded into my eyes. My brain was pounding inside my skull, and my stomach felt like it was going to go into reverse at any second. Laying in bed and slowly regaining consciousness, I made an effort not to think about those oysters that Molly had talked me into eating the night before. If that memory managed to push its way to the front, I was pretty sure it would result in my throwing up immediately.

Molly groaned in the bed next to me. "Oh, I don't want to get out of bed."

I rolled over to face her. "I know what you mean," I managed to say in a scratchy voice. "I feel like I got run over."

But today was the first day of my new job, and there was a part of me that was up and fighting through the hangover, a part of me that wanted to get out and start making money. I lurched my way out of bed and stumbled into the kitchen. I put some coffee on to brew, then into the bathroom to shower and hopefully wash away the cobwebs.

After I'd washed my hair, I dried off, feeling slightly more like an actual human being, and wrapped my towel around my waist. I went back to the kitchen, poured a cup of coffee, then back to the bedroom to get dressed. Molly was fully awake now, sitting up in bed. Out of the corner of my eye, I caught her staring at her left hand, smiling.

"Whatcha thinking?" I asked playfully.

"How much I love you," she said with a smile. "And how happy you make me."

I was still nauseous enough to where I didn't feel the urge to rip off my towel and jump back into bed with her. But it was a momentary thought, I'll be honest. She knew exactly what I was thinking.

"No," she said flatly. "If I move that much, you'll be wearing that dinner you bought me last night." She laughed. "But I love you for thinking it."

I laughed too. "Not to worry. I'd hate to see what you'd look like after you got the same treatment from me." I pulled on a pair of jeans and a long-sleeved T-shirt. "Besides," I added, "I've got to get to work."

"Seriously," she said, "get your ass out of here and start earning your keep."

I threw my towel at her as I went out the door.

"You better run, mister!" she yelled after me.

I went outside and began the painful process of getting the lawn mower into the back of the truck. In Northampton, we'd had a ramp to wheel the mower up on, but I couldn't find any boards nearby. So it was going to be a matter of just lifting it up. After some maneuvering, I managed to get it up over the tailgate and into the bed of the truck. I went back and got the fertilizer and the spreader, and put them in too. One last check to make sure that everything was there, then back inside to kiss Molly good-bye and refill my coffee. And then I was off for my first day of work as owner and sole employee of Faulkner Organic Landscaping.

Driving out to the house, I thought about Molly. I felt bad that she had to walk to work, but she said she didn't mind. It wasn't far for her to go, and she said it did her good to get some exercise. All the same, though, I wanted to get her a car. She deserved at least that much. She had done so much for me, and put up with so much from me. I decided on that first morning that as soon as I could make enough money to do it, I'd find a used car for her. Just something to get her around. If she didn't want to drive to work, that was fine. But at least she'd have the option of taking her own car instead of walking.

I stopped at a gas station on the way and bought a fuel can, then filled it up with gas. I hoped that the mower had enough oil in it to survive the day without me adding any. Two gallons of gas cost me over eight dollars. I took the receipt and stuffed it in my pocket. I decided that gas was going to fall into the category of extra expenses, and I would be billing anything and everything I could to Greg.

I got to the house in Madaket without any trouble. I was proud of myself for remembering how to get there, but the truth is that there really weren't too many turns I had to take to get there. It was basically a straight line from our house. I guess I was just easily impressed.

I got out of the truck and surveyed the spread. The first thing I was going to do was mow the grass. My hangover was going away, but it was still there, just sitting in the background. Kind of like a fog bank. You know it's there, but maybe it'll go away if you quit paying attention to it.

I managed to get the lawn mower out of the truck without too much difficulty—it was easier getting it down than it was picking it up—and pushed it through the front gate. I went back and got the gas can, filled up the mower's tank, and away I went. I was careful to mow straight lines, back and forth, making a pattern that was easy to see. I wanted to show how much effort had gone into this whole project.

In case you haven't realized it yet, I'm a big fan of doing things that make it look like you've done more work than you really have. You know, like painting. If you really want a room to look good and new, you paint the window trim and the ceiling, you tape the edges so you don't have paint splotches running over. But if you just want it to look like you put in some time and you need an immediate result, you slap a coat of paint on the walls and call it a day. It looks different than it did before, and that makes it look like you did some work when you really didn't do that much. It's just how I operate. It's a shortcut.

The lawn took me a while to mow, and that was when I realized I didn't have an edger. That was a problem, because the edges of that place looked like hell, because they hadn't been done in quite a while. There was a tool rental place on the island, and I hoped they might have an edger too. I'd check on that later.

Then I started trimming the hedges, and I pretty quickly realized that it was going to take me the rest of the day to do just that much. It was monotonous and boring work, but I kept reminding myself that I was making money by doing it, and that thought kept me going. I finished by four o'clock, which left me just enough time to rake up and bag the clippings. I'd clearly underestimated how long this was going to take me. As the sun was setting, I loaded the last of the trash bags into my truck and I called it a day.

I was tired and sore and hungry, but I'd worked an honest day. My own day. My own company. My own money. And it felt good. I looked forward to the time when I had the money to hire a couple of people to work for me, so I could show up in my polo shirt and sip on coffee while they did the work I was getting paid for. But that was going to be some time in the future. For now, it was just me.

The next day, my first job was to find an edger. I went to the tool rental place, but they told me they didn't rent lawn equipment. They told me to try a place nearby that actually sold and serviced lawn mowers, to see if they might have a used one. I stopped in and they told me it was my lucky day. They had one they'd give me for fifty bucks. It would start, that much they'd promise me. Once I'd started it, though, I owned it. And if it died ten seconds later, I still owned it.

That was fine with me. I needed it, you know. Remember my visual thing. And edging is one of those things. You can mow the grass all you want, but if the edges don't look good, it's like a bad frame on a nice picture. When you edge it, it just looks so much better. I used half of the remaining credit line on my credit card to buy it, promising to pay it off when I got my first check. I realized that I was making that promise a lot. But soon it wouldn't be an issue, because I'd have more money than I knew how to spend.

The next thing I had to do was get rid of all the clippings from the day before. The thing about Nantucket trash is that you have to use clear trash bags. They're pretty concerned about the landfill out there, and it's an issue of biodegradability, supposedly. I think it's so they can look at what you're throwing away and yell at you if you try to put recyclables in with the trash.

You think I'm kidding, but I'm serious. They've got these women out at the dump whose job it is to sit there and watch you throw out your garbage. They'll go after you if you put recycling in the trash, or even if you put a can in with the plastic. People call them the "Dump Nazis," and they aren't screwing around.

But I figured I was pretty safe. I was just throwing away grass and hedge clippings, so it should have been a no-brainer, right? You just dump it in with the rest of the trash, and it goes away. I pulled out one bag and started to walk towards the big trash dumpster when one of the ladies yelled at me.

"Wait a minute, sugar. That's gotta go in the back on the brush pile."

"Sorry," I said in a confused tone. "Where?"

"The brush pile, sweetie. It's around back. You've gotta drive over the scale and they'll tell you where to go." She pointed back to a little shack about fifty yards further in.

So I went back to my truck and drove up to the shack, where I told yet another woman that I needed to go to the brush pile. "Right back over there, honey," she said, pointing behind her. "Follow the road around and you'll see it on the right. Can't miss it." She stepped out and looked in the bed. "You a landscaper?"

I nodded. "Yes, ma'am."

"Oh, then you'll have to pay. First time out here?"

"Yes it is," I said. "What's the fee?"

"Depends on how much you're bringing out. I tell you what. I'll let it go this time, but you'll have to go out to the DPW office and set up an account for yourself. We'll just bill you each time you come through." She looked back in the bed. "And don't leave those bags out at the brush pile. You'll have to empty 'em and bring 'em back up here to throw 'em away." She gave me a smile, and waved me through.

I thanked her as I drove off, thinking that here was another expense I was going to be passing on to Greg. I hoped he knew what he was in for. I found the brush pile and emptied the bags in the general vicinity, then headed back out the way I'd come to throw away the plastic bags. It occurred to me as I was walking up to the trash can, however, that I could just reuse them. So I went back to the truck, threw the bags on the seat, and headed back to the house to do some fertilizing.

While I was spreading the stuff around, I did feel a little guilty about using non-organic fertilizer when I'd said I would use organic. But I'd been down this road before, and I knew it wouldn't kill me. I just needed to be able to cover my tracks. So I got out the spreader and emptied the bag into it. Then I crumpled up the bag and hid it behind the seat of my truck, just in case anybody happened to stop by to see what was going on.

As it turned out, I finished in the nick of time. I was putting the spreader back in the truck when Greg pulled up. "How's it going?" he asked. "I'm not checking up on you, don't worry. Just have to make sure the water's been turned on."

"Not a problem at all. Things are going well. Trying to make it look all nice and pretty for when these people get here," I said.

He looked around the yard. "Not too shabby," he said.

"Oh, you ain't seen nothing yet, kid," I said. "Wait 'til I get the mulch down. Then it'll look good enough to eat off of."

"Get after it," he said. "Don't let me stop you."

It had worked out perfectly. Greg had no idea about what chemicals I was using. What's more, he'd seen me working and thought I was doing a good job. I had to smile as I pulled out a bag of mulch and dragged it around to the back. When he came back to tell me he was done, I was on my knees spreading mulch by hand. I couldn't have timed it better if I'd tried.

"Keep it up, Billy. You're already better than most landscapers I've seen around here. Good stuff." He waved good-bye, got in his truck, and drove off.

As my second day of being a business owner came to an end, I considered myself a roaring success. Sure, I'd cut a corner with the fertilizer. But that was a one-time deal. I was committed to doing this right, to earning peoples' trust, and keeping that trust by not screwing them over. I was a changed man. World, meet the new Billy Faulkner.

CHAPTER TWENTY

Weeks went by, and I managed to get all five houses looking pretty damn good, if I do say so myself. The Madaket people who'd come in April loved the work I'd done—work that I'd billed Greg an absurd amount of money for doing—and promised me that they'd tell all their friends how great I was, and that I was totally organic. That was just the sort of advertising I was counting on, word of mouth. Rich people have rich friends, and my hope was that these rich people would tell their rich friends, who'd hire me, and then tell their other rich friends the same thing about me.

Molly and I had moved into the new cottage, and we were getting adjusted to life on the island. Molly was still working on that book of hers. She'd complain about having to go to work, because it took up her time that she wanted to spend writing. She still wouldn't tell me anything about it. Something about how it was bad luck to talk about a book before it was done.

Now that we had a little spending money, we could actually go out and meet other people. There were a couple of bars near the house that the locals went to, so we got to know quite a few people in a relatively short amount of time. There were a huge number of landscapers on the island, and a lot of them hung out at the same bars. Even though they were more or less friendly towards me, I could tell that they didn't like me very much, because I was the new kid coming in and stealing their business.

And who could blame them, really? The pay was amazing, and in a month I'd made enough money to buy a new mower and gas-powered edger, plus my own fertilizer spreader. And even more importantly, at least as far as I was concerned, I'd managed to order myself a few polo shirts with a company logo monogrammed on them.

It wasn't anything fancy, just something Molly had drawn on a piece of paper after dinner one night. But it gave me that look of professionalism, like I knew what I was doing, and was somebody to be trusted.

The great thing about landscaping work, when you look at it as a way to make a living, is that you need to keep going back to do maintenance work. You know what I mean. Weeding, cutting the grass, pruning bushes, all that stuff. So I'd drop by each of the houses about once a week, just to do a little work. The only problem was that I didn't have all that much to do after the first major visit, which meant that I didn't have that many hours to bill. But Greg didn't seem to mind that I was padding the invoices just a little bit. If he knew I was doing it, anyway, he didn't say anything. So I kept right on doing it.

Of all the houses I was currently working at, the two that were next door to one another up on the Cliff were my favorites. It was really the view more than anything else. I'd go up there and just hang out, looking out at the water. On clear days, you could really see forever, with the tip of Great Point reaching out around from the northeast, and Tuckernuck Island hanging on over there in the west. It was really gorgeous. No other word for it.

As the summer arrived, so did the people. All of my clients had the same reaction as the Madaket folks, and pretty soon my phone started ringing from Greg telling me about new people that had heard about me from his clients, and wanted to hire me. Just like I'd hoped.

A lot of them wanted to ask me questions about my organic methods, which I was glad to answer. Of course, most of what I was telling them was a load of crap that I'd gotten off of a few Internet sites. But they ate it up. I'd quote them statistics about nitrogen levels and water runoff and the benefits of composting, and they'd just listen to me like I was Moses giving them the meaning of life.

The real truth about it was—and this is the God's honest truth— I tried my best to keep to my word about using only organic methods. But here's the thing about that. Actually, a couple of things. For one, it's expensive as hell. Organic fertilizer, I was very unhappy to learn, costs a whole lot more than the chemical stuff they make in labs. And it's hard to find too. Atlantic Home Goods only sold one kind, and a lot of times, they were out of it. Buying it online didn't help much, because once I'd paid the shipping costs to get it out to the island, it was so expensive that there was no way I could justify using it. I just couldn't make enough profit if I used it. That shouldn't have really surprised me, I guess.

But the other big problem I had with organic stuff was that it worked way too slowly for these people. I learned very quickly that Nantucket summer-home owners wanted what they wanted, and they wanted it right now. It didn't matter what it was, and that included perfectly green lawns. Organic fertilizers and plant foods work by putting nutrients into the soil, and then letting the plants naturally benefit from those nutrients over time. The results last longer, but they also take longer to get. And that doesn't work on Nantucket.

The synthetic fertilizers worked a lot faster because they cut out the middle man, in a way. Organic fertilizers basically use the process of decomposition to create the nutrients, but synthetic ones are already made up of those nutrients, so you don't have to wait as long for the lawn to get green, or for the roses to bloom. As much as I hate to admit it, science beats nature in terms of the speed factor.

So I used synthetic products. I felt bad about it at first, because like I told you, I was committed this time. Really committed to doing it the right way, to doing it the way I said I was doing it. The honest way. But I just kept running up against a brick wall. So I figured what the hell, and stuck with the chemicals. I was smart about it, though. I saved a couple of organic fertilizer bags and refilled them with the synthetic stuff. Plant food, lawn fertilizer, weed control, everything. Organic packaging. It wasn't like the clients had any idea what the difference was when they looked at it, so what they didn't know wouldn't hurt them, right?

They just wanted results, and that's what they got. So long as it looked good, they didn't argue, and I kept on using the same products I was using. All the other landscapers were using the same stuff, so it wasn't like I was doing anything illegal. I was just doing it the way everybody else did. At least that's how I reasoned it in my own mind. The fact that my customers thought they were getting organic products wasn't a big deal; like I said, it was all about the results in the end.

I guess it was some time around the end of July that first year when I got the bug. The boat bug, that is. I was working up at one of the houses on the Cliff, you know, looking out on the water like I loved to do. It was a really nice day, and there were a ton of people down on the beach. But one group down the beach a little ways caught my eye. They had a boat—nothing huge, mind you, maybe sixteen or seventeen feet—anchored out off the beach, and they were hanging out on it, drinking beer and jumping in the water off the deck and all that. They looked like they were having a blast, and I decided right then and there that I was going to buy myself a boat as soon as I could.

I'd managed to get a used car for pretty cheap, so Molly at least had a way to get around that didn't involve either a bus or having to pay a cabdriver. Her job was going well, and she'd even gotten a raise. So we were really making enough money for me to be thinking seriously about getting a boat. But I didn't quite know where to start.

That night, I went online and searched for boats. I thought something about twenty feet would be the perfect size for us to use around the island. Unfortunately for me, though, anything even close to new was going to be way more money than I could afford, so I started to focus on older ones. I found a twelve-year-old center console that was over on the Cape, and the owner wanted $7,000 for it. Seemed like a perfect option.

I'd added several clients to my workload, and I was bringing in what I thought was a lot of money. But I knew, too, that dropping seven grand on a single purchase was a pretty serious chunk of change. And I really didn't know anything about boats, outside of the fact that I knew I wanted one. I had plenty of friends who knew about boats, though. That was one major benefit of living on an island. So my next step was to talk to some of them, and figure out what I should do next.

I started going to the same bar after work every evening, hoping to catch some of the guys I knew who had boats. One guy in particular everybody called Rooster. He had this flaming red hair. He drank so much that his face was covered in red splotches too. And God, did he have a temper. But he knew about boats. He'd been born on Nantucket, and his father was a commercial fisherman, so he'd grown up around boats, and had spent a lot of time on the water.

I was having a beer with Rooster and talking to him about boats one night, and he offered to take me out on his to show me how to drive it. That sounded pretty much perfect to me, so we arranged to meet the next Saturday down at the public boat ramp. He'd take me around, show me the ropes, let me drive, all that. It'd be a chance for me to really figure out if I wanted to take this plunge.

I still hadn't told Molly about this little idea. We'd been having some arguments about money lately; she actually got a little mad when I showed up with a car for her. She told me that she could keep on walking to work, and we didn't need the expense of a second car. We hadn't even set a wedding date yet, and she was already riding my ass about money. I hated to think about how she'd react if I told her I wanted to buy a boat, so I decided that I'd just do it, and let her yell. That was better than having her tell me no.

When Saturday rolled around, I told Molly I was heading out on the boat with Rooster, and left it at that. She had to work anyway, so it wasn't like she was missing out on spending time with me. I met Rooster down at the boat ramp, which sat right between a really expensive hotel on one side and a beach that was marketed specifically to little kids on the other. In other words, you were between beautiful people and perfect little families.

So there went me and Rooster, looking like a pair of local hooligans. Rooster was towing his boat behind his beat-to-hell truck, but it was a lesson in that whole not-judging-a-book-by-its-cover thing, you know? The guy knew what he was doing, and he backed it right down to the water, jumped out, and loosened the chain holding the boat to the trailer. Before I knew it, he had the boat floating in the water. He handed me a rope and told me to hang on to it while he parked his truck. Two minutes later, we were puttering out of the harbor.

As we headed out towards Brant Point, Rooster explained the buoys to me. "You want to keep the red ones on your left when you're going out of the harbor, and on your right when you're coming back in. Long as you remember that, you'll be fine. They mark the channel, so if you get outside of them, you'll get yourself stuck."

I nodded as he talked. I hated to be taking lessons in seamanship, but Rooster was good about not making me feel like an idiot. And I could see that there was a lot I was going to have to learn. This wasn't as easy as just starting the motor and driving away.

I stood next to him as he guided the boat out into the open water. The electronic GPS display was a total mystery to me. There were a bunch of numbers and lines, with a little triangle in the middle of the screen. "Is that us?" I asked, pointing at the triangle.

"Yeah," Rooster said. "It's pretty cool. You can program it to follow a line to a waypoint."

"What's that mean?" I asked. "Remember, this is my first time."

"Here, let me show you," he said. He pushed a button, which brought up a list that he began to scroll through. He decided on one, pushed another button, and the display changed. It still showed the same triangle, but now the numbers were gone. They'd been replaced with a jagged line heading off to the west. "That line," Rooster explained, "is going straight to a place that I pre-programmed on this thing. It's a spot I love to fish in the fall. If I follow that line, it'll take me straight to the spot."

"That's pretty cool," I said. "How many places do you have programmed?"

He shook his head. "No idea." He brought the list of waypoints back up and began to scroll through them, counting.

"Wait," I said, when I noticed one. "You can take this boat to Hyannis?" I asked, looking at the list of waypoints that included Hyannis Harbor.

He nodded his head. "Oh, yeah. I usually go over there twice or three times a month. Takes me about an hour and a half."

That wasn't too long. It actually seemed pretty fast. And it might actually be a way I could use to sell Molly on why we needed to get a boat. After all, if we could make a trip back and forth to Hyannis whenever we felt like it without paying for the ferry, that meant we could actually save money by buying a boat. It made sense to my mind, at least.

Rooster tapped me on the arm. "You want to take a spin?" he asked.

I slid over and switched places with him, gripping the steering wheel tightly.

"Relax," Rooster said. "Don't try to strangle it. Just like you're driving your truck on the street."

I eased my grip on the wheel and spun it slightly to the left, trying to figure out how sensitive the steering was. The boat responded pretty quickly, and I turned it back to the right. The bow angled back as the boat turned again. I straightened it out and kept it going straight ahead, letting the wind blow my hair all over the place while the spray coming over the bow hit me in the face. I was hooked.

We spent a couple of hours cruising around. I was amazed at how easy it really was to navigate, once I'd gotten the basics of it down. I figured out how to pay attention to the GPS while steering, and Rooster tried to explain to me where sandbars were, and how best to avoid them.

"Let me take over for a minute," he said. Rooster took the wheel and turned sharply, pointing the bow directly at the small island of Tuckernuck. "I'm going to show you one of my favorite things to do with a boat," he said.

He'd obviously made this same trip so many times before that he didn't even need to look where he was going. He was almost driving by feeling instead of sight. He slowed the boat down as we got close to the island, then cut the engine altogether, and let the boat slide up on the beach. The hull crunched into the wet sand below it, and he hopped out. "Open that hatch right there and hand me the anchor," he said, pointing at a small rectangular opening on the bow.

I did what he'd asked and handed the anchor to him, pulling line out of the hatch. He buried the anchor in the sand and told me to get off. I hopped off the boat and we sat down in the sand. We were the only people on the beach; the island itself didn't have very many full-time residents. "Not much out here," Rooster explained. "No roads, no stores, no electricity. Just a few houses with generators. Lots of old-money people out here. Old Nantucket families."

He stuck his hand into his pants pocket and pulled out a joint, then lit it and inhaled deeply before passing it to me. It had been a long time since I'd gotten stoned, but I took the joint in my thumb and forefinger, and sucked in. The smoke hit my lungs, and I coughed loudly. Rooster laughed at me.

"Lightweight," he joked. "You better learn to handle good weed if you're gonna get a boat."

I laughed it off and took another drag. This time I inhaled slightly slower, easing the smoke down. I held it in for as long as I could, and exhaled loudly. I passed the joint back to Rooster, and laid back on the sand. I closed my eyes and let the marijuana make its way to my brain. I stayed on my back while we passed it back and forth a few times, and when I finally sat up, I realized that I was as stoned as I'd ever been in my life. I couldn't feel my arms, and the world was going by me in slow motion.

Rooster looked at me and laughed. "What did I tell you about being able to handle the good stuff?" he cackled.

All I could do was laugh, which ended up with me coughing some more. When I could finally form a complete thought, I asked him, "Where'd you get this stuff?" It wasn't like I was planning to start a new habit or anything, but it might be a fun way to pass the time in the winter, you know?

He nudged my arm, and pointed to the boat sitting at the water's edge. "Why do you think I go to Hyannis so often?" he asked me. He gave me a knowing wink. "A few baggies of this stuff pays for the gas. After that, it's profit, baby."

CHAPTER TWENTY-ONE

I worked through the rest of the summer. I'd built up my client base enough to where I could afford—and actually needed—to hire two people. I found a couple of local high school kids who wanted to make a few bucks before school started back again, and they were cool with the money I was offering. It was nice to be getting paid myself for work somebody else was doing. Of course, I was doing plenty of work myself. Greg hadn't been kidding when he'd told me that some of these people could be very demanding. They wanted to know that they were special, and part of my job was making them feel that way.

By the end of September, most of my clients had left the island, which meant that I was at least relieved of the duty of pumping up their egos. By the middle of October, the last ones had left. I spent a few weeks doing cleanup in their yards. On their bills, it was listed as a service I called "winterizing," but which wasn't really anything more than me walking around and looking at everything. All told, I spent fifteen minutes at each house. But since it was the last bill they'd get from me until next spring, I went ahead and billed them for several hours each, plus materials. Materials that I hadn't bought, and which they'd get billed for next spring too.

I don't want you to think I'm a bad guy for doing that. You have to understand a few things about life on Nantucket. There are basically two groups out there. One is the summer people, and they've got the money. The other is the locals, and they're trying to make the money. The best way to do that is to get it from the summer people, and they don't notice if you take a little extra. And everybody does it. Hell, a lot of people out there do a whole lot worse than billing extra hours. I knew one guy who used to borrow the television out of a house he was caretaking—plus the family's car they left in the garage—while they spent their winters in Florida. So when you really think about it, a couple hundred dollars for work I hadn't done wasn't really that big of a deal, right? It wasn't like they couldn't afford it, after all.

My bank account had benefited from my little white lies, and I had managed to slip enough into my own little private savings account during the summer to buy a boat. I'd been emailing with a local guy who knew somebody who wanted to sell their twenty-six-foot center console. It was an old woman—an old summer family—and her husband had died, and none of the kids wanted to deal with the boat, so she was getting rid of it. It wasn't anything you'd see in a magazine or anything, but she was willing to let it go for $5,000 cash. And it was on the island, which saved me the trouble of bringing it over from Hyannis for its first trip with me as the captain. I had that much, and it was now just a matter of delivering the money and getting my boat.

I'd finished with my last house for the season on the first of November, and I was sitting at the house writing up the bill to send to Greg when the front door opened all of a sudden. Molly was at work, so I had no idea who it could be. But I looked up, and there she was. She looked like she'd seen a ghost.

"We need to talk," she said.

My heart jumped up into my throat. Her tone of voice sounded like she was mad about something, and my own guilty conscience gave me plenty of ideas about why she might be mad at me. "Okay," I finally managed to say. "Come sit down."

She came in and sat on the sofa. She took a deep breath, looked me straight in the eye, and immediately burst out laughing. "I'm pregnant!" she said. "We're going to have a baby!"

My heart immediately fell out of my throat and went down through the floor. Of all the things I'd expected her to say, that one hadn't even been close. I wasn't sure how to react. "Are you sure?" was the first thing to come out of my mouth. I immediately regretted asking it.

She stopped laughing. "You're not happy?"

I recovered enough of my sense to at least fake happiness. A kid hadn't been in my immediate plans, but here it was. Make the best of it. "Of course I'm happy, darling," I said. I wrapped my arms around her. "It just surprised me. But yes, I'm very, very happy to hear!"

She was satisfied, at least for the moment, that I really was happy about the announcement, and she went on to tell me about her doctor's appointment that morning. She'd thought she might be pregnant because she'd been throwing up a lot at work, but didn't want to tell me until she was sure. She hadn't wanted to take a pregnancy test, because she was afraid she'd see somebody in the store when she was buying the test. It was Nantucket, after all. So she'd waited until she could get in to see her doctor. And that had been this morning. She'd told her boss she was taking the rest of the day off after getting the news.

"You know what this means, right?"

Yeah, I knew what it meant, but I wasn't sure what Molly thought it meant. I looked at her and smiled. "What's that?" I asked.

"No more procrastination, Mr. Faulkner," she said. "You planted your seed, and now you have to make an honest woman of me."

So that was what this was about. She wanted to get married. That was a lot to take in at one time, but I didn't dare say anything like that to her. I'd been so busy that I hadn't had time to really think about the wedding we were supposed to be having. We'd been living together for so long that it was like we were married already. "Sounds good to me. When do you want to do it?"

"Very romantic, Billy," she said. "I swear to God, sometimes I think you're not yourself anymore."

I hadn't thought about it much until that moment, but I realized that she might just be right. Maybe I had changed. Maybe I didn't want to marry her. Maybe I didn't want to be the father of her child. It had to just be my nerves, I told myself. I loved this woman and would do anything for her. Just because I was now making enough money to live without her, I wasn't going to suddenly turn on her. That wasn't my style.

"I'm kidding, darling," I said in as playful a tone as I could. "It's been a pretty crazy fifteen minutes here, you know. Cut me some slack." I winked at her and gave her a hug. "I'll marry you any time, anywhere," I whispered in her ear.

That was all it took. She buried her head in my chest and started crying, telling me how much she loved me. How she was so happy. Then she pulled back and looked up at me. "Let's do it now," she said.

"What?"

"Now. Let's go downtown right now and get the justice of the peace to marry us."

I had no idea if that was even legal, but I agreed to go with her. But then I suggested we look it up online, you know, just to see what we needed to do. Just so we'd have everything we needed when we got there. I did a quick Internet search and found out that we could go apply for a marriage license today, but there was a mandatory three-day waiting period.

Molly looked at me with kind of a wry smile. "Promise you're not going to run off on me in the next three days?"

I smiled right back at her. "Pinky swear," I said.

We went downtown and spoke with the town clerk, who also happened to be a justice of the peace. She agreed to do a civil marriage ceremony in three days; Molly wanted to do it on the beach.

"I know the perfect place," I told her.

Three days later, we were married on the beach in front of my favorite house on the Cliff. It was cold and windy, and the beach was empty as far as I could see in either direction. But that didn't matter to either of us. As I listened to the words of the ceremony and looked at Molly, any doubts I'd had a few days earlier were gone. I loved this woman, I loved the child she was carrying, and I loved that we were going to be a family.

When we'd said our "I dos" and had officially been pronounced husband and wife, we went to dinner at the same restaurant where I'd asked her to marry me. Sitting there eating and watching Molly sip on a glass of water, I'd never felt more grown-up in my life. I was having dinner as a married business owner who was going to be a father. There had been a time in the not-so-distant past when that much responsibility would have terrified me. Tonight, though, I felt energized. There was so much hope. So much promise for the future.

*   *   *

A week later, while Molly was at work, I drove to a house in town where I was meeting my contact about the boat I wanted to buy. I pulled into the driveway of the house, and parked next to what turned out to be the boat in question. It looked huge as I got out of the truck and stood next to it. I'd never really thought about how much of the hull was under the water line; when you saw it all right there in front of you, it was pretty massive.

There wasn't too much to discuss, as I'd already peppered the poor guy who was selling the boat for the woman with enough questions to bury him. We'd agreed on the price—$5,000—and all the electronics and the trailer were included in that price. I'd talked to Rooster about it, and he said it sounded like a pretty good deal to him, assuming that the motor was in good shape. The guy had promised me that it was in great mechanical shape, that the GPS was brand new last year, and that the motor had less than a hundred hours of use. I told Rooster that, and he said it was a great deal.

My hands were shaking as I wrote the check. It was a lot of money. More importantly, though, I was buying it without having first talked to the woman who was now my legal wife. She didn't even know I had the money. I handed over the check and got the title to the boat. I was now a boat owner. Easy as that. I remembered something Rooster had said once: "The two best days of a man's life, Billy, are the day he gets a boat and the day he sells it."

The next trick was getting the boat trailer hooked up to my own truck, and getting it out of the driveway. The person who had left it in the driveway had thought ahead enough to at least back it in, so getting the trailer attached to my truck wasn't all that hard. From there, it was just a matter of driving away.

I'd already decided that I couldn't park this thing at my house. Not yet, at least. I needed to break the news to Molly, and I didn't think having her arrive home to find a huge boat in the front yard was going to be the best way to do that. So I decided instead to stash it at a client's house. I drove very slowly up to the house on the Cliff, the one we'd gotten married on the beach in front of. It had a circular driveway, so it made getting in and out easy. I just needed to get it out before the homeowners—or Greg, for that matter—figured out I was storing it there.

That night, back at the cottage, I paced the floor waiting for Molly to get home. I'd rehearsed over and over what I was going to tell her. I'd gone over every possible issue I could imagine her having, and managed to answer each and every one of them. Now it was time to do the real performance.

When she opened the door, I was a little too happy to see her. She knew something was up, and looked at me suspiciously. I tried to play it off as just my own excitement about seeing her, but Molly wasn't buying it. "What gives?" she finally asked me.

"Okay," I began, taking a deep breath. "I wanted to surprise you, and I wasn't sure how to do it. But I guess I'll just tell you. I bought a boat." I held my breath, waiting for one of about fifteen different responses that I'd prepared for.

She stood silently for a minute, like she was slowly processing exactly what it was I'd just said. Finally, she asked, "A boat?"

"Yeah," I began. "But listen, before you get mad . . ."

She interrupted me before I could launch into my excuse. "That's great, darling!" she said. "I have always wanted to have a boat! And since we live on an island, it makes sense, don't you think?"

I'd been totally prepared for an argument, so this was more than a pleasant surprise. That was far better than anything I could have really hoped for. "That's exactly what I was thinking," I lied. "I'm glad you agree."

"Of course I agree," she said. "Where is it?"

I told her I'd left it at my client's house until I could figure out where I was going to keep it. "Rooster and I were going to take it out for a spin tomorrow," I added.

"Isn't it a little cold out there?"

I shook my head. "Not really. The whole scallop fleet is out, and I figure if those guys can handle it, I can handle it. We're not going to go far, either," I promised her. That was a lie, too, but she'd never know.

The next morning, I went and picked up Rooster, and we drove in my truck to get the boat. He couldn't believe how well Molly had taken the whole thing; his take on things was that I'd be on the hook for some major gift down the road. Whatever. I was fine with it. I had my boat, and that was all that mattered.

We hooked the trailer to my truck and drove down to the public boat landing. Rooster had to teach me how to back the trailer down into the water; it was like learning to drive all over again. After a bunch of false starts and a lot of yelling, with a little profanity thrown in, I finally managed to get the boat into the water.

Rooster tried to make me feel better. "First time's always the toughest," he said. "Once you figure out the secret to how to do it, it's easy."

I parked the truck while he waited with the boat. When I got back, I did a quick walk-around with Rooster to see what was where. It felt a little strange having him show me where things were on my own new boat, but it was helpful stuff. The previous owner had been kind enough to sell it to me with a full gas tank, and the motor started right up.

"Purrs like a kitten," Rooster yelled over the noise. I turned on both the GPS and the marine radio, and made sure that both were working properly. When I was sure everything was operating the way it was supposed to, I slowly put the throttle into reverse, and backed away. When we'd cleared the dock, I pushed the throttle forward slowly, turning the bow away and out towards open water. Rooster guided me out of the harbor, reminding me about the buoys. As we got close to the end of the channel, he turned to me.

"Where we going?" he asked.

I grinned. "Hyannis."

He shook his head. "No way, man. Not the first time."

"Then I'm turning around and dropping you off. I'm going to Hyannis." I don't know what it was about the prospect of crossing Nantucket Sound that appealed to me so much, you know? It wasn't like I had some great plan about what to do once we'd gotten over there. But I wanted to go. Something inside. I wanted to know I could do it, I guess. Prove to myself that I'd be able to do it.

He thought about it for a second. "Fine," he grunted. "But you're buying me dinner when we get back. It's going to be damn cold out on the water."

He slid in next to me and pushed a button on the GPS. "Just making sure we get home," he said. "Setting a waypoint for right here." When he was satisfied that he'd gotten the entrance to Nantucket Harbor saved as a waypoint, he looked back at me. "Let's go," he said.

I pushed the throttle forward. We were on our way across Nantucket Sound. Next stop Hyannis.

CHAPTER TWENTY-TWO

We motored past the Hyannis Yacht Club just about two hours after we'd left Nantucket. It had been a smooth ride over, and the boat had handled really well. I'd gotten pretty good at steering it without any problem, and once you're out there on the open water, it's just a matter of hanging on, you know? I do have to admit that it was a little spooky being out of sight of land for as long as we were, but Rooster kept telling me to follow the same compass heading that was taking us pretty much due north. Once we were in the harbor, though, it was easy enough to figure out where to go.

"Head right over there," Rooster said, pointing to a dock off to the right. "That's where the public landing is. You can tie up there."

I aimed for where he was pointing, and eased up on the throttle. Even though I thought I'd slowed the boat down enough, we still slammed into the dock pretty hard. Rooster jumped out, and attached a line to one of the wooden pilings. I cut the engine and smiled. "Ten-point landing, huh?"

Rooster nodded. "Now save this as a waypoint and call it Hyannis in the GPS," he said. He was nice enough not to give me any grief about the horrible job I'd done landing at the dock.

I pushed the button on the GPS to save the destination. On the way over, we'd talked about how easy it was to run marijuana—not to mention other stuff—back and forth. I proposed the idea of being partners, and told him that I'd be happy to split the profits with him. If it was as easy as he'd said it was, there was no telling how much money we could make if we were both running back and forth. Even one trip a week—and that didn't seem like a lot to me—could make us both enough money to make the winter a lot easier to get through. And since I didn't have any landscaping business until April, I had both a lot of free time and a lack of money coming in. Rooster was cool with the idea, just as long as I didn't try to screw him out of any cash.

I promised him I was good for it, and he explained to me how it worked. He'd call his guy when he was leaving Nantucket. He'd pull up, and usually his guy was there waiting for him. Worst case, he said, he had to wait a couple of minutes. If anybody asked him what he was doing, he'd just say he was waiting for his friend, who was parking the car. Easy as that.

Rooster would give the guy an envelope that had $1,000 in it, and his dealer gave him a backpack with a bag of weed in it. It was totally on the honor system on both sides, which seemed like a strange way to do a drug deal. I'd seen plenty of movies where drug dealers shot each other over little stuff, but Rooster knew this guy, and they trusted each other. Back on Nantucket, Rooster cleared anywhere from $3,000-$5,000 for each bag, which meant he was making a couple thousand dollars in profit with every trip. If I could do that every week, even splitting it with Rooster, I'd still get enough out of it to make it more than worth my while.

Rooster called his supplier while we were sitting there at the dock, and told him about me. The guy was uneasy about bringing somebody else in, but Rooster vouched for me, so it was all good. The guy said he'd come down and meet us, and about ten minutes later, he came walking up. He was a big black guy, wearing a Georgia Bulldogs sweatshirt. He had his hands in his pockets and he was looking down as he walked up to us. At the dock, he grunted a greeting to us.

"This is the guy," Rooster said. "Billy. He's cool."

I wasn't sure how to address this guy, so I just waved. I guess that was the right thing to do, because the guy kind of shrugged at me as a way of saying hello. I never got his name; I figured that wasn't too important a detail for me to have, as long as I had his phone number. Rooster and the black guy walked away for a minute, talking quietly, and then the black guy left. Rooster came back to the boat and told me it was all set.

"I gave him your phone number, so he'll know it's you calling," he said. "I'll give you his number. When you call him from Nantucket, just tell him you're on your way. Keep it short. And don't fuck around with him. He's not the friendliest guy you'll ever meet."

That was cool with me. I wasn't too sure this was a guy I'd ever want coming over to the house anyway, and I was in this for the money, not the friendship. Rooster got back in the boat and announced that it was time for us to head back to Nantucket. I started up the boat and we eased our way out of the harbor, and when we'd cleared the last channel marker, I pushed the throttle forward and we were off.

"Pull up the Nantucket waypoint we set," Rooster reminded me.

I pushed the button on the GPS, and a little line appeared on the screen. It stretched all the way across the display, marking the path I was going to take back to the island.

We were both silent the whole way back. I was thinking the whole time about this new moneymaking scheme. It was definitely something I couldn't tell Molly about, because I had no idea how she'd react. I knew she wouldn't like it. But we needed the money, especially with a baby on the way. As much as I hated to keep secrets from her, this was one that I had to keep quiet about.

When we got back to Nantucket, I pulled up to the dock where we'd left from—my second attempt at a soft landing didn't go a whole lot better than my first—and Rooster got out. He went to my truck and backed it down the ramp, then got out and told me to pull forward slowly. He was waving his hands one way or the other, telling me to steer in whichever direction so that I could line the boat up with the trailer. It wasn't pretty, but I managed to get it on. He attached the chain to the bow, then cranked it on.

"You're going to have to learn how to do that by yourself," Rooster said when we were both inside the truck. "I'm not always going to be here to help you, you know."

I nodded as said, "Yeah. Thanks, Dad. I know."

As we drove away from the boat ramp, Rooster started talking about our new business deal. "Let's talk money," he said. "I'm the one that people here come to for grass, so I'll be the one who sells it here. You can be the mule, going back and forth to pick it up. What do you think about me paying you two grand per trip? You put up the thousand to get the stuff, so you'll make an even grand every time."

It wasn't ideal, to be sure. I'd been thinking that he and I would both sell it ourselves, which would mean I'd make that five thousand a week. But he was right. He had the customer base, and the only thing people really knew about me was that I was a landscaper. I wasn't the guy you'd come to if you wanted to buy weed. So it was probably as good a deal as I could have hoped to get.

"That's fine," I said. And that was apparently that. We were now officially business partners. Rooster gave me the supplier's cell phone number; he told me to list him in my phone as Quentin, and if anybody asked, I was supposed to say he was an old high school friend.

I drove to Rooster's house and dropped him off. Then I headed back up the Cliff to my client's house, where I left the boat.

As I drove back to my house, I kept thinking about what I'd agreed to do. Was this really what my life had become? Was I really meant to be a drug dealer? The money would be nice, to be sure, but I mean, this wasn't really the plan I had when I'd decided to move out here. The whole idea had been to leave the old me behind, you know? Make a clean break from my old life as a con man and start over. Of course, I'd pretty much picked up where I'd left off when I had the chance, since I was marketing myself as an organic landscaper.

It pissed me off that I just couldn't seem to get out of that whole mindset. It was all about the money, you know? I didn't have the brains to make a legitimate living, it seemed like, so I had to do stuff that was kind of illegal—or in the case of running drugs, that was very illegal—to make enough money to survive. It made me feel better to tell myself that I was only doing it so I could provide a better life for my family, but I knew that was a load of crap. I'd been conning people for a lot longer than I'd had my own family. This was just another con I was running, only this time I was running it on my wife too.

I couldn't keep this up. I knew that. But how many times I had I told myself that exact same thing? I guess it's like a drunk who swears he'll never do it again, you know, when he wakes up hung over and broke. But just like me, he forgets his promises pretty quick, and goes right back to drinking again. I was addicted to money, I guess. And that addiction made me do a lot of stupid stuff.

When I pulled into the driveway at the cottage, Molly was already home. I looked at my watch, and realized it was after five. I'd lost track of the time, apparently, while I was lost in my own little world. I needed to snap back into the here and now, and I needed to do it quickly. It was going to be hard enough to not tell Molly about why I was suddenly going to be going to Hyannis once a week, and I didn't need to go into the house looking like I was worried about it.

When I walked inside, she wanted to know all about my day on the boat. "I was thinking about you all day," she said. "I was so jealous that you were out there on the water without me!"

I told her it had been a great day, and that the boat was perfect. When she asked me where we'd gone, I managed to keep it vague, saying that we'd just motored around so that I could get a feel for how it handled. That was partially true, at least. It was another one of my personal justifications. And those justifications were piling up. I was really scared that it would only be a matter of time before they all came falling down around me.

CHAPTER TWENTY-THREE

I gave it a few days to get my courage up before I went back. I must have talked myself out of doing it fifty times. It was too risky, I told myself. There was too much that could go wrong. It was too dangerous. I wasn't cut out to be doing this. But there was that money to think about. The thought of what I could do with an extra $1,000 every week was nice. It meant we wouldn't be so damn worried about money all the time, for one. And with a baby on the way, God help me, money worries were only going to get worse. Especially since I couldn't work during the winter. So in the end, I finally decided to give it a shot. I reasoned with myself that if it got too hot, I'd just get out. No problem.

I planned my first trip around Molly's work schedule. Thursdays were busy for her, because it was somebody's day off at the store. That meant she had to be in at eight o'clock in the morning and work straight through to six. Ten hours would give me plenty of time to get over and back without her having any idea I'd even left the house. I called Rooster the day before to tell him what my plan was, and we decided that I'd leave Nantucket at nine in the morning, which should put me back at the dock in Nantucket no later than one o'clock in the afternoon, assuming everything went the way it was supposed to. He'd meet me at the landing to help me trailer the boat and take the delivery I'd have for him.

Thursday morning was perfect. No wind at all, which was rare for that time of year, and the sun was bright. It was a perfect day for a crossing. When she'd left the house, Molly had asked me about my plans for the day. I'd told her I'd probably head into town to get a cup of coffee, maybe read the local newspaper that came out on Thursdays. Nothing much. She kissed me good-bye and went off to work.

I waited forty-five minutes, then went out. I'd already cashed a check at the bank for the money I'd need, and I had the envelope with ten new hundred-dollar bills sealed up inside my jacket. I drove up to where I was keeping the boat. My heart was going ninety miles an hour the whole time I was hooking up the trailer. And it only beat faster the closer I got to the dock. I tried my best to relax, but there was no way I was going to be the cool customer I wanted to be. I was flat-out scared of what I was about to be doing.

Backing the boat down the ramp was a challenge, and I had more than a few screwups. It was a little bit like a bumper car ride at the fair, you know, with all the starting and stopping all of a sudden. I finally managed to get it far enough back so that the boat was in the water, then I put the truck in park and got out. I cranked the boat off the trailer, just like Rooster had shown me, and took a line from the bow and walked it back down the dock. I tied it off, then went back to the truck and parked it. I took a couple of deep breaths and, even though I'm not a religious guy, I said a quick prayer to anybody who might have happened to be listening to me at the time.

I went back to the boat, got in, fired up the motor, and turned on the GPS. I was totally stalling, checking every little thing I could think of to check. There was plenty of gas still, but I triple-checked it, just to make sure. The engine sounded fine. There wasn't any trash in the boat that needed to be thrown away. The lines were where they were supposed to be. Even the spray shield was clean. When I decided there wasn't anything else I could check to delay it any more, I untied and backed away from the dock. This was it. I took out my phone and called the number I had for Quentin.

"What?" was all the voice said on the other end after a couple of rings.

"Uh, hi. It's Billy," I said. "Rooster's friend."

Silence.

"I'm leaving Nantucket right now, and I'll be there in two hours." I tried to keep my voice steady and businesslike.

"Cool."

The call ended just like that. I hoped everything really was cool. I guessed I'd find out when I got there.

I pressed the waypoint button on the GPS and selected the Hyannis destination, then started the long, slow trip out of the harbor. My mind was all over the place. I kept wondering if what I was doing was either incredibly stupid or incredibly smart. I was risking a lot. But I was also looking at making a lot of money. I somehow managed to make my brain focus on the money instead of the risk. I'd done worse than this in my time, and the only bad thing that had happened to me was an overnight jail stay. I could handle that again, if worst came to worst. The money was just too much to pass up.

As I was rounding Brant Point, my cell phone rang. It was Rooster. He was calling to make sure I'd gotten away okay. I told him everything was fine, and that we were on schedule to meet at one. After I'd hung up, I kind of laughed. Rooster was treating me like I was his son, whom he'd just dropped off for his first day of school. He was worried about me, and he probably had a lot more to be worried about than he knew. It really wasn't until I'd gotten clear of the harbor and throttled the motor all the way up that I was really sure I was going to go through with this whole thing at all.

The faster the boat went, the better I felt. There was just something about being out there on the water, you know? It's like my focus turned to the boat, and I didn't think about what it was that I was on my way to do. I had to keep my attention on the GPS to make sure I was staying on course. As I passed Great Point off in the distance to my right, the stakes got a little higher, because I was entering what was basically the open ocean, as far as I was concerned. I was still on edge, but at least I was on edge now because I was paying attention to the boat.

About forty-five minutes later, I saw the high-speed ferry coming towards me. It made me feel better to see it, because the ferry was coming from Hyannis, and that meant I was really going in the right direction. Even though I'd been following the course on the computer screen since I'd left the dock, I still had a nagging doubt in the back of my mind that I wasn't going in the right direction. Since it was my first trip on my own, I had this vision of myself totally screwing up. I'm not sure where I thought I might have been headed—maybe to Portugal?—but whatever, it made me feel better to see the ferry. And it was a connection to people out here in the middle of the ocean, even if there weren't very many people on it at the time.

I passed the ferry and waved. Not sure who I thought was saying hello to, but it seemed like every time I passed another boat, the captain waved to me. So I figured it was something you just did on a boat. I didn't get any kind of response. But just then, I hit the ferry's wake, which was pretty big. Going full-throttle wasn't the best idea, I learned, because my boat jumped up out of the water and slammed back down. It repeated that little process three times as I went through the wake. With each wave, it was like everything in the boat—and every bone in my own body—rattled and shook like we were in the middle of an earthquake.

On the third time I slammed back down into the water, the door to the little cabin under the console flew open and slammed into my knee. I eased up on the gas and put the engine in neutral so I could close it. When I looked, I found out that the latch that held the door shut had apparently broken, so there was no way to keep it closed. I thought for a minute, then stuck my hand in my pocket and pulled out a quarter. That would work, at least for a little while. I pushed the door shut again, and then wedged the quarter in between the door and the frame. The extra width managed to keep the door shut.

The rest of the trip was uneventful, and I pulled into Hyannis Harbor right on schedule. I slowed up as I got close to the dock, and I could see Quentin's car. He apparently saw me too, because the driver's door opened, and he stepped out. He was carrying a backpack over his shoulder. I slowly pulled up to the dock. Or at least I thought I was going slowly. I misjudged the distance and slammed into the dock. So much for third time being the charm.

I tried to look cool, like I'd meant to do that, just in case anybody happened to be watching me. My heart was about to explode from fear. I left the engine in neutral as I went forward and exchanged the envelope for the backpack without getting out of the boat.

"Where's the other one?" Quentin asked.

I thought he meant Rooster, so I said, "He's back on Nantucket."

Quentin shook his massive head. "No, dumbass. My other bag. Where's it at?"

"Rooster has it," I said. "I didn't know I was supposed to bring it back."

He kind of laughed in that way that says you're an idiot. "You bring it with you next time," he said. "And make sure you bring this one, too. I'm not gonna be buying more of these damn things."

"You got it," I said. He grunted and walked back to his car. "I'll see you next week."

He didn't respond. I immediately wished I hadn't said it. The less we talked, the better off we both were, and here I was trying make small talk like I was setting up a date.

But it was done. I'd done my first drug deal. Or at least half of it. Now I just needed to get back and hand it off to Rooster and get my $2,000. The way I had it planned, I'd put the original thousand I'd taken out the day before back in the bank this afternoon, so even if Molly decided to check on the balance, the money would be there. I was starting to feel like I could do this.

I changed the waypoint on the GPS back to Nantucket, and motored away. I'd learned a few lessons on this first trip, and I kind of thought that every time I did it, I'd get better, you know? So by the time I'd done it for a few weeks, I should be pretty much on autopilot the whole way. I was already patting myself on the back, and I hadn't even gotten out of the harbor to head home yet.

Before I really throttled up, though, I thought it would be a good idea to stash the backpack in the cuddy cabin. With a little bit of effort, I managed to pull the quarter out, and the door fell open. I threw the backpack in, closed the door, and replaced the quarter. Now I was just a guy out for a little boat ride. Nothing to see here. I pushed the throttle all the way forward and headed for home.

It was just about twenty minutes before one when I slid around the lighthouse at Brant Point. I was home again. I'd made it. I felt like Christopher Columbus right then, like I'd just done some journey that everyone said was impossible, and I'd proven them all wrong.

As I slid past the Coast Guard station, my heart all of a sudden started beating really fast again, because the whole idea of what I was carrying came flooding into my brain. I tried to calm myself by taking deep breaths, but it didn't work. The big boats sitting there outside the station looked like they were aimed right at me, ready to come grab me, and throw me in jail. But I motored by without anybody so much as appearing on the dock.

I turned my attention forward again, and saw Rooster standing on the dock waiting for me. He looked casual, like he just happened to be hanging out there. As I got close, he called out and asked me if I wanted any help. I played along, and yelled back that I'd love some help getting my boat on the trailer. My mind now focused on not slamming into the dock as I got close, and I cut the engine sooner than I had in Hyannis. No luck. The momentum took me hard into a piling. Rooster just laughed at me.

"First time on the water?" he asked when he finally stopped laughing.

"Yeah, something like that," I said. "I do that every time. What the hell is the secret to do it without killing yourself like that?"

"You need to remember you've got reverse on that thing, too," he said. "Put it in reverse when you get close, and you'll have a lot softer landing."

"Thanks," I said. That was good information to have, actually. It might actually keep me from breaking anything else on my boat.

He took the bowline and tied it off as I got out and went to my truck. He guided me as I backed up to the ramp, and it went a lot better this time around. We got the boat up on the trailer, and I told him to follow me. He nodded without saying anything. It was like we were spies trading classified secrets, and we were sure that everybody was watching us. I got in the truck and slowly drove away, pulling the boat out of the water. I stopped and waited for Rooster to get to his own truck. When he was behind me, I turned out and started to make my way up to the Cliff.

I drove slowly, making sure to keep Rooster in my rearview mirror. When we got to the house, I got out of the truck and couldn't help but smile. The deal was done. I'd pulled it off without any major problems. I climbed up into the boat and got the bag out of the cuddy, and threw it down to Rooster. He unzipped and looked inside, something that hadn't occurred to me to do when I'd gotten it. I was glad to see Rooster smile when he saw what was there.

"Looks good," he said up to me. "Nicely done. How was the trip?"

"Easy stuff," I said. "Not a problem at all. This is going to be the easiest money I ever made."

"Don't get cocky," he warned me. "You start getting cocky, you screw up. You screw up, shit goes wrong. And that's bad for everyone."

"Got it," I said flatly.

He zipped the backpack and put it in his truck, then took out a wad of cash from his pants pocket. "Two grand," he said, handing it to me. "Pleasure doing business with you. Same time next week?"

I nodded, trying to keep from showing how excited I was about my sudden income bump. "Sounds good to me. Oh, by the way. I need that other backpack from last week. You've still got it, right?"

"Yeah. I'll get it to you," he said.

Rooster got in his truck and left, and I just stood there for a minute, thinking about how easy it really all had been. Even taking into account the cost of gas and the $1,000 I'd had to use to get the weed in the first place, I was still making a lot of money. I did a little quick math in my head, and figured out that I was probably taking in $900 for what amounted to about five hours of my time. That was a hell of an hourly wage for a guy who'd only managed to squeak by in high school, and graduated by the skin of his teeth. I was pretty proud of myself.

And even though I couldn't really tell anybody how I got the money, I didn't care. I had it, and that's what mattered. I know it's easy for somebody to sit where you are and judge me for doing it, but put yourself in my position before you get too high and mighty. You know, Nantucket is a really expensive place to live, like I told you. Hell, nowhere is cheap when you think about it. Especially when you've got my past.

Throw a family into that mix, and it can get pretty damn hard to survive, quite frankly. But here was a way for me to support my family. And really, I wasn't hurting anybody. It's not like people would smoke weed because of me. I was just helping out a friend. If I didn't do it, either he'd get somebody else, or he'd do it himself, right?

That's what I kept telling myself as I drove to the bank. Nobody was getting hurt, and I was just helping out a friend. I repeated it over and over in my head, like some kind of mantra. I deposited $1,000 in our account to replace the money I'd withdrawn the day before, and then drove home. By the time I'd gotten back to the house, I think I'd actually convinced myself that I wasn't really doing anything wrong. Just helping out a friend. Victimless crime. Providing for my family. All that sort of thing.

CHAPTER TWENTY-FOUR

I made the Nantucket to Hyannis run once a week through the winter. Every Thursday, I'd head over in the boat with an empty nylon backpack and an envelope with $1,000 in it. I didn't care if it was raining, snowing, or blowing like hell. A lot of the local scallopers—the only other guys who were out there on the water at that time of year—thought I was nuts to be going out in some of the weather I did. They thought I was just out joyriding in my boat while the wind whipped and the water temperature was in the forties.

But I didn't care. The money was too easy, and that temptation was just too much for me to resist. The thought of that extra cash warmed me up like a heater, and I just gritted my teeth and went. By the first of April, I'd done the trip so many times in so many different kinds of weather that I got to where I thought I could pretty well do it blindfolded if I had to. I began to recognize certain landmarks on the horizon, and could tell you where I was almost exactly based on how long it had been since I'd left. I was really getting good at making the crossing.

Molly still had no idea what I was doing on her busy days. And she never asked about how it was that we could afford to do things like go out to dinner every once in a while, even though I didn't have any actual landscaping work at the time. I was happy for that, because I still wasn't quite ready to come clean about my side business. She had enough to worry about, with doctor appointments and all the other stuff that came with being pregnant. I knew there would come a time when I'd have to tell her, but again, that time wasn't just yet.

About that time, we made another addition to the old family, a little beagle we got from the local animal shelter. I wasn't really excited about it at first, to tell you the truth, but Molly thought he was too cute to pass up. We saw his picture in the paper, and then went in to visit with him. His name was Arthur, and I have to admit that he was really cute.

We cleared it with the landlord to make sure it was okay, and he said he didn't have a problem with us having a dog as long as we understood that we'd have to pay a pet deposit in case he destroyed anything or pissed on the rug or whatever. It was part of our original lease, he reminded me, that if we did decide to get a pet, it'd require that deposit.

That was fine with me. If it made Molly happy to have Arthur around, then so be it. After a couple more visits to make sure everybody got along okay, we got to bring him home. It was good for Molly to have something to focus on other than the fact that she was pregnant. I'd heard just about all I could take about how big the fetus was, and how I needed to keep my voice down because I was upsetting the baby. The dog gave her something to distract her from all that, so Arthur was okay in my book.

The change in season forced me to get back to my real job, which meant I'd have to work a little harder to get in my trips back and forth to Hyannis. My client list was up to sixteen houses, and I'd already hired a couple of Bulgarian kids to work for me. I'd gotten hooked up with a service on the island that paired foreign kids who came to the United States on H-2B visas that let them work through the summer. The kids were set to start on the first of May, so I had to work by myself for a month, getting yards and gardens ready.

The only catch was that they were only legally allowed to work until their visas expired, and then they had to leave the country. I'd talked to enough people to know that a lot of the ones who came over on those H-2B visas stayed long past the dates when they were supposed to go home, but nobody seemed to care enough to find them and ship them back.

I began the year pretty much abandoning the whole organic concept. I made sure to keep enough organic products in plain sight in my truck, so that in case anybody happened to look in, they'd think I was doing everything as advertised. Old dog, new tricks. It was the only way I could make enough money to make this operation work, and I figured the Bulgarians wouldn't care. As long as they got paid, they'd keep their mouths shut.

It was kind of nice to have a little time to get used to working again. Before my clients got in town, I could work without them looking over my shoulder and telling me all the things they thought I was doing wrong. I did a little work, billed for a lot more work, and gave Greg my invoices. He paid them, then billed his clients directly. The more I thought about it, the more I decided I liked the position of being the middleman. I had it in both my jobs; it was like Rooster and Greg were my bosses, and I was more than happy to let them make a little money off my work if they kept paying me for the work I did. I guess maybe I was little bit like the Bulgarians in that way, you know? Just give me my money, and I'll do what you need done, without asking a lot of questions.

I got all of the spring work done on all of the houses by myself, but I'll cop to the fact that I didn't do all that much work. Of course, the invoices I submitted said I'd worked like a slave nonstop, but the reality was that I didn't do all that much. Human nature is a funny thing, you know? People see something for the first time in a long time, and it doesn't really matter how bad it looks. They're so excited to be back in their little summer paradise that they think it looks great.

The Bulgarian kids showed up on the first of May as planned. Their names were Stanislav and Georgi, but I just called them Stan and George. They didn't seem to mind. They spoke pretty good English, so it was easy enough to explain to them what I needed them to do. I taught them how to use the lawn mower and the hedge trimmers, and showed them how to fertilize the plants and lay down mulch. Landscaping isn't rocket science, so it wasn't too hard to teach them. And they were pretty bright, actually, and they figured out everything that they needed to do.

Having them there was great, because it made it a lot easier for me to do my weekly Hyannis runs through the summer. Summer in Hyannis is a lot like summer in Nantucket. One day the harbor was empty, and I was in and out without seeing another boat. The next week, though, it was like somebody flipped a switch, and boats appeared out of nowhere. It made me a little nervous to be surrounded by that many people the first time, but I hoped that my boat was generic enough, and that I was there for such a short time, that nobody would remember me.

Another thing about the summer that I hadn't really thought about before was the fact that all those summer kids that show up on Nantucket have all kinds of money to spend, and a lot of them want to spend it on weed. So suddenly Rooster's business—like every other business on the island—went crazy. He asked me if I'd be okay with doubling the amount I picked up, and I told him I'd be happy to do it as long as he doubled the price he was paying me. In other words, four grand per trip. I'd shell out two thousand to Quentin, and Rooster would pay me four when I gave him the week's delivery. He was fine with that, and I was happy beyond belief.

Money was rolling in. But by the end of July, Molly was just too pregnant to work anymore. Or at least that's what she said. She'd even stopped working on that book project she'd been so excited about when we first moved to Nantucket. I guessed that the baby had taken all of her creative energy. And even though she wasn't due for another couple of weeks, she said she just couldn't stand being in the store all day dealing with people when she was as pregnant as she was. So they let her take time off—unpaid, of course—so that she could have the baby. They'd give her the job back once she was ready to come back to work, whenever that was.

That made my life a little harder, because it meant that I'd have to make my weekly trip across Nantucket Sound while she was at home. It was actually pretty easy to get around that, because I had the Bulgarians. I scheduled work so that Thursdays were what we called "maintenance days," which meant it was just mowing lawns and pulling weeds. I'd drive them to whatever house we were working at for the day, and then I'd leave them and take off in the boat.

One issue that did come up was a place to keep the boat once summer rolled around. The clients who owned the house where I'd been keeping it were back in town, and that meant finding a new place to store it. Rooster was a huge help there, because I really had no idea what to do. He talked to some people he knew that had a mooring, and they agreed to let me rent it from them for $500 a month. It cut in to my profits, but not enough to be a problem. I chalked it up to the cost of doing business. They were nice enough to let me use their dinghy to row out to the mooring. I told Molly yet another little white lie, and said that a friend of Rooster's had let me have their mooring for the summer because they weren't using it.

Everything was going perfectly, to my mind. Molly wasn't asking too many questions, and my weekly trips weren't screwing up my landscaping schedule. I was cutting corners and lying a little bit with my business practices, but not enough to cause any kind of moral conflict in my own head, you know? But then, all of a sudden, everything changed in a snap. It was like the turnover at the beginning of the summer, when everybody kind of showed up all at once. It was that same kind of immediate change.

On August tenth of that year, Molly gave birth to our daughter, Caroline, and she was absolutely perfect. I'd heard stories about how having a child changes your life forever, and makes you feel a love that you never thought was possible, but I'd always thought it was bullshit. But then it happened to me. It wasn't easy for Molly, but the second that the doctor put that kid in my arms, my knees buckled, and I had more love in my heart than I ever thought was humanly possible. In that single moment, everything in my life changed. From that point forward, I promised—and I meant it this time—that I was done with lying of any kind, because my daughter deserved to have a father who was an honest man.

But as soon as I'd made that promise, the justifications started. I wasn't going to give up my side job as a drug smuggler, because I was only doing that to make sure that my child had the best life possible. So drug running wasn't included in my whole-new-life resolution. And the realities of the landscaping business meant that if I wanted to keep my rates reasonable, I couldn't spend as much as I'd have to in order to buy all the natural, organic stuff. So by using non-organic chemicals, I was actually doing my clients a favor, right? But other than those little issues, I was going to stop the lies to my wife. She and Caroline both deserved that much.

But where was I supposed to start? I mean, my whole life story was made up of a bunch of lies, starting with my life in Vermont. If I wanted to come totally clean, I'd probably have to admit to cheating on a couple of tests when I was in high school. And the more I thought about it, the more it looked like I was pretty much a con man from birth, with one lie leading into another one. And it went all the way up to the person I'd become today: a self-described organic landscaper who was cheating his customers by using non-organic products that he charged them for, all while moonlighting on the side as a drug runner. It wasn't a pretty picture.

I kept reminding myself that my new family needed to know the truth, and I spent the next week working up the courage to unload my whole story on Molly. It was a Wednesday night. I remember it pretty clearly. I'd worked all day while Molly was home with the baby. I called her to tell her I was working late—I promised myself this would be the last lie I'd tell her—and stopped off at a bar instead. I started doing shots and drinking cheap draft beer, trying to give myself a little liquid courage. I had a pretty good buzz on by the time I pulled myself away and headed home. Drinking and driving on Nantucket isn't looked at quite like it is in other places. It's pretty common, really. Some people get caught, but most manage to make it home without any problems.

I fell into the group that made it home that night. When I walked in the front door, Molly was sitting in front of the TV, rocking the baby in her arms. I took a deep breath, and told myself it was all for the best. I sat down next to her and gave her a kiss.

"You smell like you've been drinking," she said after a second.

"Yeah. I stopped off and had a beer." I paused for a second. "Actually a few beers." There, that wasn't so hard to tell the truth. She didn't seem too upset by that news, and I got a feeling of strength, like I could tell her everything without worrying. So I opened the floodgates.

"Molly," I began, "there's some stuff that's been bugging me lately, and I just need to get it off my chest. So let me talk for just a minute so I can get it all out."

Her expression changed, like she was a little scared about what was coming next.

"We're married now and we have a child, so it's time you knew everything about me, about my past, and about what's going on now." I started with the maple syrup scam, trying to explain it away as a need to make money when there weren't any other options for me. She actually laughed about that one. Then I told her about my arrest, and how I'd moved to Connecticut, where I got a job selling insurance. I explained how Victor had sucked me into his own scam, trying to paint myself as a victim in the whole thing. She didn't laugh this time. Instead she interrupted me in mid-story.

"Do you think they're still looking for you?" she asked, her voice sounding a little worried.

I shook my head. "No, it's been too long," I assured her. "They must have given up by now. But there's more you should know."

She sighed, and I could see her whole body sort of slump, like she didn't know how much more of this confession she was up for. I told her about the fact that I wasn't always using organic fertilizers all the time, because it was just too expensive to buy. But I explained to her that I had the organic stuff in my truck, so if anybody came looking around, they'd think I was using the stuff I was claiming to use. So I wasn't in danger of getting busted on that.

She got up and put Caroline in her crib, then came back to the sofa and sat down next to me. She put her hand on my knee and looked at me. "Billy," she said softly, "I know you're a good person, and I know you've got the best intentions. It's hard to make a living out here, and I know you're doing the best you can. All I ask is that you just keep being the good person you are, and working as hard as you do for us. We love you no matter what, and we always will."

As she talked, I felt worse and worse about myself. This woman had put her trust in me, and had fallen in love with me, and now she was learning that I wasn't the man she thought I had been. But she was still willing to see past it. My eyes went down to the floor, but she ducked her own head around so she could look me in the eyes.

"It's okay, darling," she said. "Thank you for telling me."

I smiled, despite feeling like the world's biggest jackass right then. "There's one other thing you have to know," I said softly. "I've been making trips to Hyannis once a week in the boat. I go over and pick up a shipment of weed that I bring back to Rooster for him to sell."

Molly was dead quiet now. She took her hand off my knee and sat back in the sofa, now looking at the wall above the TV.

"I'm only doing it for the money," I said, now pleading with her. I knew this was a big bomb to drop on her. "It's just so that you and Caroline can have everything you need."

She still didn't say a word. Just sat there staring at the wall.

"Please, Molly. Say something."

Finally she spoke. "Billy, I don't know what to say. The thought of it scares the shit out of me, quite honestly. What if you get caught? What then?"

I took a minute and explained the process to her, trying to show her that there was no chance of me getting caught, because it wasn't like I had to go through any police checkpoints or anything. It was just a quick in and out in Hyannis, and then another quick handoff to Rooster. "And then there's the money," I told her. "Right now, I'm making $2,000 every week. That's a month's rent plus groceries for the week, with a little left over. Every week."

She shook her head. "I don't like it, Billy. Not at all."

I reminded her that she was out of work and not getting paid, which meant that the three of us were living on just what I brought in, and my landscaping income would be barely enough to scrape by. "And I want more for us," I said. "I want us to have the life we want to live. I want Caroline to have everything she could ever want."

I felt a little awful about blaming my own greed on my newborn daughter, but the truth was that I did want to give that child everything. I didn't want to be the father who had to tell his kid she couldn't have something because we couldn't afford it. But honestly, the real truth was that I'd gotten used to having a little extra cash in my pocket. Giving that up was harder work than I was willing to do at that moment.

We went back and forth for a while, her telling me that it was too dangerous, and that I shouldn't be doing it, me saying that it was easy money, and that nobody was getting hurt.

"Obviously you're going to do it no matter what I think," she finally said. "But I do want to ask you something, and you have to swear to me that you'll do it. Be careful out there, and if it ever starts to get dangerous, promise me that you'll stop doing it. We'll survive without the extra money."

"I promise," I said.

She exhaled heavily, and that was the end of it. She'd finally given in, and I could feel my whole body straightening out, like I'd been hunched over for my entire life to that point, and I was just figuring out that there was a more comfortable way to live.

"We're okay?" I finally asked her.

She nodded. "Yeah. But remember your promise."

"I won't forget," I said.

She took my hand in hers. "We're going to make it," she said. "I'm sorry you're having to do all this for us." She paused for a second. "I'm not sure whether to thank you for doing what you're doing, but I guess I need to. You're only doing it for us, and that means a lot to me. So thank you."

I'd never loved her more than I did at that moment.

CHAPTER TWENTY-FIVE

The trouble really started that fall, and it was all because of that goddamn house with the pond in back. Everything was great with the landscaping, but the people who lived in the house apparently thought that there was some kind of algae growing in their pond that didn't look good. I guess there was something about aquatic growth that screwed up their view of the sunset or something. Anyway, they started by asking me to see what I could do about it, so I told them I would. But what do I know about that stuff? I mean, I mowed lawns for a living. I didn't know what was making this stuff grow in their pond. But I pretended to go down there and look at it, like I had any idea what I was doing. They sat up on their deck and watched me, so I bent over and studied it real close and scratched my head a lot. I spent about ten minutes doing that, then came back up.

"I'm not sure what's causing it," I said. That was actually true. I had no clue.

"Well, do you think . . ." the husband began, but his wife interrupted him.

"We're going to have to get somebody in here to look at it and figure out what to do," she said. "We're leaving right after Labor Day, but I want this cleared up as soon as possible." Clearly she wore the pants in the family where that damn pond was concerned. "That's just unacceptable."

I apologized for not knowing more about what to do, and the husband gave me kind of a sympathetic look, like this was something he dealt with all the time, and that I shouldn't take it too personally, you know? So I didn't. I left it at that, and figured they'd take care of the problem, and just let me do the job they were paying me to do.

It took a few weeks for whatever lab they hired to get out to the island and sample the water, and then a few more weeks for them to get the results. The wife, naturally, was the one who called me to tell me about what they'd found. I was at one my clients' houses, working with the two Bulgarian kids, getting the garden ready for the winter. Even though she was somewhere in Maryland, it was like she was standing right next to me while she yelled at me.

"Apparently there's a nitrogen overload in the pond," she said. She sounded a little pissed, like this was something I could control. When I didn't say anything about that, she went on. "The lab said it could have come from one of a couple of different sources. One of the first things that they mentioned was using too much fertilizer."

Now we were back in the land of things I could talk about, so I decided to speak up. "I've been following the schedule of putting fertilizer on your lawn that we agreed to," I said, "so it shouldn't be that. But if it's too much, I can cut back."

"It's not that," she said. "At least not in the way you're thinking."

I was confused now. "What do you mean?"

"Well, I told them that my gardener uses all organic products." I hated that she called me her gardener. It made me feel like an illegal alien. "So they did another test. This one tested for other chemicals, just to make sure. Chemicals that are specific to commercial, non-organic fertilizers."

My stomach started to do a few somersaults. I was nervous about what was coming next.

"Suffice it to say that they found a lot of those chemicals that shouldn't be in organic fertilizers. I, of course, told them that there was no way it had come from my lawn, and that they must be mistaken."

"You are absolutely correct, ma'am," I said, trying to get back in control of the conversation. "I only use organic fertilizer." So much for my no-lying promise.

"I wish I could believe you, Billy," she said. "But there's a little more to the story. You see, they apparently took soil samples from our yard, too. Care to guess what they found?"

Now I was screwed. There was nothing I could say, so I kept quiet.

"That's what I thought," she finally said. "Consider this your termination notice." She hung up.

My whole business plan was about to come crashing down. There was no way to get around that. Nantucket is a small place, and word gets around fast when something happens. Your neighbor gets in a fight with his wife, and everybody on the island seems to know it before they even kiss and make up. And the bigger the scandal, the quicker the news seemed to spread, so I was pretty sure this one was going to be all over the place soon.

When I heard my phone ring a half hour later, I think I knew who it was and what he was going to say before I even saw the number. Sure enough, it was Greg. I answered, but didn't get a chance to say anything before he launched into his speech.

He'd just gotten an angry call from a client who had discovered that I wasn't using the organic methods I'd claimed to be using—and charging a pretty penny for using too—and that I was officially fired from all of my other clients, effective immediately. He told me that any currently unpaid invoices would be paid, but that after that, I shouldn't expect to ever make another dime in landscaping on Nantucket again as long as I lived.

After he'd hung up, I started to think about what I was still owed. Less than $1,000 in total, which wasn't going to take me too far. I called Stan and George over from where they were working, and told them to stop. I explained that I'd just been let go, without giving away too much information about why it was that I'd been fired. I told them that I hated to do it, but I had to lay them off. They took it in stride, actually. Apparently they'd met some other Bulgarians on the island who were working at different jobs and making more than I was paying them, so I guess they looked at the whole thing as a blessing in disguise. I wish I could have shared that feeling.

The good news in all of this was that we had enough cash on hand to get us through the winter, even if Molly didn't go back to work. I knew I didn't have a business to run anymore, and I knew that I'd never be able to pass myself off as a business owner again on Nantucket. But I did hope that between my weekly runs to Hyannis and the money we had saved, we'd have enough to get by. And who could tell? Maybe by next summer, things would have blown over, and my sins would be forgotten.

And then there was Molly, and how to tell her about this. She'd been under enough stress as it was with the baby. And just to add insult to injury, the place she'd been working had told her that they'd filled her position, and she didn't have a job anymore. The only good news in that was the fact that she could collect unemployment, but that was only a couple hundred dollars a week.

That was actually a pretty standard thing on Nantucket, you know, for people to collect unemployment during the winter. Whatever business they worked for would close down after the crowds had gone, so they didn't have a job anymore. But bills kept on coming in, and people had to eat, right? So they'd call the unemployment office and tell them they got laid off, and the business would say that yes, they had gotten laid off. And that was all it took. They got paid for doing absolutely nothing all winter long. It's not bad work, actually.

All things considered, we were doing okay. I didn't tell Molly about me getting fired. I'd just leave the house like I always did and tell her I was going to work. I'd kill the morning sitting in a coffee shop, and then grab lunch somewhere. I'd spend the afternoons drinking beer at a bar, watching whatever TV show was on, and shooting the breeze with the bartenders.

I kept going to Hyannis, but the load had gotten cut in half back to what Rooster called the winter level. So that was making it easier to pay the bills. But the shit really hit the fan in December. My God, it was cold. People were saying it was the coldest December they could ever remember, and the harbor had ice patches in places.

Then one day I woke up and turned on the TV. All kinds of alerts were flashing on the screen about the weather. There was a major storm front coming in, and we were going to get hammered. Sure enough, that afternoon, it started snowing hard. And it kept on snowing all through the night and the next day, and when it was finished, there was about three feet of snow on the ground. On top of that, it got so cold that the harbor froze over entirely, and they canceled all the ferries to and from the island.

Most people took it in stride, you know? It was part of life on an island. Sometimes you got stuck and couldn't leave. That just happened, and people dealt with it. But that frozen harbor meant I couldn't get my boat in the water, much less out of the harbor. So I couldn't make my weekly runs. Life was starting to get real all of a sudden.

You know that saying about when it rains, it pours? Let's just say it started pouring right about then. My truck needed a new fuel pump, and it seemed like the baby was at the doctor's office every week for another checkup or shots or whatever the hell else she needed.

On top of all that, Arthur got sick. He started throwing up one night, and Molly started freaking out because she thought he was going to die. I told her he'd probably eaten something out in the yard. But when she gets it in her mind that something is wrong, she doesn't let up until whatever it is gets better. So the next morning, I took him up to the animal hospital, and they ran a bunch of tests. They said the same thing I'd said, that he'd probably eaten something that upset his stomach. He was, they reminded me, a beagle, and beagles will eat anything that doesn't bite them first. Even then it's a fight to the finish. So they told me to feed him rice for the next couple of days, and just let whatever it was get through his system. Then they handed me a bill for $400 and change.

I was all too aware of how much money we were spending. Molly had gotten used to having the money that I'd been bringing in, though she still wasn't real happy about how I was getting it. But she kept quiet as long as she could keep spending it. Diapers, baby clothes, formula, all that stuff. And those damn doctor visits. We didn't have insurance, so it was all pay-as-you-go, and she was going a whole hell of a lot.

It took several days for the harbor to clear up enough to where they could get the ferries in and out, but everybody said it was still dangerous out on the water because of the ice. I guess it was like the Titanic, you know? Hit a patch of ice at full throttle, and your boat is going to sink out there. And every so often, we'd get another cold front that came through and froze it back up again. So I was stuck. All I could do was sit there and watch our money run out.

By March of that year, Molly's unemployment benefits had run out, and she still didn't have a job. At least the water had finally warmed up enough to where I could get across in the boat, but our money was pretty much gone. I'd had to have some work done on the motor, which had cost a lot more than I thought it should have, plus the cost of gas was going up and up. I still hadn't told her that I didn't have a landscaping business anymore, so Molly didn't really have any idea how bad our financial future was looking.

When it came time that I would have usually started back to work, I still hadn't worked up enough courage to tell Molly that the business was done. So I went back to my routine of coffee in the morning and beer in the afternoon. I was drinking a lot more than was good for me, and I knew it. But it was a way to stay warm, and to kill the time. Of course, it was costing me money too, but I hoped Molly would be able to find work somewhere soon, since summer was coming fast.

That was about the time she told me that she didn't think she'd go back to work. It didn't make sense, she said, because I was making so much money. That way, she could stay home with Caroline, and we'd save the money we would have had to spend on day care. That way, she'd also have more time to refocus her creative energy on her book. Even though it was the perfect chance for me to come clean about the fact that I'd lost my business, I still kept my mouth shut. I was just too scared to admit to her that I'd gotten caught. I hoped I could make enough money by running dope to keep us fed.

I guess if I had to point to a day when the wheels officially all came flying off, it was May the seventh. I was sitting at a bar having my afternoon beers when my phone rang. It was Rooster. He needed to talk to me in person, and he needed to do it now. I had no idea what was wrong, but told him where I was, and he said he'd come meet me.

When he walked in, I immediately knew something bad had happened. He looked like he'd been hit in the face with a board. He sat down next to me and ordered a beer. After he'd taken a couple of swigs off it, he turned to me and in a really quiet voice said, "Quentin got busted. We're done."

He might as well have put a gun to my head and pulled the trigger. That was my only source of income, and now it had been taken away too. But it got worse.

"The cops have our phone numbers," he said. "They went through his phone and looked at all of his contacts. We're fucked."

That sounded like the understatement of the year to me. Not only did I now have no money coming in, the cops knew that I'd been in contact with Quentin once a week. It wouldn't take them too long to figure out what I'd been doing. And once they did figure it out, Rooster was right. I'd be fucked.

I swallowed hard. "When did it happen?" I managed to ask.

"I just heard about it. They got him a few days ago. Apparently they'd been watching him for a while."

The word "watching" sounded like it had come through a microphone, like Rooster had yelled it. If they'd been watching him, it wasn't too crazy to think that they'd also seen him go to the dock in Hyannis to meet me, which meant that they could have seen me too.

"But look," Rooster said after a minute, "he had plenty of people he was dealing to on that side. They're going to be busy cleaning that up over there. We've got time to figure this out."

That was just great. We had time. Super. What the hell did he think we'd be able to do in that time? Make a time machine and go back and erase our phone numbers out of Quentin's phone? Warn him to be careful because the cops were on to him? What? What exactly did he think we could do with all of this time we supposedly had?

"Don't worry, man," Rooster said. But it sounded like he was trying to convince himself as much as he was trying to convince me. Like if I could believe that there wasn't any reason to be scared out of my mind, it would mean he didn't need to worry, either. We both knew that wasn't true, though. There was enough worry to go around. This was serious.

We sat there for a little bit longer, but I couldn't focus on anything Rooster was saying. I was too freaked out. I paid my tab and left without saying so much as good-bye to him. I think he was too distracted to notice that I'd gone, actually. Driving home, I was totally thinking only about what I was going to tell Molly, because I knew this wasn't something I could keep from her. The more I thought about it, though, the more I felt like this was all part of some greater cosmic plan, you know? By the time I'd gotten to the house, I'd managed to convince myself that there was a force out there that had made this whole nightmare come true as a way of making me tell my latest secrets to my wife. It was, it occurred to me, becoming something of a pattern. I got myself into a world of shit, and I finally had to tell Molly about it all.

When I walked inside, I startled her. I was supposed to have been at work just then, so she hadn't expected me. She immediately knew that something was up. She didn't waste any time.

"You're home early. What's wrong? You feeling okay?"

Just like Molly. Her first concern was whether or not I was sick. She was worried about my health, not about whether or not I was about to get thrown in jail.

"No, I'm fine," I said. "But I do have to tell you something." I sat down next to her. "Okay, here's the thing," I started. "Greg fired me because one of our clients found out that I was using non-organic fertilizers." I told her about the pond, leaving out the fact that it had happened the year before. When I'd finished telling her about it, she looked me straight in the eye.

"Okay. We'll figure it out," she said. "Anything else?" Her voice sounded hopeful, like that was all that was on my mind.

"Um, yeah, actually. One other thing." This was going to be hard. I took a couple of breaths, and then let it rip in one long roll. "The guy I was buying grass from in Hyannis got busted, and apparently the cops might have my cell phone number now."

Molly's face went pale. It was the first time since I'd met her that she couldn't speak. She looked terrified. She was breathing fast. "So what does that mean?"

I didn't quite know, exactly, but I figured I'd try to soften it. At this point, I didn't have a lot to lose. "I'm not sure. Rooster said that he had a bunch of people he was dealing to in Hyannis, so if they even get as far as Nantucket, it won't be for a long time."

"Rooster," she said. She almost spat the name out. "All of this is because of him. I never liked him from the start, and now he's gone and gotten you in trouble with the police."

I immediately got defensive of my friend. "Rooster didn't do anything to get me in trouble," I said. "I did what I did, and we spent the money together. So let's just leave Rooster out of this."

Molly got up and started to pace around the living room. "What are we going to do, Billy? You could go to jail, and I'm going to be left to raise our daughter by myself. Our daughter, Billy. Our daughter. Did you ever think about her?"

"Of course I did. She's the whole reason I was doing what I was doing."

Molly was fuming. "Oh, right. I forgot that," she said sarcastically. "You were just providing for your family by running drugs. Jesus, Billy." She stormed towards the front door and grabbed her car keys. "I've got to get out of here before I say something I regret."

She slammed the door behind her, and the noise woke up Caroline. She started crying, and I went to get her. Molly was upset, and she needed to get out. I got it. I heard her peel out of the driveway, and she gunned the engine as she drove away. Caroline was screaming, and no amount of my telling her everything was going to be okay seemed to help. I started to walk around, bouncing her in my arms, trying to get her to shut up. The truth of the matter was that the longer she screamed, the only thing I really wanted to do was throw her out the window and disappear. I didn't want the responsibility, I didn't want the life I had just then. All I wanted was to be somebody else.

I don't know how long it was before I heard the phone ringing. It might have been thirty minutes, it might have been six hours. It was getting dark outside; that was about all that I knew in terms of the time. And Caroline had finally stopped crying. I pulled my phone out of my pocket, but didn't recognize the number. I had a sinking feeling that it was the police, so I let the call go to my voice mail. When the message notification finally beeped, I called my voice mail to see what my future held.

When I heard the message was from the Nantucket Cottage Hospital, it was a relief. But only for a second. I wasn't sure I'd heard it right, so I replayed the message. The second time through, though, I figured out that I had heard it exactly right the first time. My wife was in the emergency room. She'd run her car into a telephone pole, and I needed to come to the hospital as soon as possible.

People always talk about how they see their lives flash in front of their eyes when major things like that happen, and I had one of those moments myself. All I could see was Molly dying in a hospital bed, leaving me with Caroline, and then I'd get thrown in jail, and Caroline would go into some kind of foster care or whatever. It was another one of those damn worst-case-scenario-thinking things, you know?

I put Caroline in her carrier and strapped her into the truck, then went racing up to the hospital. I flew through the door into the emergency room, with Caroline hanging off my arm. I grabbed the first person in a uniform I saw and told her who I was, and she directed me to the triage desk. The woman there told me to sit down, and explained the situation.

"Your wife was in a serious accident," she began, "and we're currently evaluating her to determine the extent of her injuries. She has a cracked pelvis, which we can treat here. But if she has any internal injuries, we'll have to transfer her to a trauma center on the mainland."

"Oh my God," was all I could say. "When will you know? Can I see her now?"

"It will be a few hours, Mr. Faulkner," she said. "And I'm sorry for that. And I'm afraid you can't go in just now. We need to make sure everything is okay first. She's been sedated, so she's comfortable for now. If you'll have a seat in the waiting area, I'll let you know as soon as I hear anything." She shuffled some papers on the desk in front of her. "While you're waiting, could I ask you to fill out some paperwork? It's personal information, plus insurance."

I didn't want to tell her I didn't have insurance, so I took the papers and a pen, and took Caroline with me into the waiting room. It was incredibly uncomfortable. Plastic chairs bolted to the floor, and a bunch of out-of-date magazines. It was like a total cliché of hospital waiting rooms. But I didn't really care. My brain was now totally focused on my wife. I just wanted her to be okay. All my earlier thoughts about wanting to be somebody else were gone. I just wanted my wife to be okay.

I sat in the waiting area for two hours, unable to do anything besides worry about her. Caroline was quiet, thankfully, and people who were sitting around us got a kick out of cooing at her and waving, and all the stuff you do to babies. I was happy to have them do it.

Finally the nurse came up to me. "Can you come with me, please?" she asked softly. It wasn't real reassuring. I figured this was the part where she told me how sorry she was, and that they'd tried everything they could, but that her injuries had been so bad that there had been nothing they could do. When we were back at the triage desk, she sat down, and told me to take a seat across from her.

"Good news," she said.

That was all I needed to hear. Everything after that didn't matter. My wife was alive and was going to survive, whatever injuries she'd gotten.

"Like I told you earlier, she cracked her pelvis. She's in a lot of pain, but there is no internal bleeding, mercifully. She has a lot of bruising but, all things considered, she came out of it pretty well."

I heaved a huge sigh of relief. "Thank you," I said. "Thank you so much for everything."

She smiled. "I'm just glad this one had a happy ending. Can I get your insurance information?"

I handed her the papers I'd filled out. "We don't actually have insurance," I said. "We're both unemployed."

The happiness went out of her face pretty quickly. "No insurance?" She paused for a second. "Um, okay. We'll send you a bill with an installment payment plan option." She turned away to put the papers in a folder.

"Can I see my wife now?"

It was like she'd forgotten that I was there to see her in the first place. She turned back to me. "Yes. You can. Just give me a second, and I'll take you to her room."

She moved some papers around on the desk, and then motioned for me to follow her. We went down a long, bright corridor, passing several closed doors along the way. She stopped at one and looked back at me. "I need to warn you before you go in," she said, "that she looks a little rough right now. Remember, she's been in a serious accident."

I nodded and she opened the door. I looked in and almost threw up. Molly was in bed, machines behind her beeping. There was an IV tube going to her arm. Bruises made her face and arms look almost black, and I could see scratches across her forehead and cheeks. She looked dead.

I sat down in a chair next to the bed and looked at her. She looked so peaceful lying there, and I almost started crying as I thought about everything that I'd put her through. I felt like this whole thing was my fault, her lying there with whatever injuries she had. If I'd just been a better person, a better husband, a better father. If I'd just been a better man, she wouldn't be lying there in that bed.

"Hey there, good looking," I said softly. "What's new?"

She opened her eyes slightly and cracked a smile. "You're lucky you're so damn cute."

I started to cry a little. "I love you so much, darling. I can't tell you how sorry I am that I've put you through all of this."

"Not your fault," she said. "I know you were just trying to help."

That was all it took to get me crying for real. I didn't care. I sat there and cried, and just let all the emotion that had built up inside me go. It was the first time in as long as I could remember that I'd cried like that, and it felt so good. For that moment, just for that little time I was sitting there, nothing else in my life mattered. I had my wife and daughter, they were both going to be okay, and we were going to make it. I was sure of that.

CHAPTER TWENTY-SIX

Her recovery was a lot more involved than I'd thought it was going to be. I guess it never occurred to me that a cracked pelvis was more than a broken arm. You know what I mean? You break your arm, you get a cast on it, and a few weeks later, they cut the cast off and you're good to go. But Molly was in bed for three weeks, in a ton of pain. She was popping pills every couple of hours to try to keep it in check, but she was still hurting. When she was finally able to get out of bed, she had to use a walker to get around. I joked that she looked like a grandmother.

While she was in bed, the house duties were all on me, and that included taking care of Caroline. That's a nice way of saying it looked like a hurricane had gone through the inside of our home by the time Molly was back on her feet. Even then, she still had a lot of physical therapy to go through before she'd be anywhere close to being able to take over for me. If you want to know the truth, I never realized how much she really did when I was out of the house. I couldn't have ever taken care of it all nearly as well as she did.

The bill for her hospital stay came in the mail while she was still recovering in bed, and I almost needed an ambulance of my own when I opened it and read "$8,628." Damn near gave me a heart attack. I couldn't even believe it. Part of me wanted to drag Molly's ass out of bed and slap her for running her car into a telephone pole. The police report said that she'd come around a curve at what they said was a high rate of speed—higher than the speed limit—and slammed into the pole without even hitting the brakes. So it was basically her own fault. They canceled her car insurance and, since the thing was totaled anyway, it didn't matter.

But then there was the other part of me, the part that remembered she'd gotten in that accident because of what I'd done.

That part of me wanted to protect her from all the bad stuff in the world, and an $8,000-plus tab for hospital care pretty much fell into that category. In the end, that was the side that won, the side that wanted to protect her. So I didn't mention the bill. I just wrote a check for the first installment payment, and that was that.

When Molly was able to get out of bed, I told her that I was going to head out and start job hunting, assuming she was okay with taking care of Caroline for a few hours. She said she thought she was up to it, so I headed out. I picked up a paper in town, and scanned the classifieds. I had to laugh at the number of landscaping jobs that were being advertised, but I didn't have a chance there. The word about me had gotten around, and no landscaper on the island would even talk to me, let alone give me a paying job.

One of the local airlines was hiring for baggage handlers. I figured I could do that. The pay was described as "industry-competitive," whatever that meant. Applicants had to be able to lift fifty pounds. I knew I could do that. They also had to be able to pass a drug test. No problem there. And finally, an FBI background check. That might be a problem, given my history in Connecticut. And it might be a little problem with my former life as a drug runner, too. Moving on.

A few other listings that didn't fit me for whatever reason. Then I found something that looked perfect. A shop in town that sold T-shirts to tourists was looking for counter help. It said that no experience was necessary, and they needed somebody to start right away. I had both of those things, and the place was only a couple of blocks away from where I was right then. So I made my way over and walked in. The girl behind the counter couldn't have been more than seventeen, but she said she was the manager. I told her I'd like to apply for the job, and she gave me an application. I filled it out and handed it back. She looked it over, then turned her attention back to me.

"You're a little older than the people we usually get applying here," she said after a second.

"Yeah, I figured that. But—" I stopped short. "Can I be totally honest with you?"

She nodded.

"I live here year-round. My wife was recently in a pretty horrible car accident, and she can't work. I've got a daughter who's going to be a year old in August. I really, really need a job. And I can start right now, if you want me to. Literally. Right now."

The girl looked at me like a charity case, which was pretty much what I was going for. She thought for a second, then said, "I'm so sorry. That sounds rough. We're only paying ten dollars an hour."

"That's something, at least," I said.

She looked at my application again. "Okay, you look like you can probably do this job." She put the papers down and reached across the counter to shake my hand. "You're hired, Billy."

"Thank you so much, " I said. "I can't even tell you how much this means to me. And don't worry about the pay, you know. Like I said. Something is better than nothing."

It was not going to be much money, but I meant what I'd said. If I could pull forty hours a week at ten dollars an hour, I'd be getting four hundred a week. That would at least pay the rent. At least for the summer. Molly's physical therapy bills were going to be another matter, but we'd figure that out somehow. I could only focus on one thing at a time. I just had to cross my fingers that we didn't get too many surprises any time soon.

I spent that summer selling T-shirts for twenty-four dollars a pop. These people were paying more than twice what I was making in an hour for a T-shirt that said "Nantucket" on it. It struck me as an insane amount of money to pay for a shirt, but customers were in and out of the store all the time. Tourists, all of them. Kids screaming about wanting this shirt or that, and parents arguing with each other about how overpriced all this crap was. I kept my head down and just took their money.

The thing about the tax policies in Massachusetts is that they don't charge sales tax on clothing under $175, for some reason. So we didn't have to account for it in the sales price, which meant that every twenty-four-dollar shirt was just that. Twenty-four bucks. When I was in the store alone, I'd occasionally make deals with customers, and sell five shirts for a hundred dollars. Pretty simple trade. You give me a C-note, and you can take five shirts.

And because I didn't have to calculate the tax on it, I didn't have to put it in the register. I'd just hit the button to open the cash drawer without making a sale and put the hundred dollars in. After they'd left,

I'd open the drawer again and take that hundred right back out and slide it into my pocket. Oldest trick in the retail employee handbook for ripping off your employer. I managed to justify it in my mind that the shirts themselves only cost four dollars apiece in the first place, so if I sold five at full price, that covered my hundred-dollar theft. Nobody was any the wiser, and those extra little cash bumps came in handy at the grocery store every week.

I was working as many hours as I possibly could—and stealing as much as I could, too—but it still wasn't enough to keep up with the money we were spending on doctor visits for both Molly and Caroline. We were barely scraping by, and what little money we had left in the bank was running out quick. One night after work, I sat Molly down to explain the situation to her.

"We can't keep this up," I told her. "I can't find a job that'll pay me enough money to afford all the bills."

Molly looked guilty. "I know it's hard, honey, but we'll figure out a way. We always do."

I shook my head. "Not this time. We're getting buried. I don't see any way to get out of it."

"So what do you suggest we do?" she asked. "It's not like we can just start over without the baby, you know."

"I don't know, Molly. I've just been worried about it, and I wanted to talk to you."

She told me to relax, and gave me a hug. We'd work it out, she said. We'd figure something out. She'd find some work she could do as soon as she was able to move around. She'd finish her book and sell it to a publisher for a big advance. She did her best to make me feel better. It didn't help much, but I tried to put on a good face. That night, though, I couldn't sleep. I tossed and turned in bed, but the more I thought about how much I wanted to sleep, the more awake I was. Finally I gave up and got out of bed. I sat on the sofa and turned on the TV.

Late-night TV is always some weird stuff. You get ads for DVDs showing girls taking their shirts off at spring break, and usually some weird, not-quite-real medical wonder drugs that they tell you can help you lose weight or get laid or whatever. But every so often, you come across a pretty cool movie. And tonight, I happened to get lucky. I forget the name of it, but it was something about a guy who wanted to leave his wife, but didn't want to go through the whole divorce thing. So he transferred all his money to an offshore bank account, and then faked his own death. Told his wife he was going camping, but never came home. He made it look like he'd fallen off a cliff into a river, and when they couldn't find his body, they eventually decided he must have died. The truth was that he was sitting on a beach in Bermuda, and nobody had any clue.

That was when the first thoughts of my plan started to form. I could stage an accident pretty easily, and it wasn't like we had a lot of roots on Nantucket. So leaving was the easy part. The only hitch was the money. I didn't have a lot of disposable cash on hand like the guy in the movie, so there wasn't much to transfer into a Bermuda bank account that we could live off of after we'd disappeared. It was a stupid idea. I tried to put it out of my mind, and turned my attention back to the TV.

I guess I must have fallen asleep—the last thing I remember was some guy showing how his blender could crush ice in a matter of seconds—because the next thing I knew, Caroline was crying, and Arthur was howling. You'd have thought the house was on fire with all of the noise. I went and picked the baby up out of her crib, and started to walk around the living room with her in my arms. Arthur had, thankfully, quieted down, and was now following behind me. I opened the door to let him out in the yard.

I was groggy, and my brain wasn't really firing just then. The life of a new parent, you know? But it was like there was this light flashing in the fog, sort of hidden, but I could still see it. I started to remember what I'd been thinking before I fell asleep, my plan to disappear. It wouldn't work. It couldn't work. I reminded myself that I didn't have that bankroll stashed away somewhere, money to live off of once I'd relocated. And then there was the baby. What would we do with her, since I was playing out this fantasy in my head?

Caroline was a mixed blessing. I loved that child with every ounce of my soul; I would have done anything for her. But at the same time, I couldn't help but think that this whole mess had happened because of her. If I hadn't been forced to provide for her, then I wouldn't have had to do the things I'd done. If it was just me and Molly, you know, the way we'd planned it, things would have been different.

It was easy to rationalize it that way. Granted, when I look back on how things happened today, I understand how wrong I was to even think that. I mean, I was running drugs before Molly was even pregnant, so it wasn't fair of me to try to blame the baby for everything. But she was an easy target. She couldn't defend herself, she couldn't argue with me. Hell, she couldn't even talk. And she had no clue about what her father was going through, and the shitstorm that he'd managed to turn his own life into.

And I guess that was the moment it hit me. When I started thinking about the fact that I'd turned my own life into a disaster, it occurred to me that it wasn't my own life. It was Molly's life too. And Caroline's. We were all in this together, and it was all because of me being stupid. I'd been the one who screwed up my business, and it was because of me that I was probably the target of a police investigation. I'd gotten my family into this mess. And as hard as it was for me to admit, it was going to be up to me to take the responsibility for fixing it, no matter what I had to do.

I heard Arthur scratching at the door, which was his signal that he'd surveyed the backyard, and decided that everything was cool out there. I opened the door and let him in. I was envious of him, in a way. He didn't have to deal with things like paying rent or buying food. He just sat around all day and had his needs taken care of for him. Yeah, he was somebody else that depended on me to make sure he had a happy life. Who would have thought that a little dog could be the thing that made me feel totally depressed about my situation?

By the time Molly had woken up, I was pretty much right back where I'd started. I was in a world of hurt, depressed about the future, and scared about what I was going to do. But I had no idea of what to do, or how I was going to wake up from this nightmare. All I knew was that I had to do something. And the clock was ticking.

CHAPTER TWENTY-SEVEN

The first stroke of anything that looked like good luck I'd had in a long time came about a month after I'd started selling T-shirts, when I met a guy named Richard. He was a local builder, and we met one day while I was walking Arthur at what passed for the unofficial Nantucket dog park. It was a big open space that was maintained by one of the local nature conservation groups. There was a path that made a big loop around the area that took twenty minutes or so to walk. The dogs loved it, because they could run all over the place without anybody getting irritated about them.

Richard was a big guy, six feet plus a few inches. He was originally from Alabama, and still had the accent to prove it. Dark-brown hair that was starting to go gray, and a face that just told you he was friendly. When I first met him, he told me he'd had a beagle once, and that he loved the breed. So my dog was what broke the ice for us, and we became fast friends. He walked every morning at the same time—he had a yellow lab named Otis—and invited me to join him. I didn't have a lot else going on at that hour of the morning, so I took him up on it, and started walking with him.

It was nice to have somebody to talk to other than the dog, and he told me all about how he'd ended up on Nantucket. He'd left Alabama after high school, and gone to college in the Northeast. After graduation, he'd been living somewhere in Massachusetts and fallen in love; the girl had wanted to move to Nantucket. It sounded a whole lot like my own story, and I actually told him so. Anyway, Richard's relationship with the girl fizzled out, but he learned pretty quick that he could make good money building houses. So he started his own company. He'd buy empty lots that he thought were reasonably priced, and then build a house, which he'd sell for a profit. Then he'd start the whole thing all over again with another empty lot.

I told him my own little story, leaving out the parts that didn't necessarily put me in the best light. He agreed with me when I said that I thought Nantucket was an impossible place for a guy like me to make a living and raise a family, especially on ten dollars an hour.

"I don't know how a lot of these people make it," he said once. "They struggle like hell, and a lot of them end up getting their houses foreclosed on, or evicted from their rentals. There's a certain point when you have to wonder if it's worth it."

I had to agree. "I'm kind of at that point myself," I admitted. "I'm wondering if it's worth it. But I don't know how I can get out."

And so it went. Every morning at eight o'clock, we'd meet up in the parking lot and walk the dogs. I liked him a lot. He was a really nice guy who seemed to have a really good head on his shoulders, and the more I told him about our situation, the more sorry he felt for me. He and I would meet for lunch every so often, and he'd always offer to pay. Like I said, just an all-around really good guy. And then one day in early August, he offered to help me out.

"Listen," he said. He loved to start conversations by telling you to listen, like if he didn't specifically tell you to, you'd just totally ignore him. "I can put you to work, if you want, once the T-shirt shop closes. I've got a project that's going to be starting up about then. Nothing spectacular, just building a house out in Madaket."

Hearing that name again brought back the memories of the house with the pond, the one that had made me lose my business.

"I can let you help, if you want," he continued. "It's not charity. I want you to know that. I'm doing this because I could use somebody to do some work. Say five hundred a week, cash?"

I didn't even think twice. "I'll do it. Absolutely."

"Okay. Let me know what the shop schedule is. I should have a better idea about when we're going to pour the foundation in the next couple of weeks. Once that's done, you can start."

At the time, all I knew was that this opportunity was going to be a lifeline that would help me pay the bills through the winter when I didn't have a lot of other job opportunities banging down my door. And just maybe I could start yet another chapter of my life with a new career.

Plus, if Molly could get back to work, we might just survive. I had no way of knowing it at the time, but that job was going to be my escape from Nantucket.

Despite my luck with job opportunities, there was a huge black cloud hanging over me, one that had nothing to do with finances. That cloud was the constant threat of a knock at the door. I'd open it to find a couple of police officers who had come to arrest me. I felt like I was constantly looking over my shoulder, and I always seemed to hold my breath and walk a little faster whenever I passed a cop on the sidewalk. The anxiety was worse than going to jail, or at least that's how it felt at the time.

A few weeks later, when Molly could actually walk around a little bit without having to use the walker, I thought it might be nice to take the boat out, just for old time's sake. A little sunset cruise, just the three of us. We picked a Tuesday, because I had the afternoon off from work at the shop, and went out on the water. Molly had made sandwiches, and we took a six-pack of beer with us. Caroline was wide-eyed the whole time. This was a new adventure for her. I took it slow and easy out of the harbor, and headed west once we'd cleared the end of the jetties. I kept it slow the whole way, both for Molly and Caroline. We didn't need any more trips to the emergency room.

Off to the south, you could see all the houses on the Cliff. I pointed out to Molly the ones where I'd done work. She looked up at them, lights shining through the windows. "I wish we lived that life," she said softly.

"I know. It would be nice, wouldn't it? Not a care in the world."

I cut the engine, and we just floated around out there, watching the sun set off in the distance as we ate our dinner. It was one of the most peaceful times I could ever remember having in my life, just floating around out there on the ocean. There wasn't much breeze, and there wasn't a cloud in the sky at all, so the sunset was really gorgeous. We finished our food, and I decided to head back before it got too dark to see. The whole time we were driving back, Molly never took her eyes off those houses on the Cliff. It was almost like she was in a trance. Part of me was scared, though, that it was the last time we'd ever be able to do this as a family.

When we got home that night, Molly put the baby in her crib, and then came and sat with me on the sofa in the living room. I was totally lost in thought, and didn't realize she'd sat down until she poked me.

"Penny for your thoughts," she said with a smile.

I sighed, not really wanting to tell her what I was thinking. "I'm worried, Molly," I finally managed to say. "I'm just worried."

"But you said you had a new job offer for the winter. And I'm really making some progress on the book, too. I feel really good about my chances of selling it. Plus, I'm getting to where I feel like I can go back to work too."

I shook my head. "It's not that," I said. "It's this whole thing with Rooster and Quentin and the cops. I just know something bad is going to happen. That I'm going to end up in jail, and leave you guys alone. I just have this feeling."

"Darling," she said softly as she put her arm around me, "I hate that you're so worried about that. There's really nothing you can do at this point. If something is going to happen, it's going to happen. I know I was upset about it before, but I'm over it now. We'll be okay. I promise."

I just couldn't bring myself to agree with her. I'd been thinking about it so much and for so long that I couldn't see any way that things were going to be okay. And that's when I mentioned the movie.

"What if we could just disappear, you know? Move to some island somewhere where nobody's ever heard of us, and where the cops can't find us. Just you, me, and Caroline. What about that? I was watching this movie one night when I couldn't sleep, you know, and . . ."

She laughed, cutting me off. Apparently she thought I was making a big joke. "Sounds great. Should we take our private jet or the yacht?"

"I'm not kidding, Molly. I know it sounds crazy, but I can't think of any other way to keep us from getting separated, and you having to raise Caroline by yourself."

"Billy, you can't be serious about this. There is no way you can really be seriously thinking about this."

I turned to face her. "I'm totally serious. And I think I have a plan for how we could do it."

While we sat there on the sofa, I told her what I'd been thinking about for the last week. I would teach her how to drive the boat, and we'd make the trip to Hyannis. From there, I'd get out and take a bus to the Boston airport, where I could fly pretty much anywhere in the world. She'd come back to Nantucket by herself, then tell everyone I'd fallen off the boat on the return trip. They'd search for me, and when they couldn't find me, they'd declare me dead. Then Molly and Caroline could come meet me, wherever I'd happened to land, once everything in Nantucket had been settled.

She waited a few seconds to let it all sink in. "You've obviously given this a lot of thought," she finally said. Then she laughed a little. "But it's absolutely crazy. Sorry, but there's no way in hell we can do that."

I didn't realize how serious I'd been before, because I kept going at her. I was on a roll, and now that I'd brought it out into the open, I was not giving up that easy. "It can work, Molly. We've got enough in the bank still to where we can live for a long time somewhere that's cheap. We wouldn't have to work even. Some place where they couldn't find us."

"And what then, Billy? We just live happily ever after?"

"Yes. We do exactly that." I was feeling stronger the longer I talked. "We can make this work, and it would solve all of our problems."

"Billy, there is so much wrong with this idea that I don't know where to start. Let's just drop the subject. We had a great time on the boat, so let's don't screw that up."

I let the conversation go at that, but I wasn't going to let it die forever. Since this was the first time I'd ever talked about it to somebody else, I hadn't ever fully explained it. But now that I had, it really sounded like it could work. There were a lot of details to work out. I knew that. And it wouldn't be easy. I knew that, too. But I had to believe it would be easier than Molly trying to raise our daughter alone on Nantucket while I sat in a jail somewhere.

During the next couple of days, I thought about my plan, working out the specifics in my own mind. I wasn't concerned about convincing Molly to go along with it. I figured that there was going to come a point when she didn't have a choice. So that didn't factor into my plans.

The first real issue I had to figure out was getting Molly from Hyannis back to Nantucket. It wouldn't be too hard to teach her how to steer a course on the GPS. The bigger issue I had, though, was how to make it look like I'd fallen off the boat somewhere and that she hadn't noticed. After all, if she'd been standing there with me and I fell off, she'd have enough sense to stop the boat and get me back in it. So it had to seem like she'd been completely unaware.

I turned a few ideas over in my mind, and decided that the best way to pull it off would be to have her tell people that she was sleeping in the cuddy while I was driving the boat. That would work. If she was asleep, she'd have no way of knowing that I'd fallen off. Problem solved.

But that solution actually created another problem, namely the fact that a boat without a captain wouldn't be able to follow the GPS course. And I knew that once they started looking into it, one of the first things they'd do was look at the GPS, to see what course the boat had followed. We didn't have an autopilot; it was strictly manual steering.

I did a little research on the subject, and learned that a boat without somebody driving it will actually go in circles. So there was going to have to be some creative steering going on, which added an extra degree of difficulty to the whole idea. But it wouldn't be impossible. If Molly steered in kind of a corkscrew way, it would make it look like nobody had been driving, I hoped. And she'd also be able to land safely on Nantucket, as long as she steered the course the right way.

Where to have her come ashore was still another issue. It needed to be somewhere easy to get to, so she wouldn't have too much trouble getting away. I mean, if she landed up at Great Point, she'd be all the way out at the far tip of the island, and that wouldn't be easy for anybody. I needed this to be easy.

I settled on the beach in front of the Cliff. She could call Rooster on her cell phone, and he could come pick her up in his truck. That way, she could get in to town to report me missing. From there, it was just a matter of her waiting out the search that would go on. But all the time they were looking for me, I'd be on a plane out of the country. The more I planned it out, the better the idea began to sound. I was starting to think that this might just work.

The next question was where I would go. The guy in the movie I'd watched had gone to Bermuda, but that looked pretty expensive. So I started looking for cheaper places. Mexico sounded good, but it was too close for me. I wanted to be some place way far away, some place where they could never find us. Or at least far enough away that if they did find us, it would be too far to bother coming to get us.

After looking at a ton of maps, I saw one for Vietnam. I'd heard of the place in movies and books, you know, because of the war and all. I never thought of it as a place to live, though. But it turns out that they have some pretty amazing beaches. And it was cheap. American dollars went a long way there. So we'd have enough time to get settled before money became too much of a problem for us. And as an added bonus, Vietnam didn't have an extradition treaty with the United States, so even if the police did find me, they couldn't do a damn thing about it.

The plan, at least in my mind, was coming together beautifully. Plane tickets wouldn't be cheap, and we'd need passports, but I wrote that off as part of saving my own ass. Now it was time to convince Molly that we had to do this. There was no other way. And I was sure I could make her see that. When I laid out all the details of how we could really and truly do this, she'd have to go along. I didn't see that she had a choice in the matter.

CHAPTER TWENTY-EIGHT

I started hammering away at her as soon as I got home from work every night. I tried to make her see the alternatives, which were basically her starving to death while she tried to live alone with Caroline, or the three of us living together in Vietnam, where we'd be safe and happy. Even if I didn't get caught by the cops, I still didn't have any way I could think of to make a decent living. If we did it right, there would be absolutely no risk to anyone. Nobody was going to find out we'd done it. I'd take a little money out of the bank to help me live once I got there, and she and Caroline would come later, after things in Nantucket had died down. When they found out I was dead, the cops would stop looking for me, and we'd be safe. If we really wanted to, we could even come back to the United States one day.

I kept at it and kept at it. We had some of the loudest, longest arguments I'd ever had with another person. She started going on walks alone, leaving me and Caroline behind. She'd tell me she needed to think about things, you know, and needed to clear her head.

Whatever it was she was doing on those walks, one night she came back from one of them and told me that she'd at least let me take her on a practice run between Hyannis and Nantucket, even though she wasn't making any promises about doing it for real. She just wanted to see what it would be like. I took it as a great sign that she was finally coming around to my way of thinking.

We agreed that on my next day off, we'd go to Hyannis. When the day finally got there, it was a nice one. That worked in my favor. If it was a nice day, I'd told myself, it would make it that much easier for her to learn how to drive the boat. If she felt comfortable, she might even figure out that I was right, and it wouldn't be a big deal. The nice weather would also mean we could take Caroline with us, which would save us from having to get a babysitter.

I drove the truck down and launched the boat, something I'd gotten pretty good at. She wasn't going to need to worry about how to put it back on the trailer, if everything went the way I was thinking it would. As we were leaving the harbor, I let her drive as I stood behind her. I showed her how to use the GPS, and how to get the different waypoints to bring up the line for her to follow. I wanted her to be comfortable with driving it.

All things considered, she picked it up pretty quickly. She actually looked like she was having fun. And Caroline was sleeping peacefully, sitting in her little carrier inside the cuddy. I'd poke my head in there every so often to make sure everything was okay, but she was fine. It had been a long time since I'd made this trip, and it felt good to be back out on the open water, cruising across the Sound.

Once we'd gotten near the harbor on the other side, I took over. I took her to the same dock where I'd always meant Quentin, and explained that she'd drop me off there. From that point, she'd pick the waypoint for Nantucket on the GPS, and then follow that course back. We didn't stay at the dock for more than five minutes before I started to feel weird, like at any minute police cars would come screaming up with sirens going.

"Okay. Let's see you go back to Nantucket," I said to her. "Pretend I'm not on the boat."

"Aye, aye, Captain," she said with a smile. I wasn't sure if she was just humoring me by doing this, or if she was actually getting closer to the point that she agreed with me that we didn't have another choice.

I told her how to back the boat away from the dock, and then how to get headed in the right direction to go home. I pointed out the buoys that she needed to stay between in order to stay in the channel. From there, I let her drive. She did beautifully, I have to say, and steered the boat like she'd been born to do it, following the line on the GPS perfectly.

We were about halfway back to Nantucket when I told her to stop. She looked confused for a minute, but did what I'd asked, slowed the boat down, and put the throttle in neutral.

"Okay," I said. "Let's say that right here at this point, I have to go to the bathroom. You're asleep in the cuddy, and I don't want to wake you up. So I just go to the back of the boat, drop my pants, and go. But while I'm going, I fall off the back, and the boat is now steering itself."

"Got it. What does that mean?"

"It means that, if nobody was driving, the boat would start doing circles. So you need to steer a corkscrew that leads towards Nantucket, because that GPS will record the path you steer. And they'll want to look at that when you report me missing. So what I want you to do is look at that line on the screen there and steer circles that keep it in the middle. Make sense?"

She nodded. "I think I can do that."

She pushed the throttle forward slowly, and steered off to the west.

"Perfect," I said. "Now bring it back around."

She turned the wheel back to the east, bringing the boat around. I looked down at the GPS screen, which now showed two distinctly different lines. One cut straight across the screen. That was our programmed course back to Nantucket. The other line was sort of an oval shape, and that was the course that Molly had steered.

"Awesome. Now just keep doing that. Make sure that straight line stays in the middle of the circles. That way, you know you're staying more or less on course."

She got into a rhythm, and pretty quickly was steering a perfect corkscrew that was taking us right to Nantucket. I just sat next to her and followed our progress on the GPS. Every circle she did brought us closer to the island. And every circle she did also made me more confident that our problems were going to be solved.

After about three hours, we were getting close to Nantucket, and Molly looked over at me. "So what now? How does an unmanned boat get back to the dock and on a trailer?"

"I've got it covered," I said. "You're not going to go into the harbor. When you get close enough, you're going to find a place on the beach right up there where you can land." I picked out a beach in front of us. "Right about there looks good," I said, as I pointed ahead. "Just keep doing your circles all the way into the beach."

We were about a hundred yards away when I realized that there were a lot of people both on the beach and in the water. "Okay," I told her, "go ahead and stop here. When you do it for real, we'll time it so there won't be people on the beach. So you'll just go all the way up onto the beach."

Then we talked a little bit about how it had gone, and I was a little surprised when Molly told me that she thought it had been pretty easy. That made me happy. The fact that she didn't say anything about how impossible it was going to be meant that there was a chance she might just be cool with it. I went on to tell her that once she'd gotten to the beach, she would wait a little while, and then call Rooster. He'd come pick her up, and from there she could call the cops and tell them that I'd obviously fallen off the boat.

"I still think this is a crazy idea," she said.

"Have you got a better one?" I asked.

She shook her head without saying anything.

"I didn't think so. This will work. I've got it planned down to the last detail. It's perfect."

I took over driving, and steered us back to the dock. After we'd gotten the boat on the trailer and got back in the truck, Molly was quiet. She was obviously thinking about how things were going to work out, but the silence was killing me.

"What do you think?" I said.

She was looking out the window while she was talking. "I don't know, Billy. I mean, do we have enough money to do this?"

"Yes, darling. We do. We'll have enough to survive for a while once we get there, and we can find jobs. I mean, since we don't have health insurance, the damn hospital bills are going to bankrupt us before we even get them paid off, at this rate."

And then it hit me. Insurance. Why hadn't I thought about that? A life insurance policy could give us enough money to live comfortably. Even a $500,000 policy would mean we'd be on top of the money world. We would be rich for the first time in our lives. I mentioned the idea to Molly.

"What, you want to add insurance fraud to this whole thing? Now you're scaring me."

"It wouldn't be a big deal at all, Molly," I said. I sounded a little like I was pleading with her. "We could get the policy now. I could work for Richard for a few months during the winter. It wouldn't look like we were planning anything, you know? We'd wait a few months then do it."

"Billy, let's take a little reality break here. You're already in trouble with the law, and this ridiculous plan of yours is risky as hell. I'm not even totally on board with it, even. Now, let's cut out the fact that you're suggesting we break another law with the insurance. Forget that part for a second. What happens when they can't find you and everyone thinks you're dead? You think the insurance company is just going to cut me a check? They're not idiots, Billy. Until they see your dead body, I'm not getting shit from them."

I had her there. She didn't remember, apparently, that I had once sold insurance for a living. And even though it was a scam for the most part, I had learned a few things about the business. Ordinarily, in a case of death in absentia, the provider would wait for seven years to pay the claim. But I knew that there were actually ways around that rule. Case in point, there was a specific life insurance policy I remembered reading about where the beneficiary could get the money even if there was no body. That policy covered a death at sea.

They were originally meant for guys who worked on boats all the time. If someone like a commercial fisherman fell off his boat five hundred miles offshore, they weren't going to ever find that body. But back at home, his wife and kids needed to eat, right? So after a few days, the guy would be declared legally dead, and the insurance company would pay his wife the benefits. If Molly could play it off that I was dead, she'd get the insurance money, since I'd died at sea. That would erase any thought of money problems we might have. I didn't care what Molly might say about the law.

The next day, during my lunch break from work, I went for a little walk. I went down to the ferry dock and just wandered around, trying my best to fit in with the crowd of tourists. I stood there for a few minutes, then pulled out my cell phone. I'm not totally sure how I remembered the number; maybe it was just tattooed into my memory or maybe it was just like a reflex action. Whatever the reason, my fingers dialed the number without my even having to think of it. He picked up after three rings.

"This is Victor."

"Victor, listen, it's Billy. Billy Faulkner. I need some help."

"Billy fucking Faulkner," he said. "You got some nerve calling me, you know that?"

"Yeah, I know, Victor. What I did wasn't cool."

"Wasn't cool? Listen, you motherfucker, you damn near got my ass thrown in prison. It's a whole hell of a lot worse than uncool. Now what the fuck you want from me?"

I told him I needed life insurance. The only catch was that the policy would have to include a provision to cover death at sea.

"What the hell you got planned, boy? Actually, you know what? Don't tell me a Goddamn thing. I don't care and I don't want to know. If I do this for you, you gotta do something for me."

"Anything, Victor. Just say it."

"Never call me again. You got it? I'll send you a policy and you send me your money every month. Other than that, I don't ever want to hear from your sorry white ass again. We clear?"

"Crystal, Victor."

He grumbled something about my being a pain in the ass. "It's gonna cost your sorry white ass two hundred fifty bucks a month. No questions asked."

I knew he was screwing me on the premium. The number he quoted me was at least five times more than it should have been. But I didn't care. I needed the policy. "That's fine, Victor."

"Right answer. Soon as you send me a money order—no checks, you hear me?—I'll send you the policy. Give me your address."

I told him our mailing address. "One other thing, Victor. My wife, Molly Faulkner, needs to be listed as the primary beneficiary."

"Fine. You can fill out the paperwork however the fuck you want. Don't call me again. Just send me the damn money." He hung up the phone.

I put my phone back in my pocket and looked out at the water. That had gone better than I'd hoped. Things were falling into place nicely right about now. I laughed to myself when I thought about how this whole idea had started one night when I couldn't sleep, and had happened to turn on a late-night movie. Now it was like I was falling down a mountain, going faster and faster every day. If I made it safely to the bottom, I'd be a free man. But first I had to survive the fall.

CHAPTER TWENTY-NINE

Victor made good on getting me the insurance policy. Molly was pissed when she found out what I'd done, but I promised her that there was no way we'd get caught. The policy was good for $350,000, and that was a lot of money, especially in Vietnam. We could live on that for ten years, if we played our cards right. As long as we could avoid any major emergencies, we'd be fine. Hell, by the time that money was gone, we'd probably be able to come back to the United States without any issue, and we'd be able to start life all over again with new jobs. I was getting more and more optimistic every day.

By the end of the summer, Richard had broken ground on his new building project, and the timing was perfect. The T-shirt shop where I'd been working closed right after Labor Day, and even though I was only pulling in a few hundred dollars a week when it was open, it hurt not having that income. So it was a huge relief to have the job with Richard start when it did.

The first day I worked for him, I felt completely self-conscious. I had no idea what I was doing, and it was totally obvious to anybody who was paying any attention at all. "You can use a paint brush, right?" he asked me.

I hadn't ever painted anything, but I figured it couldn't be too hard. I'd seen it done. Up, down, left, right, brushes, rollers. "Sure."

He walked me over to a Jamaican who was painting the trim around a bank of windows on a wall. "This is Stafford," he said. "He'll put you to work."

The Jamaican put down his brush and shook my hand. "Good to meet you," he said. "You going to paint some shelves in a closet upstairs for me. You cool with that?"

I nodded. Boards in a closet? Piece of cake. I followed him up a flight of still-under-construction stairs that seemed a little dangerous. But he went up them like a cat, so I figured they were safe enough. He handed me a little can of white paint and a brush, and pointed at a closet.

"Those shelves," he said. "Top and bottom. Easy."

"Easy," I agreed. He left and went back down the stairs. I looked at the shelves. There were only three of them, which seemed like it wouldn't take me all that long. I started at the top and worked my way down, first painting all the tops and then all the bottoms. I thought I pretty much had done it perfectly until I put down the can and stepped back to admire my work. It looked like I'd painted the entire floor under the shelves in addition to painting the shelves. Maybe nobody would notice. It was a closet, after all.

I went down the stairs to tell Stafford that I'd finished. He took one look at me and burst out laughing. "Did you get any paint on the shelves?" he asked. "You got more on your face than I got in this can."

Just then, Richard appeared. He looked me over, and then joined in with the laughter. "Guess you're not a painter, huh?"

I started to blush. I was embarrassed to even be there. So much for first impressions with my construction-work talents. "I guess not," I managed to say, trying to play along.

"Don't worry about it," Richard said. He could tell I was uncomfortable, and being the good guy he was, he wanted to try to make me feel better about the fact that I'd just screwed up royally. "We've got plenty of other stuff you can do around here."

He gave me a plastic container of white paste; the label said it was window glazing. I had no idea what that meant, but didn't want to look even more stupid than I did after the painting fiasco. He walked me over to a doorframe and pointed at the spots where finish nails had been used to attach the wood to the wall. "You see those little holes? Take some of that stuff—just a pinch—and push it into the hole. Then smooth it over with your fingers." He reached his fingers into the plastic tub and pinched off a piece, then filled a hole to show me how it was done.

I nodded. "Got it," I said.

This I could handle. Mindless, easy, no way to get myself covered in white goop. I did the first one while he looked over my shoulder. He approved of my first attempt, and went back to talk to Stafford. As I stood there filling nail holes, I could make out bits and pieces of their conversation. It was about me, naturally. Apparently Stafford had a nephew that Richard hadn't hired, and Stafford was a little pissed that I'd gotten a job when I clearly wasn't qualified. I felt like a leper.

I survived the first day without any further incidents. When I showed up the next morning, though, Stafford was in a mood. He'd discovered the disaster I'd left on the floor of the closet. He stopped painting the wall he'd been working on to let me know how pissed he really was.

"You know we're going to have to re-sand that floor up there because of you? What, did you spill the whole damn can?"

I tried to laugh it off. "Like I said yesterday, man, I guess I'm not a painter."

"True dat." He turned back to the wall he'd been painting when I'd arrived. I didn't ask him any questions about what I was supposed to do. I figured anything I said would end up with my looking even worse, and just irritate him more, so I picked up the plastic tub of glazing and went into a different room, looking for nail holes to fill.

And that was pretty much the routine I settled into. I'd meet Richard at the dog park and we'd walk a few laps around the path, then I'd take Arthur back to the house and head off to work. I wasn't much help that I could see on the job site. When all of the nail holes were covered over—which took three days—Richard had me sweep floors and pick up loose nails outside. The longer I spent working there, the less useful I felt. And even though Richard was nice about it, I could tell that he was basically giving me money because he felt sorry for me.

But I kept coming back. And every Friday, he'd hand me five one-hundred-dollar bills. He said he didn't want to write me a check, just because then there was a paper trail, and he'd rather keep it just between us. I was fine with that. I'd been used to having a cash-only income, and the arrangement worked well. Molly had started looking for work, but because the summer was over and the crowds had gone, most of the shops on the island were closed, and there just wasn't a lot of opportunity. She never mentioned the book anymore; I was starting to think it would never see the light of day.

She'd go back and forth between being depressed and frustrated when she couldn't find a job, and those emotional swings really started to work in my favor. The longer she looked for work without finding anything, the worse her outlook on life got. And the worse things looked, the better my plan sounded to her. She was going for a lot of walks on her own. She'd always tell me she just needed time and space to think, you know? I'd be more than happy to give her whatever she needed, if it got her to go with my idea. And she was getting closer and closer to that point.

We'd spend weekends out on the boat. I let Molly drive so that she could get more experienced with how to handle it. Her confidence as a captain grew, and one evening while we were just outside the harbor cruising around, she suddenly made a sharp turn in towards the shore.

"What are you doing?" I asked, startled by her sudden change of course.

"Practicing," was all she said.

She turned the wheel so that the boat started doing the corkscrew turns we'd talked about, and as she got close to the beach, I got nervous.

"You're about to be in really shallow water," I warned her.

"I know. I want to see how it's going to be when I do this for real."

My heart skipped a beat. I wasn't sure I'd heard her right. "When you do it for real?"

She nodded. "Billy, as much as I hate to say this, you're right. We can't keep living like this. It's impossible. I've fought it as much as I can. But now, I can't fight any more. I'm done. We're going to do it."

She slowed the boat down and scanned the shoreline. Without saying a word, she steered it right onto the beach, the engine still going. Suddenly, an alarm started blaring. It was telling us that the propeller was digging into the sand on the bottom, and the motor was starting to overheat.

Molly looked over at me. "That's the noise that's going to wake me up," she said with a smile. "I'm going to be napping in the cabin. You were driving. That alarm woke me up."

My eyes lit up. She was really serious. She was taking charge, and figuring out the details that were going to make our plan work. She turned off the engine and went into the cuddy, shutting the door behind her.

"So I'm asleep in here," she said from inside. "If I look out the windows, I can see lights up there in the houses on the Cliff. So I know we're somewhere that there are people."

I was confused. "So what? Who cares what you see?"

"I need to think I'm safe here," she answered. "Think about it. If you get woken up all of a sudden, and you're not sure what's going on, you're going to panic, right? But if there are people around, there's no reason to panic."

I waited for her to complete the thought, but she apparently thought she'd said enough. "And?"

"And that means I have no reason to think you've gone overboard. I can just think that you went to get help, you know, because the boat ran up on the beach and you need someone to help you push it off. As far as I know, you might be right up there in that house asking to borrow their phone, and you'll be right back. So there's no need for me to go to the cops yet."

It was brilliant. Playing that idea out in my head, I tried to play the part of the devil's advocate, you know, to find the holes in the story. I reasoned that if she didn't think anything was wrong, it would make my disappearance seem that much more real. Like we hadn't planned it down to the last detail. You know what I mean? If you'd planned this disappearance, it would make sense that you'd want to get the word out quick. So if she waited—like she was just waiting for me to get back with help because we ran aground on the beach—it made it seem that much more real.

And when she did finally report me missing, she could say that she thought I was on the island trying to get help, but she didn't know exactly there. But all that mattered was that they searched for me on land; that would delay their search over the water. Any delay in a search for someone in the ocean is bad, because the longer you wait to start looking, the better the chance they're dead when you find them. If you find them, that is. So by delaying the search, it would make it more likely that I was dead. Meanwhile, I'd be on a plane out of the country.

"You might just be a genius," I said to her as she came out of the cuddy. The door slammed back against the frame, and I remembered the fact that it didn't shut. That gave me yet another idea. "What about this? I wedge a quarter into that door to keep it shut. It flies open otherwise. What if you tell them that I'd put the quarter in there when you'd gone to sleep so that the door wouldn't disturb you? You know, if I'm here and you want to come out, I could just open the door for you."

She smiled at me. "Who knew my husband was such a criminal mastermind?" she asked with a laugh.

So it was a go. I was going to disappear. Eventually I'd be presumed dead, and Molly would spend a little time on Nantucket. But soon she'd get so depressed about being there—you know, with everything reminding her of her now-dead husband—that she just had to leave. Not sure where she was going to go, just had to get out. Maybe leave the country. She wasn't sure. Wherever she happened to land, she'd start a new life with Caroline. Once she was in her new location, she'd meet someone who reminded her of me so much that she couldn't help herself from falling in love and living happily ever after with this new mystery man.

That winter, we applied for passports and started making the final preparations for my disappearance. After looking at a calendar and talking about it, we decided on a day in the middle of March to do it. The weather at that time of year could be a little unpredictable, which would work in our favor. Maybe the boat hit a wave and that's what caused me to fall off. Maybe we got caught in a storm. There were plenty of forces of nature that could have caused me to fall off. And there wouldn't be anybody on the beach at that time of year, so there wasn't any risk of Molly being seen before she was ready to be found.

The plan was for Molly to discover that I was missing, but to first think that I'd just gone off to get help, like we'd talked about. When I didn't come back after a while, she was going to get bored with waiting for me. She'd call Rooster to come pick her up in his truck. He could get his truck on the beach and drive right up to where we were planning for the boat to end up. He'd pick her up, she'd tell him that I was off getting help, and she'd try to call me. I wouldn't answer, of course, but that wasn't a big deal. I was probably on my way back to the boat. I'd figure out that she'd gotten a ride home, and we'd catch up with each other back at the house.

After a few hours when she still hadn't heard from me, she'd start to get nervous. At that point, she'd call the cops and tell them that I was missing, but she was sure I was on the island. They'd start searching for me there first. When they couldn't find me—and this was the only real wild card in the deck—they'd eventually start to believe I might have fallen off somewhere between Nantucket and Hyannis. The question was how long it would take them to figure out I wasn't on the island.

Once they did start their ocean search, it was going to be a big area they were looking in. Twenty-six miles is a long way to go, and that's just point to point. That doesn't take into account the fact there are hundreds of square miles of ocean just between Nantucket and Hyannis, maybe even thousands. But they'd probably first want to retrace the trip from the GPS plotter, and they'd see that twenty-six mile course from one side to the other. And when you're looking for a person in that big ocean, twenty-six miles might as well be the whole universe.

CHAPTER THIRTY

I bought a one-way ticket to Hanoi, departing out of Boston on Sunday, March the seventeenth, at eleven fifteen at night. Our plan was to have Molly go to Hyannis the Friday before. She'd tell people that she was going back to Northampton for the weekend to visit some old friends. She'd spend the weekend laying low over there, staying in a cheap motel. On Sunday afternoon, she'd call me to say that she was in Hyannis and would be taking the ferry over, but I'd suggest that I just come over in our boat and pick her up. It was an easy trip, after all, and one that plenty of Nantucket people did all the time. So it wasn't anything that would draw much attention. Once I got to Hyannis, I'd get out and we'd switch places. She'd get in to make the return trip alone. And I'd be on my way.

You remember me telling you that my name got me here? Here's what I meant. My real name is Adam, but nobody on Nantucket knew that. They all knew me as Billy. The way it all worked out, I thought it was pretty much a genius move on my part to make the reservation under my real name. In case there was anybody who thought there was something suspicious about me going missing, they might be smart enough to check flights to see if I had actually gone somewhere. But since everybody knew my name was Billy—even if they thought it was William—they'd be looking for me under that name. Nobody would make the connection that some guy named Adam Faulkner was me. Adam was just a person who'd flown from Boston to Hanoi on a nonrefundable, one-way coach ticket. Kind of a coincidence that he had the same last name, but again, no red flags.

But hopefully before anybody knew I was even thinking about being gone, I'd walk to the bus station and get on a bus to Logan to catch my flight to Vietnam. We decided that she'd have to wait until the life insurance policy paid off before leaving Nantucket, so she would buy tickets for herself and Caroline once she got that money. She'd spend her time tying up loose ends, paying the last month's rent, finding a new home for Arthur, all that stuff.

Arthur was my only regret in this whole thing. I had really grown to love him, and it killed me to know that I was going to have to pass him off to some new owner. But I had to do what I had to do. He'd get over it, I was pretty sure. So long as he got fed and got to go on a walk every once in a while, he'd forget about me in no time flat.

I'd done some research, and found a youth hostel where I could stay in a dorm for eight dollars a night. We still had several thousand dollars in the bank, so eight bucks was no problem. I spent the better part of the month leading up to the big day making withdrawals at the ATM, being sure to leave enough for Molly to live off of until she got the insurance money. I spread it out over a long time, so it would just look like I was taking out money to live on. I really didn't want anybody to think I'd drained my bank account all at once. I bought some prepaid phone cards so that I'd be able to talk to Molly while we were apart. I didn't want to email with her, because I was afraid that those could have been traced. So it was going to be calls made from pay phones, and nothing more. I wanted to make sure we could make a clean getaway.

Everything seemed like it was perfect. I'd managed to get a tourist visa to travel to Vietnam without too much trouble. The boat was full of gas. Molly was ready to do what she had to do, and so was I. Everything was ready. We had the script for the play. Now we just had to wait for the curtain to go up.

As the day got closer, I was on edge. I tried to go through my daily routines as normally as possible. I'd walk the dog every morning with Richard, then report to the worksite for my daily dose of humiliation. Time went by so slowly. It was driving me crazy, you know what I mean? Like being a kid and waiting for Christmas. Only a hundred times worse.

And then it was finally March the fifteenth, the day Molly was going over to supposedly visit her friends. It was a Friday. She and Caroline boarded a morning ferry before I went off to work. We made a big show of it, just in case anybody might notice us and remember it later. We stood near the cop who was on security duty, because I thought that would just make things that much better. You know, local law enforcement would see us saying our good-byes. Just another witness to vouch for Molly's story when it came time for her to tell it.

I told her how I'd miss them, and that I'd see them Sunday night when they came back. I asked if she had her return tickets, and she announced very loudly that she did. I stood on the dock and watched the ferry slowly pull away. The next time I saw my wife, I'd be pulling off the biggest con job of my life.

That day at work, nothing bothered me. Stafford gave me his usual ration of shit, pointing out everything I did wrong, and telling me how his nephew could have done it better in half the time. But I just let it slide off me. Nothing could touch me. Not even his constant insults. I was about to be a free man, in every sense of the word.

Richard didn't come in until just before I was about to leave for lunch. He apologized, and said something about having to go in front of a town committee to get approval for some addition to the house that his clients wanted. "Looks like you're going to have some more nail holes to fill," he said with a laugh. He handed me my pay for the week. "We'll keep you busy through the rest of the spring."

"Thanks very much," I said to him as I slid the bills into my pocket. "I can't tell you how much this helps out."

"Don't mention it. I know how hard it can be. I'm glad I can do it for you guys."

I felt the first tingling of guilt. Richard had been so good to me. He was the kind of guy who'd give you the shirt off his back if you needed it. And here I was, taking money every week for doing nothing, and I was going to leave without saying a word to him. Like Arthur, I'd really grown to like him a lot. He had been a good friend. He'd listened to me tell him my stories about how things were always going wrong, and how we never seemed to have enough money. He'd been like a therapist on those morning walks. I was going to miss him, too.

That night, the house felt like a tomb. It was so quiet and empty. I turned the TV up full blast, just to have some noise. I packed all of my clothes into a duffel bag, and then drove myself crazy with checking and re-checking stuff. I had to force myself to sit down and actually watch television, just to distract myself.

I woke up early the next morning, still sitting there on the sofa with the TV blaring at me. It was weird being in the house without Molly and Caroline. Even Arthur seemed a little weird. It was like he knew something was up. I took him for his usual morning walk with Richard, but instead of going straight home afterwards, I stopped off at one of the houses I'd used to work at, the one on the Cliff that overlooked the ocean.

I left the dog in the truck and walked around to the other side of the house. I looked down at the beach, and realized that it was almost exactly the spot where Molly was planning to run the boat aground. It was kind of ironic. I mean, that house had always been my favorite of all the houses I'd worked at. The location was perfect, and I'd dreamed about what it would be like to wake up to that view every day. And now my wife was going to be helping us start a new life by ending up right there.

I spent the rest of the day trying to keep myself busy doing little stupid stuff around the house. I think it was probably the longest day of my life, but somehow I got through it. I couldn't sleep at all that night, thinking about what was going to happen the next day. I finally got out of bed at about five o'clock, made some coffee, and turned on the TV. The weather was going to be nice, a perfect day for a crossing. Twenty-six miles to go. Just like running a marathon. Actually, it was a lot easier than that. All I had to do was go twenty-six miles in a boat, and I was home free.

That morning, during our walk, I told Richard that I might go over and surprise Molly. She had been visiting friends in Northampton, I told him, and was scheduled to come back tonight. But I thought it would be fun to take the boat over and pick her up myself.

"Sounds a little nuts to me," Richard said. "It's going to be damn cold out there on the water."

The air temperature was in the forties, so yeah, it was going to be chilly. "I'm not worried about it," I joked. "I'm a Vermonter, remember. I like the cold."

We made small talk for the rest of the walk, but I wasn't paying too much attention. I'd planted the seed with one of the only people I had regular contact with. He knew I was going to go over in the boat, and as far as he knew, it would be a surprise to Molly. And he had believed it. That made two witnesses.

At two o'clock sharp, my phone rang. It was Molly. "Let's do this," was all she said.

"I'm ready. Give me a couple of hours and I'll meet you at the dock."

"Can't wait to see you," she said. "Be careful. I love you."

"Will do. I love you too. See you soon." I hung up the phone.

It all sounded really businesslike to me. Like we were talking about grocery shopping or watering the plants or something like that. It sure as hell didn't sound like we were talking about what was really going to happen.

I looked down at Arthur. His eyes looked sad, but he was wagging his tail. It was kind of how I felt too. I was happy that I was finally going to be able to live without worrying about who was coming for me. But I was really going to miss the little guy. I took a minute and scratched his head. I gave him a hug. "See you when I see you, little man," I told him.

He just looked at me with those big brown eyes. I really wasn't ready for how emotional I felt, you know? I guess I hadn't thought about the fact that leaving all this behind was going to be as sad for me as it was. Maybe it means I'm actually human after all.

I made sure he had some water, and I put a little extra food in his bowl. That distracted him. He buried his face in that bowl and started eating like he hadn't seen food in a week. I grabbed my duffel bag and headed out the door without another word. I had to wipe a few tears out my eyes when the storm door snapped shut behind me. It was a really ugly sound.

I did everything I could think of to relax while I drove. My heart was pounding out of my chest, but I had to be clearheaded and focused. But nothing worked. Deep breaths, thinking about other things, singing along with the radio. None of it helped. My hands shook as I attached the trailer to the truck, and I had trouble keeping steady pressure on the gas pedal while I drove to the boat ramp.

When I got there, I had to stop and force myself to go slowly as I backed the boat down the ramp for the last time. It wasn't pretty, but I eventually got it in the water and parked the truck, just like I always did. Nothing out of the ordinary. That was key. Do everything the way

I always did it so nobody would think there was anything strange. I left the key under the driver's-side seat, and went down to where the boat was tied up.

Once I was underway, I could feel my heart rate slowing. I puttered slowly away from the dock and, as I passed the lighthouse at Brant Point, I reached into my pocket and pulled out a penny that I'd been saving for this exact moment. There was an old Nantucket legend I'd heard about from a guy who said if you tossed a penny off the ferry as you rounded the point, it meant you'd come back one day. And while I wasn't necessarily interested in coming back to live here, it had occurred to me that I'd need to be alive and out of prison in order to be able to. So I figured it was a way of hedging my bets, and making sure I remained free and alive. I tossed the penny off the side of the boat towards the lighthouse. "Adios," I said softly as the coin hit the water. "It's been real."

I pointed the bow of the boat north, and brought the Hyannis waypoint up on the GPS monitor. This was it. There was no going back. I was still idling pretty slowly when I got to the end of the jetties and passed the foghorn. Part of me was going to miss the place, I have to admit. But the part of me that wasn't had won out. I took one last look over my shoulder towards the beach, the same beach where Molly was going to be landing in a few hours. "Keep her safe," I said out loud. I pushed the throttle forward, and I was on my way.

A little over two hours later, when I pulled up to the dock in Hyannis, there was Molly. She looked as gorgeous as I'd ever seen her, like the time away had been at a beauty salon, and not in some roach motel with stains on the blankets. We'd agreed ahead of time that if there was a crowd on the dock, I'd circle around and wait until everyone was gone, but she and Caroline were the only signs of life. I cut the throttle about a hundred yards from the dock, and put my duffel bag over my shoulder. Then I slowly accelerated, just enough to get the boat moving. I edged up to the dock perfectly. It might have actually been my best landing ever, come to think of it. Molly handed me the baby, and then hopped in. I gave her a kiss—I tried to make it a good one, since I didn't know exactly how long it would be until I got another chance—told her I loved her, kissed the baby, and then got out.

"You have everything?" she asked me. Again it sounded way too casual, like she was making sure I had my lunch before sending me off to work.

"Yep. Got it all. Ready to rock and roll."

"See you soon, darling. I love you so much," she said. She put Caroline down in the cuddy. She was such a good little kid. Didn't make a sound the whole time. I stood on the dock alone, watching my wife back away from the dock. She blew me a kiss before she turned the bow away from me. I watched as she headed out of the harbor until she was out of sight.

I took a deep breath as I turned to go. "Game time," I said to myself.

CHAPTER THIRTY-ONE

Now, you have to understand that this part of my story is pretty much based on what I read about it. I wasn't there, obviously, so I can't tell you exactly what went down. All I know is that Molly and Rooster pretty much fucked up what I thought was an unfuckupable plan. You know what they say about making something idiotproof, right? The world goes and invents a better idiot. I just didn't know that my best friend on Nantucket and my wife happened to be the two better idiots that the world happened to invent.

I did what I was supposed to do. I walked over to the bus terminal and bought my ticket with cash. I got on the bus and went up to Boston, just like we'd planned. I got on my flight and flew to Hanoi, just like we'd planned. I got to the youth hostel, just like we'd planned. Like I said, I did everything exactly the way it was supposed to have been done.

And from everything I read online about the incident—and there was a whole hell of a lot of information about it—Molly did what she was supposed to do when she left Hyannis. She ran the boat up on the beach like she was supposed to do, waited a few hours, and then called Rooster to tell him that she needed him to come pick her up. And Rooster, for his part, did that. He came and got her, then took her and Caroline back to the house. But that's when things went wrong. Really, really wrong.

From the stories I read, she got back to Nantucket some time that Sunday night. She managed to stay on the boat overnight, then called Rooster once the sun had come up. He came and got her, and everything to that point had gone according to the plan. Rooster took her back to the house and dropped her off. So far, so good. But then Rooster went rogue, you know, and tried to be helpful.

He decided to go look for me, and he started at the boatyard. He asked those guys if I'd come by, and they said no. So he explained what he knew, namely that Molly had called him and said she'd woken up on the boat, and I was gone. She'd assumed I was off getting help. But if they hadn't seen me, he wasn't sure where else I would have gone. The guys at the boatyard got nervous, and told Rooster to call the cops. So he did.

It must have been a slow day at the old police station, because those guys went into full-blown search mode, and brought out all the troops to look for me. They went and got Molly at the house, and she took them down to the boat. She didn't have a choice but to tell them what she'd planned on. It was just a little earlier than she was supposed to let that cat out of the bag. She gave them the story about how she'd gone to take a nap, and as far as she knew, I had been driving the boat all the way back to Nantucket.

That was when Rooster decided to be even more helpful. He called Molly on her cell phone while she was standing there with the cops, and told her that he'd just talked to me, and said that I was looking for a new propeller for the boat because I thought ours had gotten damaged when the boat ran aground. Where he got the idea to do that is still a total mystery to me, and if I had the chance to kill him for doing it, I'd drive an axe into his head.

Molly had no idea what the hell he was talking about, because that wasn't a part of any plan we'd discussed. But she played along, and said how relieved she was. It turned out to actually be a good thing for a little while, because it meant that I was, in fact, on the island somewhere. It didn't occur to any of them to ask Rooster where I was when I called, and nobody seemed to think it was weird I'd called him and not my own wife to tell her. But they all just figured I was fine, and called off the search. That was a silver lining, at least for a little while.

When the boat was still there that afternoon and I hadn't shown up, the cops decided to talk to Rooster again. They finally asked him if I'd said where I was when I called, and he said he couldn't remember. What time had I called him? He couldn't remember. Had I said anything else? He couldn't remember. It wasn't adding up for them, and they said so. All of a sudden, Rooster cracked. He admitted he'd never talked to me. He'd made up the whole story. He couldn't explain why he'd said it. He was trying to make Molly less worried.

Then the cops went nuts. Instead of just a boat on the beach, now they had a disappearance on their hands. They went back to the boat and started going over it. The first thing they checked was the GPS. They got a guy from the boatyard to look at it, and he told them that the boat had left Hyannis on a straight shot for Nantucket, but had started doing circles about nine miles from the island. The only way he could explain that change in the course was that I must have fallen off halfway back to the island. I was probably floating around out there, nine miles offshore, no doubt freezing to death.

And just like that, the Coast Guard was involved. Now they were searching for me out in the water. Helicopters were flying around, and a couple of boats were out there, too. The newspaper got wind of the story, and they started issuing updates on their website. Within a few hours, the whole island knew I'd fallen off my boat. And just as soon as those stories broke, everybody was an immediate expert on everything, including me.

People who'd never met me were telling reporters that I was an excellent boat captain, and that they were sure I would be found alive. The only thing they couldn't figure out was how it happened. Most people figured I'd gone to take a piss off the back, and fallen off. Then were the conspiracy theorists who thought Molly had pushed me. I even heard of one guy who claimed we were probably having sex and I lost my balance during the act. I never quite figured out how that one would have worked, but it did give me a good laugh.

They searched for a couple of days, but finally had to call it off. The search area was just too big, and the chances of my surviving for that long in the water were next to impossible. It took a few more days, but the authorities finally declared me officially dead.

Molly became a target for reporters from all over the Northeast. She told the story just like we'd rehearsed. She'd been headed back to Nantucket and called me to tell when she was coming home, and I'd said I'd come pick her up in our boat. She'd gotten on the boat in Hyannis, and was pretty worn out from the weekend, so she and Caroline went into the cuddy to take a nap. I'd put the quarter in so that the door would stay shut. She fell asleep, and didn't wake up until the alarm started going off.

She didn't know what was wrong, but she'd looked out the cabin windows, and it was dark outside. She saw lights in the houses, though. So she knew that she was safe, because they were near people. She couldn't be sure it was Nantucket, but at least she knew that people were nearby. So she didn't panic. She thought I'd gone up to one of those houses and asked for some help.

Because she thought there wasn't any reason to get all worried and get the baby upset, she tried to go back to sleep. She must have dozed off, because the next thing she knew, the sun was up and light was coming in the cabin windows. She noticed that the alarm wasn't still going off. She figured that meant I was there, and had turned it off. When she tried to open the cabin door, though, it was still wedged shut. She knocked on it and called my name to get me to open it, but I hadn't responded.

She tried to push it open, but couldn't. That scared her, so she kicked at the door to get it open. When she finally got out, she saw that I wasn't there. That really scared her. But then she still thought that I must have gone to get help, so she tried calling me on my cell phone. When I didn't answer, she called Rooster to come get her. End of story.

As I was reading her accounts, they all sounded pretty believable at the time. Looking back on it, though, I realized there were a few holes we hadn't thought about when we were concocting the whole idea. For one thing, the fact that an unmanned boat managed to bullseye that beach was pretty lucky. Actually, it was impossibly lucky. Nantucket is basically a dot on the globe, but an unmanned boat happened to safely land on a beach that just happened to be one of the only safe spots she could have ended up? The fact that she hadn't missed the island entirely was amazing enough, let alone the fact that she'd hit the perfect beach. When we'd worked out the plan on paper, it sounded a lot more reasonable. But reading it in the news stories made it sound impossible. Kind of like listening to a teacher read something you wrote for a class, you know, and it sounds ridiculous.

It also stuck out in my mind that she wouldn't have seen any lights on in the houses on the Cliff. When we did the practice run in September, there had still been some people in those houses. But now, in March, none of those people were there. They were all off in their winter homes, and all those houses were empty. In other words, there wouldn't have been any lights on in any of them. Nobody called her out on that, though, luckily enough.

The other thing that was weird was the fact that she told everyone she went back to sleep when the alarm was going off. Who goes back to sleep after their boat runs aground, right? We hadn't talked about that part before, and when I read it, I couldn't believe she'd said it. But like the lights thing, nobody mentioned it. I guess they were all too focused on the tragedy that was my apparent death. There really is a sucker born every minute.

The other big problem she had was that she told her story so many times, facts started to change. In the first version, the engine had been off when she finally managed to get out of the cuddy. In another version, the engine was still going and she actually had to turn the key to get it to shut off. A third story had her saying that she couldn't remember if the engine had been on or not. She claimed she'd been confused when she first got out, and just wasn't sure. But nobody paid much attention to those little changes, either.

About a week later, Molly organized a memorial service for me. It was terribly tragic to read about. And the pictures were great too. They had a wreath made of flowers that they dropped into the water, and a bunch of people I didn't recognize where there to pay their last respects to me, all of them crying. Really sad. And Molly was in the middle of them all, looking like the perfect grieving widow whose husband had died suddenly and left her with a baby. She played the part perfectly. I would have had her as a lock for an Oscar if it had been a movie.

I gave it ten days before I called her, because I was nervous about making contact with her. But I went to a pay phone and used one of my calling cards. The second I heard her voice, I totally forgot that I was going to yell at her for all the stuff she and Rooster had done wrong. I was so happy, I forgot all of it immediately. We couldn't talk long, but I got the rundown. Caroline was fine, Arthur was fine, Molly was fine. She'd been bombarded by people who wanted to do things for her, and everybody had been so nice. She felt a little bad about lying to everyone, but she knew it was for the best.

The best news was that they were about to issue a death certificate, which meant that she could start working on getting the insurance company to pay her on my policy. She didn't know how long it was going to take, but as soon as she had heard from them, she'd let me know. That was music to my ears.

I gave her a quick update on me, telling her that I wasn't in love with the place where I was staying. I had to share a room with three other guys, and none of them spoke English. And I had to keep my stuff locked up, because people in the hostel didn't have any problems with going through your bags and stealing your clothes or your money. I promised her, though, that she wouldn't have to live there, that we'd find our own place, and that we'd live the life we'd dreamed of once she got there. Somewhere nice, on the beach.

And that was it. A six-minute phone call was all I was willing to risk then, so I told her I loved her, and asked her to kiss Caroline for me. We said our good-byes, and I hung up. As soon as the call was over, I felt worse than I'd felt in a long time. I missed her so much, and just wanted her to get out of Nantucket and get to Vietnam so we could be together again. I didn't have a lot to occupy my time, so I was doing a lot of sitting around and thinking. Thinking about Molly, mostly.

The story about my death pretty much fizzled out about as quickly as it had erupted. There were five or six updates a day when the news first broke; after two weeks, even the Nantucket paper had quit focusing on it. They had other things to talk about, like an argument about zoning ordinances, or what the high school lacrosse team had done in their latest game.

And that struck me as the best possible thing that could have happened. I wanted to disappear, and the easiest way to do that was to have people stop talking about me. I was banking on the whole idea that if people forgot about me, my life would go on without any further incidents.

I called Molly again a week later, but she didn't have any update on the insurance payment. That sucked, but I was still hopeful. It was typical, actually. The insurance company was dragging their feet, because any time you ask them to pay out that much money, they fight it like hell. But in the end, Molly would get her money. I was sure of that. And once she did, she and Caroline would be on their way to be with me.

That thought was what kept me going, knowing that some day soon, my wife and daughter would be there, and we'd be a reunited family. I started to fantasize about our lives together. I figured we'd move to the coast somewhere. Find a little village near the beach, and get a small place to live. It was going to be perfect. It was hard to wait, but my daydreams helped me pass the time.

I did try to get out of my own head by walking around Hanoi, seeing all the tourist places. A lot of the stuff to see in the city was art museums and cultural places, which didn't interest me a whole lot. But there were a bunch of historic places too. One of my favorites was a prison, which I guess is kind of weird. It was the place they used to call the Hanoi Hilton, where they kept a bunch of prisoners of war during the Vietnam War. It's got some scary stuff in it. Nightmare kind of stuff, actually. But it was still cool to see.

I tried calling her a few days later, but the call went to her voice mail. I left a quick message, and said I'd try again later. But when I called three hours later, she still didn't answer. It wasn't like her not to have her phone with her, so I started to get a little worried about things. Had she gotten in trouble? Had somebody figured out what we'd done? My mind started to go off in a thousand different directions, and none of them were good.

As much as I knew, on some level, that I was just doing the same thing I always did—making something out of nothing, basically—I couldn't shake the feeling that something horrible had happened. While I had thought that coming here was going to be the solution to all of my problems, the truth was that I felt just as insecure and worried here as I had when I'd been in Nantucket. The fact that I couldn't talk to my wife, and I didn't know what was going on with her, was driving me crazy.

I called her again the next day. She finally answered, and my stomach did a bunch of backflips. "Are you okay? I've been totally worried over here," I said as soon as she answered.

"We're fine," she said flatly. "Sorry. I've just been busy. There's still a lot to do around here. How's everything over there?"

"It's fine. I just miss you guys so much."

"We miss you too," she said, though her voice sounded a little different. Like she wasn't really listening to me. "Still no word from the insurance company, though."

That upset me. She should have heard something, at least an acknowledgement from them or something, by now. "I'll call Victor," I said.

"No, don't do that, honey," she said quickly. "I'm sure it's nothing. And remember, the fewer people who know where you are, the better. So I really wouldn't bring Victor into it. And besides, what are you going to do? Call from beyond the grave? Remember, Billy, you're dead, as far as anybody else knows. I'll keep on it and get the money. Don't worry."

She was right. My new life was based on nobody from my past knowing where I was. It was like the witness protection program. I had to become somebody entirely new, with no past relationships. So calling Victor was out. I didn't have a choice but to let Molly handle it from her end.

After a few more minutes of chatting, it was time to go. I hated to end it, but I didn't want to waste the phone card time. I told her I loved her and hung up, but I couldn't help but want to get Victor on the phone and figure out what was going on. But I couldn't do that. Like Molly had said, I was supposed to be dead, so it would be really weird to have me calling him. Once again, I had no choice but to sit and wait. I could literally feel myself losing more and more of my mind with every passing second.

CHAPTER THIRTY-TWO

Weeks went by, and every time I talked with Molly, I got the sense that she was less and less excited about the prospect of coming to live with me. She'd always say she loved me, which made me feel a little better about the situation, but her voice just seemed distant somehow. You know how people sound when it's like they've got something else on their mind? Yeah, it was like that. But she was my wife, you know, and I missed her so much. But she sounded like her mind was someplace else the whole time. My brain wouldn't give it up, no matter how many times I tried to convince myself that everything was fine.

But after two months and still no word from the insurance company, I got mad. I didn't tell her what I was going to do, but I thought I could get the information I needed without telling them who I was. I decided to skip over Victor, and go straight to the company that had issued the policy. I went to an Internet café and got their contact information.

When I called the number for the company, I told the secretary that answered that I was Molly's father. I was concerned, I told her, because my daughter had tragically lost her husband in a boating accident and, even though there had been a death certificate issued, they had yet to pay her the insurance money. Didn't they know that my daughter and granddaughter needed money to survive? This was inhuman treatment on their part, and I demanded an explanation. It took me about fifteen minutes worth of lying to get her to finally agree to talk to me about it at all. There was nothing that could have prepared me for what she was about to tell me, though.

"Sir, I have to inform you that I'm not supposed to tell you anything, because you're not the policyholder or the beneficiary."

I cut her off immediately. "I understand that, but my daughter is literally starving to death, and as her father, I have to step in and get the ball rolling, because you people can't seem to do what you're legally obligated to do." I hoped I sounded intimidating enough to get her to talk.

She paused a minute before continuing. "I understand your frustrations, sir. As I was going to say before you interrupted me, I'm not supposed to tell you anything. But since you're the father of the named beneficiary and the circumstances are what they are, I will go ahead and tell you that we've already paid the claim. We sent her the check almost three weeks ago, according to my records here."

That little piece of information hit me like a brick to the stomach. It took me a few seconds to regain the ability to speak. When I'd recovered enough to do it, I thanked her for her time, and apologized for the misunderstanding. My daughter, I said, had failed to tell me. But it was my fault, because I was out of the country and hadn't been so good about keeping tabs on her recently. I hung up, and immediately went into my worst-case scenario thoughts again.

Molly hadn't mentioned getting the money. In fact, just the opposite. She'd specifically told me that she hadn't gotten the money yet. So what was going on? I went straight to a pay phone and called Molly, but got her voice mail. Now I was really upset. I left her a message, but tried to stay calm. I said I was just checking in to see if there was any update on the insurance money, and left it at that. I told her I'd call her again in a few hours, and I hoped she'd be able to talk.

I didn't know what else to do, so I went to a bar and started drinking. I was the only American in the place, but I wasn't in the mood for conversation, so I didn't care about that. I wanted to drink myself stupid, to get the thoughts out of my head. I didn't want to believe that my wife had gotten the money—money that she was supposed to use to come here with my daughter to live, and money that we were going to live off of. I mean, it was our money. Our money. What the hell was she doing with it if she had actually already gotten it? What I knew was probably true was worse than anything I could have imagined. The more I thought about it, the more upset I got. And so I drank.

By the time I got around to calling Molly again, I was drunk. I knew it would be a mistake to call her that way, but I was on a mission.

So I dialed the number. She answered on the first ring, and I laid into her. "I've been worried about you, dammit," I said. "I know you've got things to do with the baby and all, but seriously. I need you to answer when I call you."

"Billy," she said, "take it easy." She sounded annoyed. "I was taking a nap when you called. I'm tired. Remember, I'm the one who's raising a baby by herself here. So you need to relax a little and try to be more understanding of what I'm going through."

She was right, of course. Taking care of Caroline was exhausting when it was both of us sharing the duties; I couldn't imagine how bad it was for her to do it by herself. But even though I'd been drinking for the better part of four hours, I wasn't so drunk that I couldn't remember my main reason for calling. "I'm sorry. I just miss you guys so much and I can't wait to have you here. Speaking of that, did you get any update on the insurance money?" I was trying to give her an intro to tell me she'd gotten the check.

"Nothing good," she said. "I actually called them yesterday, and they said that they're going to contest it. They told me that until your body was found, they wouldn't pay it for seven years. They said it was in the policy. But don't worry, honey. I'm going to fight it. I'll get the money soon."

She was lying to me, and I knew it. The question was why. I sighed heavily into the phone. "Molly, I know you got the check. Now what is going on?"

I could hear her catch her breath on the other end of the phone. "What are you talking about, Billy?"

"I'm talking about the check you got from the insurance company. Three Goddamn weeks ago. I talked to them, Molly. I know you got the money."

"You did what?" she screamed. "I told you not to call anybody!"

"I told them that I was your father, and the woman I talked to looked up the claim for me. She said they paid it three weeks ago. What the hell, Molly? What's going on?"

"I don't know what to tell you," was all she said before she hung up.

*　　　*　　　*

The whole world around me started spinning. I have a vague memory of stumbling my way back to the hostel, and then throwing up in the bathroom. I guess I passed out in my bed right after that, but I don't really remember that part at all. I woke up the next morning with a splitting headache, feeling like I'd throw up again any second. I was dizzy, and there was no way I was going to be able to stomach any food. I sat there in my bed, staring at the ceiling, thinking about everything that had happened the night before.

It was obvious that Molly had changed her plans. Even though she'd said before that she had been all on board with using that insurance money to live with me, obviously that was no longer her idea. I hadn't logged on to my Facebook account since coming to Vietnam because I was afraid of getting caught, but I thought maybe I could find out something about what she was doing. So as soon as I could muster the strength to pull myself out of bed and get dressed, I went to the Internet café again and logged on, only to discover that she had unfriended me. That meant I couldn't see anything about her. She was blocking me out, apparently. Keeping me out of her private life. Keeping everything secret.

My own page was covered in people telling me that they couldn't believe I was really gone. I scrolled through them and, to be honest, got a little teary-eyed at a few of them. A girl I'd grown up with in Vermont said something about always loving me, and Rooster had posted that he'd give anything to have me back. And that post gave me an idea. I knew it was risky—it might even be suicidal, for that matter—but I was desperate for information about what was going on with Molly. I could call Rooster and ask him. It was the only thing I could think of. I had to know, even if I already knew. I just needed to hear it from somebody else, and Rooster was the only person I knew I could trust.

I spent the day wandering around the city, trying to work up the courage to call him. I didn't know what I'd say to him. How do you announce to your friend who thinks you're dead that you're actually alive and well, only living in a foreign country? Oh, and by the way, you think that your wife—who was in on the plan from the start—is now screwing you over. I knew it was going to shock him, I just didn't know how much. I was kind of scared that it would scare him into going back to the cops, you know. In the end, though, I decided it was a risk I was going to have to take. I needed to know what was going on with my wife, and I couldn't see any other way of finding out what I wanted to know.

I went to a pay phone and dialed his number, my fingers shaking uncontrollably, and my heart racing. I knew he wouldn't recognize the number, which meant he wouldn't answer. But I thought that if I left a message and told him I'd call back in a few minutes, he'd answer the second time around. The phone rang once and, as I'd guessed, went straight to his voice mail.

"Rooster, listen. It's Billy Faulkner. I know this sounds crazy, but it's really me. Honest to God. I'm not dead. It's a long story, and I'll explain the whole thing. But right now, I need to talk to you. You can't call me, though, so listen. I'll call you again in ten minutes. Do not tell anybody you heard from me. Please. Don't tell anybody. I promise I'll explain everything. I'll call you in ten." I hung up and started pacing around, trying to make the time go by faster.

After waiting for ten minutes—it felt more like four days—I called Rooster's number again. It picked up again on the first ring, but this time it was Rooster himself. "This better be good," he said. "Start talking."

It was great to hear his voice. "Rooster. Hey, man. Holy shit, I don't know where to start. Molly and I worked out this deal to collect on a life insurance policy by faking my death. I can't explain the whole thing right now, but the idea was for us to leave the country. You know, trying to get away from the cops and start our lives over." I paused for breath.

"Hold on. Are you serious?"

"Yeah, I'm serious, Rooster. But I don't have time to bullshit right now, okay? I need a favor from you. I'll tell you the whole story some other time. Right now, I need to know what Molly is doing. She's supposed to be coming to meet me, but now she seems like she's lying to me. I need to know what's going on, and you're the only one I trust there."

There was a long pause on the other end of the phone. Finally, he cleared his throat. "Dude, I . . . I don't know what to tell you. I can't believe I'm talking to you. I thought you were dead, you know?"

It was like talking to an echo, and I was getting more and more frustrated. I tried to keep my voice calm. "Yeah, I know, and I'm sorry about all that. I mean it. But seriously. I don't have a lot of time here. I'll call you again some time and we can catch up, but for right now, I need to know. What's going on with Molly? Do you ever see her?"

Another pause. "Yeah, he said. "I've seen her out a few times. She's been palling around with a cop. One of the guys who investigated your . . ." He stopped short. "Your death, I guess you'd say."

"What do you mean when you say she's been palling around, Rooster? Like she's going out with the guy?"

"Dude," he said, "we all thought you were dead, you know? So I didn't think about it. But yeah, man, she's dating a cop."

It didn't take her long to get over that whole mourning period, huh? Nobody thought to say something to her about the fact that her husband hadn't really been dead long enough for her to be screwing somebody else? Out of sight, out of mind. Now I was mad.

"Son of a bitch," was all I could manage to say.

"I'm sorry, man. I . . . I'm just sorry."

"Thanks, Rooster," I said. "Tell you what. I'll call you in two weeks. You see this number on your phone, you answer it. Got me?"

"Yeah, Billy. I got it."

"And don't tell anybody you talked to me. Please. Like I said before, I really need you to keep it to yourself. Don't tell anybody."

"I'll take it to the grave, bro."

"Thanks, man. Talk in two weeks."

That was a lie. I knew it then, just as soon as I said it. I didn't have any use for Rooster now. I didn't want to chat about life on Nantucket, I didn't want to take any walks down memory lane with him. If he tried to tell people he'd spoken to me on the phone, they'd think he was crazy. It would, if I was counting right, be the second time he'd claimed to talk to a dead man on the phone, and the second one would be about as believable as the first one. As long as I never called him again, nobody would ever believe I was alive. Rooster had already proven himself to be a little touched in the head, you know, so I figured I was safe.

There was a gnawing feeling in my stomach as I hung up the phone. It spread up and throughout my body, and I thought I was going to pass out. My eyes watered, but not from sadness. It was pure fury building up inside of me. An anger like nothing I'd ever felt before. I wanted to put my fist through a wall. The facts came crashing in on me. My wife had basically stolen our money from me, money we'd worked together to get, and was sleeping with one of the cops who'd been trying to figure out what had happened to me.

Right on cue, my brain kicked in with all of the negative thinking. I started to analyze every conversation she and I had had, going back to when I was still living on Nantucket. Had I missed something? Was she having an affair while I'd been at work? What about those walks alone she was taking? Was she going over to meet this guy? Or was this something that had just started recently? Maybe they met during the original investigation for the first time. But in the end, did any of that really matter at all? No. The only thing that mattered right then was that my wife had chosen to abandon our relationship, and keep the insurance money. That, and she was apparently sleeping with a cop. That was a fact.

Other than that, though, I'd never know what had actually happened. I wouldn't ever know how they'd met, or how long they'd been seeing each other. I'd have no idea how he treated my daughter. I was completely alone, with no way of reconnecting with my old life. And if Molly chose to cut me out of her life—which seemed to be the direction she'd gone—I would have no way of getting back in. That was also a fact.

I stewed in my own anger for a few days, trying to get my mind wrapped around the idea that Molly had actually done what she'd done. I'll admit to you that there was a lot of booze involved, and a lot of screaming at trees. I'm a little surprised I didn't get thrown into a psychiatric hospital. I know I probably looked a few steps away from being completely sane and normal.

I've heard of the whole idea about the five stages of grief. You know what I'm talking about? There's something about starting off denying whatever it is, then working your way up to anger, then bargaining, then depression, and then you finally get to the point where you accept it. I went through all of them, if only in my own little world.

At first, I tried to convince myself that it couldn't really be true. But it was hard to argue with the evidence, so that was denial. And then

I got mad. Very, very mad. That would be the part when I was yelling at trees in a drunk fury. For a few minutes, I even told myself I'd be willing to sacrifice whatever I had to in order to get back with her. Call that bargaining. But that was a pretty short conversation. I was supposed to be dead, remember, so going back wasn't an option. When I realized that, it did exactly what it was supposed to do, according to the model, and made me totally depressed. My life was basically over, at least as I knew it.

After a massive, four-day drinking binge, I realized that there was nothing I could do. There wasn't any way for me to change what had happened, and that was that. Molly and I were done, and I was on my own. I'd never see her again, and I'd never see my daughter again. It was a shitty moment, I promise you that. It killed me to fully accept the fact that I no longer had the family I'd had in Nantucket. But I'd accepted it, so I was done with the stages of grief.

The thing about those stages of grief, though, is that I think they left one out. At least in my mind they did. I'm sure whoever came up with the idea was a smart guy and all, but he still forgot an important stage. And that was the stage I'd already started focusing on. And since I didn't have much else to occupy my time, my focus was pretty intense on that last stage.

The one he forgot was revenge.

CHAPTER THIRTY-THREE

There's one thing you ought to know about me, and that's that I can hold a grudge longer than most people you know. Just in case you were planning to try to screw me over too. Call this your fair warning. Some people might call it a character flaw, but I don't care. It's kind of a source of pride for me. Bear in mind, I can be the best friend you ever had too. I'll do anything for my friends. But you screw with me, and I'm coming after you. And I'm not going to quit until I hurt you worse than you hurt me. That's just the facts. So if you can't handle that, don't screw me over in the first place. Simple as that.

Molly would have been very smart to have understood that before she jumped into the sack with another guy, and left me high and dry. You'd think that since she was married to me, she'd have gotten a clue about how I could be. But apparently not. Now it's her turn to understand what it means to feel that pain of having someone you loved—or at least someone you claimed to love—turn their back on you, and make your life hell. You know what I'm talking about?

The bitch had the nerve to send me a letter after our last phone conversation. She typed it out. I guess that she didn't want me to be able to prove that she'd actually written it. Anyway, she told me in the letter that she was sorry it had ended the way it did, and that she was sorry that I'd found out about it the way that I had. She'd been waiting for the right time to tell me. She never meant to hurt me, and she missed me, and would always love me, and all kinds of other bullshit. I read it, then set it on fire. She'd get hers. I'd see to that.

And that's pretty much the long and the short of it. That's my story. The good, the bad, and the ugly. But it's not over just yet.

I moved out here to China Beach about six months ago. Hanoi was just too much for me to deal with, and I'd always wanted to move out to the coast with Molly and Caroline. But that wasn't going to happen after she did what she did. Once I'd gotten over the shock and the sadness, I figured it was time to move on with my life, so I went with my original idea.

And here we are. I'm a bartender, which is cool with me. The bar owner is an American expat living here. Hell of a surfer too. He taught me to surf, and I've gotten pretty good at it, actually. He's got a restaurant and a bar, and employees get to eat free when they're working. So I get to eat for free six days a week, drink as much as I want, and surf whenever I'm not working. Life is pretty good, when I sit and think about it.

I don't have all the worries I had in what I call my first life. I'm not running any scams, I'm not ripping anybody off. I'm pouring drinks, and meeting a lot of great people. People like you. I'm getting laid on a regular basis, making enough money to live on the beach, and having a great time. I'm living a life that a lot of people would love to be living. You know, it's like Molly said that night when we were on the boat and she was looking up at those expensive houses on the Cliff. She said she wished she could live like that. Well guess what, you bitch. I'm living like that now.

As for Molly, I don't know what she's got planned for herself. I don't really care, to tell you the truth. I'm over it. But I do have a suspicion or two that the cop she's with probably kept her out of a lot of the trouble she should have gotten in. Come to think of it, it wouldn't really surprise me if he was the reason nobody asked a lot of those questions that somebody should have been asking—you know, about how she saw lights in houses that were empty, or how a boat without a driver made a perfect landing on a calm beach with easy four-wheel-drive access. If he was part of the investigation, he could have done a whole lot to keep her out of trouble. I don't know it for a fact, but I'd bet you good money that he helped her cover the whole thing up. And now she's probably spending my life insurance money on that son of a bitch.

For the most part, I've put it out of my mind. You know, like I've been saying to you, I can overthink anything. Give me a situation— hell, give me a word—and I'll tell you fifteen different ways you can interpret it, and fourteen of them will be bad for you. So yeah, I still think about it every now and then, but I've pretty much made peace with it. But there's still one thing about that whole thing with Molly and cop that still bugs me.

Molly had a pretty major change of heart about my idea for coming here in the first place. It was out of the blue. She was totally against it for the longest time. Didn't want to hear about it. And when I mentioned a life insurance policy, she damn near lost it on me. But then, it was like somebody flipped a switch on her a few weeks later, and she was all about it. At the time, I thought it was because I was so convincing. But today I wonder. I wonder if she wasn't with that cop even then, telling him exactly what I had planned. I can't prove it, of course, but I just wonder. Maybe I'll find out one day. Karma has a way of catching up with you in the end, I've found.

Oh, yeah. Before I forget. About that whole sixth-stage-of-grief thing, the revenge stage. I don't have any plans to ever go back to Nantucket, that much is for sure. I doubt I'll ever even go back to the United States, for that matter. My visa expired a long time ago, so I'm technically an illegal alien living here. But they don't seem to be all hell-bent on tracking me down. A bartender in China Beach living in the country on an expired visa is a pretty low priority, I guess. So I'm not going to get my revenge by showing up on Molly's doorstep and killing her, or anything like that. I mean, that wouldn't really be my style. I like to be more subtle than that. More passive-aggressive.

But don't you worry. She'll get hers. And with any luck, her boyfriend will get something of an ass-kicking too. The funny thing about my situation is that, even in the United States, I'm a low-level guy. It's like my situation here, as the bartender on the expired visa. Low priority. Back in the states, I'm a nobody, you know? When you really think about it, there's no way they could prove I actually broke the law. I mean, Molly was the one who got the money. I just went for a boat ride. And my past insurance crimes? I'm not even sure you could call them that, but just in case you want to, I'm sure that's all gone away by now. They've got to have some bigger fish to go after. Starting with Victor, that bastard.

Same thing with the drugs. There wasn't much they could hang on me when I lived there, when I think about it now. But even if they did have something, it wasn't a real big deal, in the overall scheme of things. I was just running the stuff. I wasn't even selling it. So I'm a former low-level drug carrier and current estranged husband of a woman who committed insurance fraud when she claimed that her husband died.

It really doesn't add up to a major crime spree. So no big thing. And I have to believe that they aren't going to try to track me down all the way over here. Even if they did try to, you have to remember that Vietnam doesn't extradite to the United States. That, my friend, is what they call winning at life. Finally. I'm a winner at this little game.

But Molly, on the other hand—she's a different story. Since she's the one who got the money from the insurance company, I'd have to say that she's the one who ought to get her ass thrown in prison for insurance fraud. And if I'm right about the fact that she was diddling that cop when we were still living together, then there's the whole issue of tampering with a police investigation that would fall on the pair of them. If they were working together like I think they were, then both of them have got some problems.

The thing is, as a bartender, you end up talking to a lot of people. I had a guy here one time, a lawyer from somewhere in Indiana. Here on vacation with his wife. He sat at the bar drinking rum punch while his wife went shopping. Turns out that he was one of those guys who specialized in defending drunk drivers that had gotten popped for driving under the influence. I asked him how you defend something like that. You know, the Breathalyzer doesn't lie, right? Either you're drunk or you're not. The little machine tells the whole story.

He looked up at me and laughed. "Billy," he said, "facts are funny things. They're always open to interpretation."

Then he told me a joke. This guy's working late one night at his office, and there's this temporary secretary working there. Just filling in for the regular girl. Anyway, this guy thinks she's looking pretty good, so when the working day is finally over, he goes back to her place, and has his way with her all night. The next morning comes around, and he gets all nervous. Starts talking about how his wife is going to kill him. Then he gets an idea. He goes into the girl's kitchen, opens up a beer, and pours it all over his head. Then he goes into her bathroom and throws baby powder all over himself. Then he tells the girl good-bye, and he drives home. When he gets home, well, there's his wife waiting for him, ready to kick his ass. So he looks at her and says, "Honey, I'm not going to lie. There was a gorgeous secretary at the office, so I went home with her last night and we did things I'd never even dreamed about." She looks at him, takes a couple of whiffs, sees that baby powder on his hands, and says to him, "You bullshit liar. You've been out playing pool with your buddies all night. Now get your ass in this house."

Just like that lawyer said. Facts are always open to interpretation, you know? And that stuck with me, what he said. He was right. You tell your side of the story, and whatever facts you tell the other person are the ones you choose to tell. And when you're telling that story, you can leave out the facts that might make you look bad. And even then, you can always spin them around so they make somebody else look worse, you know? You can pretty much control how the other person interprets the facts.

And that's where I can finally get to that sixth stage of grief, so I can finish the process and get on with my life without her once and for all. The way I'm going to get revenge is pretty simple, actually. As a bartender, I've gotten pretty good at talking to people. And I don't mean talking like a salesman. I mean just plain talking. Like we're doing now. I've gotten pretty good at telling stories.

And that's just what I'm going to do too. Get my story out there. My version of things. The version where Molly is the self-serving bitch that I know she is now, and her little boyfriend is just as guilty of breaking the law as she is. The version that I just told you here.

You see, that story I just told you is about to get around. And it's going to get out the way I want it to get told. I spent awhile writing it out. The same way I told it to you here. I typed it all out on my boss's computer. Then I printed it, and sent it off to a few people just last week. Reporters, mostly. I made sure to get a copy to a guy I know who writes for the Nantucket paper. Oh, and a few other Nantucket people. You know, the chief of police, the chairman of the Nantucket Board of Selectmen, people like that. And Molly got a copy too. I thought she might like to read the story from my perspective. Make her squirm a little bit while she waits for her world to come crashing down around her, the same way mine did. The insurance company that had paid her the life insurance money got a copy of it too. I figured they'd find it interesting reading.

Nantucket's a small place, and as far as I know, Molly is still living there today. Rumors spread around that island like wildfire. Literally. It's like a spectator sport, you know? Somebody gets arrested, everybody knows it. Somebody beats their wife, everybody knows about it.

Now, I just wonder what would happen if word got out that somebody helped her husband fake his own death, then collected on the insurance policy with help from a local cop, the same local cop who'd hidden facts during the investigation. It'd be a real shame if they both ended up in a word of shit because of what they did. There's just no telling what all might happen. I guess we'll find out once the rumors start flying around, won't we?

Thanks for listening. I feel a lot better now.

For sales, editorial information, subsidiary rights information
or a catalog, please write or phone or e-mail

ibooks
1230 Park Avenue
New York, New York 10128, US
Sales: 1-800-68-BRICK
Tel: 212-427-7139
BrickTowerPress.com
ibooksinc.com
email: bricktower@aol.com

www.Ingram.com

For sales in the UK and Europe please contact our distributor,
Gazelle Book Services
White Cross Mills
Lancaster, LA1 4XS, UK
Tel: (01524) 68765 Fax: (01524) 63232
email: jacky@gazellebooks.co.uk